TEMPTING THE MONSTER

A MIDNIGHT STALKERS NOVEL
BOOK ONE

HAYLEY FAIMAN

HAYLEY FAIMAN BOOKS, LLC

ALSO BY HAYLEY FAIMAN

Rough & Rich

Rough & Real

Cash Bar Series —

Laced with Fear

Chased with Strength

Flamed with Courage

Blended with Pain

Twisted with Chaos

Mixed with trouble

SAVAGE BEAST MC —

UnScrew Me

UnBreak Me

UnChain Me

UnLeash Me

UnTouch Me

UnHinge Me

UnWreck Me

UnCage Me

Unfit Hero Series —

CONVICT

HERO

FRAUD

KILLER

COWBOY

Zanetti Famiglia Series —

Becoming the Boss

Becoming his Mistress

Becoming his Possession

Becoming the Street Boss

Becoming the Hitman

Becoming his Wife

Becoming her Salvation

Prophecy Sisters Series —

Bride of the Traitor

Bride of the Sea

Bride of the Frontier

Bride of the Emperor

Astor Family Series —

Hypocritically Yours

Egotistically Yours

Matrimonially Yours

Occasionally Yours

Nasty Bastards MC —

Ruin My Life

Tame My Life

Start My Life

Dance into My Life

Shake Up My Life

Repair My Life

Sweeten My Life

Wrap Up My Life

Underworld Sinners—

Stolen by the Sinner

Bound to the Sinner

Caught by the Sinner

F*cked by the Sinner

Stripped by the Sinner

Rejecting the Sinner

Loved by the Sinner

Devil's Hellions MC —

Dirty Perfect Storm

Cocky Perfect Storm

Taboo Perfect Storm

Wicked Perfect Storm

Midnight Stalkers—

Tempting the Monster

Enticing the Monster

Watching the Monster

Awakened Curses —

Vow to a King

Vow to a Tyrant

Vow to a Rogue

Offspring Legends—

Between Flaming Stars

Beautiful Unwanted Wildflower

Esquire Black Duet Series –

DISCOVERY

APPEAL

Forbidden Love Series —

Personal Foul

Kinetic Energy

Standalone Titles

Royally Relinquished: A Modern Day Fairy Tale

STAY CONNECTED

Linktree: https://linktr.ee/AuthorHayleyFaiman

Website: http://hayleyfaiman.com

Facebook: https://www.facebook.com/authorhayleyfaiman

Facebook Reader Group: https://www.facebook.com/groups/433234647091715/

Goodreads: https://www.goodreads.com/author/show/10735805.Hayley_Faiman

Signup for my Newsletter: https://view.flodesk.com/pages/63e6bf4b0f93ed601fa2a3d9

TikTok: https://www.tiktok.com/@yourauthorhayleyfaiman

Instagram: https://www.instagram.com/hayleyfaiman/

Temptation is a woman's weapon and a man's excuse.

— H.L. MENCKEN

INTRODUCTION

TEMPTING THE MONSTER

A Midnight Stalker Novel

A Life for a Life.
The family has one motto and a list of rules.
The family isn't something you join.
You can only be born into it.
The family is mine.
I am the family's.
Until I see her.
She doesn't see me.
But I must have her.
I need to own her.

PLAYLIST

You can listen to the Tempting the Monster playlist here

Animals : Maroon 5
Heart of Glass: Blondie
Karma: Taylor Swift
Closer: Nine Inch Nails
I feel It Coming: The Weeknd, Daft Punk
Unstable: Justin Bieber, The Kin LAROI
Bad Habits: Ed Sheeran, Bring Me The Horizon
Intro: The xx
Bad Medicine: Bon Jovi
Fix You: Coldplay
Prisoner: Miley Cyrus, Dua Lipa
Latch: Disclosure, Sam Smith
Like A Wrecking Ball: Eric Church
Circles: Post Malone
Midnight Show: The Killers
Everybody Wants To Rule The World: Tears for Fears
Criminal: LEOWOLF
Needed Me: Rihanna

Chills - Dark Version: Mickey Valen, Joey Myron
I Feel Like I'm Drowning: Two Feet
Flawless: The Neighbourhood
Bad Guy: Billie Eilish
Sinners: Ari Abdul, Thomas LaRosa
I'm Yours: Isabel LaRosa
Where are you?: Elvis Drew, Avivian

THE FAMILY

A LIFE FOR A LIFE

Mafia is a bit strong of a definition. It also suggests that we have a structure that can be infiltrated—ours cannot.

We are not the same.

Family is somewhat defined as a group of people related to one another by blood and/or marriage. That is indeed what we are, so family it is. And that is what we are. A family bound by blood and/or marriage. There is no in-between, and you cannot be part of the family unless you are related in some way.

"Do you take this oath?" my father asks.

He is only my father outside of this room. Inside, he is the director. He has no name. He has no other title. He's just Director. *My oldest brother is a manager, as am I. My younger brother and several of my cousins are leaders.*

Then there are the corps. Those are cousins who have just been initiated into this side of the family. They're younger, greener, newer to the life that we live, to the oaths that we take.

They all have a lot to learn and much to do to prove themselves.

They must also complete four steps to work their way up to being leaders. Then, when they are leaders, they will have three more steps to become a manager.

I was initiated when I was fifteen. It took me ten years to become a leader.

"I do, Director," my youngest cousin whispers.

He's trembling, his thin, gangly teenage body visibly quaking in front of us. We cannot speak to him, though. We cannot encourage him in any way. We must stay silent. Only the director and the initiate may speak.

Standing in a circle around him, we wait for instruction from the director. We don't need to wait, though. We all have been exactly where our cousin sits. We know exactly what happens next, but ceremony is important to all of us, so we wait.

The sacrificial slaughter is brought into the room moments later, our circle only breaking to allow the man to pass through. He is blindfolded. Gagged. His hands are tied behind his back before he is kicked behind the knees so that he is forced to fall to them on the concrete floor with a whimpered cry.

"A life for a life," the director states.

It is always a life for a life.

An eye for an eye.

A tooth for a tooth.

A hand for a hand.

This is our motto: Life for a life. It is simple, but it explains who and what we are with four little words.

"A life for a life," the new initiate whispers.

"Stand." The simple direction is all he needs. The boy stands, taking two steps forward, gripping the blade in his hand.

"Go ahead."

And with those two words, he lifts the blade and slides it deeply across the tied man's throat. The gurgling sound is all that is heard. The spray of the blood coats the boy's face and torso. The deed is done.

"Bring in the women. Clean him up."
The initiation complete, now the boy can begin his training.
But tonight, we party.

CHAPTER
ONE

PARKER

I CHEW ON MY BOTTOM LIP AS I STARE AT THE SUPPOSEDLY calming blue wall ahead of me. It's not calming at all. In fact, it makes me want to scream. Everything makes me want to scream lately, though. Which is why I'm here. Trying this... again.

I'm a nervous wreck.

Anxiety to the moon and back, but I'm here. I've never made it this far before. Last week, I walked to the door but couldn't actually open it and come inside. All my previous therapies have been virtual.

Actually, walking into the building does something to me. It makes me feel sick to my stomach in a million different ways. But today, I came inside, and now I am seconds from standing up and walking out of the room, then the building. I don't think I can go any farther.

Reaching across from me, I grab hold of the coffee table

magazine and stare at the cover. It's old, by at least ten years. If I were somewhere that didn't make me feel like I wanted to scratch my skin off from the inside out, I might laugh at the fashion and beauty tips, all of which are so outdated it is actually hilarious.

My knee bounces, I'm unable to concentrate on the pages, and I jump to my feet.

Nope.

I can't do this. Spinning around, I take a single step and realize I'm fleeing in the wrong direction just in time to run into a brick wall. Tilting my head back, I look up at the man who stares down at me.

I try to take a step back, but my legs slam into the little coffee table that's covered with old magazines, and I fall backward, my ass landing on the top. I slide a little on the glossy magazines.

The man doesn't reach for me to help me to my feet. Instead, he watches me, a smirk playing on his lips as if he finds my falling on my ass amusing, which I guess it is, but I don't think it's very kind to actually laugh about it.

I scrunch my nose, and my eyes find his. "I know it's hilarious that I fell," I mutter as I stand. "Such a gentleman."

He snorts, then, without another word, walks past me and out of the room. Smoothing my hands down the front of my clothes, I hear the little bell over the door chime just as a soft voice calls out my name.

I blink, then my gaze focuses on the woman who is standing in the office doorway. She has a kind smile on her face. She's probably in her early fifties. Her blonde hair is pulled up into a simple big bun on the top of her head, and she's even wearing pearls. She looks distinguished.

She's wearing a beautiful navy pantsuit and what I can assume is a white silk blouse underneath. On her feet are nude pumps that I can tell just by looking at them are designer. In fact, everything she's wearing is designer and doesn't have a single wrinkle.

"Parker Nichols?" she asks.

I brush my hands down the front of my jeans again, trying to wipe off the sweat from my palms. "That's me," I quip brightly in an attempt to appear cheerful and hide the absolute terror I'm feeling in this moment.

Her smile doesn't waver, but I can tell she doesn't believe my faux bright and cheery disposition. "I'm Doctor Brenda Hamilton. Please come in and sit down."

What I want to do is turn around and run far, far away. I don't do that, though. It's almost as if she has a hold on me. I watch as she takes a step backward, a silent invitation into her office. Inhaling a deep breath, I hold it for a moment, then force my feet to move.

They don't move quickly. Instead, they shuffle forward, and after what feels like a lifetime, I finally make my way into the office. There is a nice buttery deep-brown sofa on one side, a desk with a dark-teal rolling chair pushed in, and then two deep-gold chairs that face the sofa.

I love the style. It's classically eclectic.

"You can sit wherever you like. There is no assigned seating," she says, her tone soothing, and I wonder if this is how she gets people to open up to her because I'm instantly relaxed.

I sink down to my ass on the sofa, and although it's more luxurious than anything else I've ever sat on in my life, it doesn't keep my anxiety at bay. Now that I'm sitting in this room, facing this woman as she sinks down in one of the gold chairs, I want to do nothing more than run.

This is so different from virtual counseling. She can see my little tics and habits. She will definitely be able to read me better this way. She'll know if I'm holding back. I don't like it. I feel far too vulnerable.

"You don't have to tell me anything deep and dark today. This is our first meeting. I'm good with whatever you feel like talking about."

"I want to leave," I whisper.

She doesn't say anything in response. I'm not sure if she's trying to read me, think about what to say, or if she's attempting to get me to talk. None of it works. Staring at her, I tilt my head to the side and wonder if I should just get up and walk away or actually respond.

Instead of leaving, feeling like that would be rude, I shove my hands beneath my thighs, sucking in a deep breath, and I speak. I'm not sure what I'm going to say. I have nothing planned, so I just go for it.

"I dream a lot," I blurt out.

"You do?" she asks, her voice almost a soothing song.

I nod, my teeth sinking into my lip, then I chew, my teeth scraping across to find a piece of dead skin and tug on it until it comes off. Then I do it all over again. I can feel a piece tear and begin to bleed, and only then do I speak.

"I do," I whisper. "It's always the same dream," I confess. "I'm about six years old and asleep in bed. I feel something or someone watching me, so I open my eyes, and he's there."

"Who is there?" she asks, although I'm not sure if she's curious or happy that I'm talking, so she wants me to continue.

I do anyway, no matter her reasoning. It doesn't matter. It feels kind of good to tell someone this. Even if she doesn't give a rat's ass and only cares because she's getting paid to care. Which I'm sure is part of the case anyway.

It doesn't matter. I continue talking, whether it's because I love this sofa or because she makes me feel comfortable. I know the words need to be said. They consume me, and they shouldn't.

"It was a man. I'd never seen him before. He stood above

me, wearing a nice black suit and sunglasses. I couldn't see his eyes or anything. He had dark hair and just stood there. Watching me. Then he took a step backward, turned around, and walked away."

She dips her chin in a single nod, then clears her throat and shifts in her chair. "This bothers you. That you don't know who he was, that he was watching you, or that he walked away without saying a word?"

"My parents were killed that night," I whisper. "That's what bothers me."

I stare at her, watching her reaction. It's genuine. She winces slightly, then straightens her composure and lets out a heavy sigh, though it's not out of boredom, more like she's trying to put everything together.

"And you think this man was involved?" she asks.

"I don't," I reply softly. "I don't know why, but he didn't scare me or anything. I just can't get him out of my mind. He stood there, watching me, then he left. My parents were gone, and that was that."

"Are you sure he was real?" she asks. "Maybe you were looking for answers?"

I hate how everything is a question because I don't know the answers to any of them. I've always dreamed of him as if he were a living, breathing thing, a man who stood over me, who watched me. But it was the single worst traumatizing night of my life. What if he was just made up?

"I'm not," I whisper. "Certain that he was real, that is," I clarify.

She half smiles and dips her chin, her eyes searching my own before she speaks again. "Why don't you tell me about your life now. Your parents are gone, but who do you live with? What do you do for fun?"

And that is how the session goes until the very end. She asks me questions that are superficial in an attempt to calm me down. I answer them, and by the end of the session, I feel much calmer, like maybe I can walk into this room again and do this another day... not tomorrow, but another day.

WELLS

BIG GREEN EYES.

The likes of which I've never seen before.

Of course, they belong to a patient of my mother's. No perfectly normal and sane girl looks at a man that way. The way she stared up at me. She was beautiful, complex, and broken. I could see behind her eyes. They were far too open. She is far too vulnerable. Far too broken.

I've always gone for cheap, easy, and vacant. This woman was a far cry from all three of those things. In fact, she's the exact opposite of every woman I've ever fucked. I want to know what haunts her, not because I want to fix her, but because I want it to be me.

Leaving the counseling office, I jog toward the car. Coleman is driving, waiting for me in the driver's seat. I open the door and sink down in the passenger side as his fingers grip the steering wheel tightly. Slamming the door behind me, I jerk my chin in a silent order for him to go ahead.

"What happened?" I demand.

He doesn't speak immediately. Instead, he shifts the car into *Drive* and slams his foot against the pedal before he throws us into traffic. I should probably be concerned. My brother doesn't typically drive erratically. He's one hundred percent the safe big brother. When in doubt, we can always rely on Coleman.

There is also the fact that he is a manager in the family. We are not allowed to do anything charged with emotion, and this definitely feels like that. It's confusing, to say the least, and I can do nothing but watch him and wait for an explanation.

As soon as we're out of the city and on the interstate, and he still hasn't said anything, I turn toward him. My gaze flicks up and down his body, noticing just how rigid he is, and I tilt my head to the side. He isn't going to tell me, so I'm going to have to bug the shit out of him about it.

"You want to talk about it?" I ask.

"No," he says, his teeth gnashing together.

I hum, and he lifts his hand from the steering wheel long enough to flip me off, then replaces it quickly to ensure he doesn't lose control of the half-a-million-dollar machine. A half-of-a-million-dollar car that was a gift when he became a leader. When we became managers, we were given a penthouse condo in downtown Dallas.

"Then you want to tell me what the fuck?" I ask, changing my tone and question.

"Dad," he snorts. "Fucking asshole."

Arching a brow, I don't say anything, knowing he will continue shortly. Thankfully, he does. It's nice that I'm not the one on Dad's shit list today, so I'll take joy in this drama over my own. He inhales deeply, then lets it out on a long, exhaled breath before he engages the cruise control and begins to move in and out of traffic with a much calmer ease.

"He found out about that girl I was fucking."

Fucking is not what Coleman was doing. Coleman was falling in love with her. She was also the daughter of one of our father's business associates.

Personally, I didn't think it would be an issue. What if it worked out? Nothing wrong with mixing business with pleasure and intertwining the companies, but who knows why our father does anything, really?

It's not like he ever explains himself.

Sure, he's our father, but he's also the director, and those two roles have a very fine line between them.

"So he wanted you to break it off?" I guess when he doesn't continue.

Coleman snorts. "He wants me to marry her."

His words come out sharp and bitter. I stare at him, unsure why he's so fucking pissed off. He's been practically crying over this bitch for weeks. Sounds like a good deal to me, plus he's almost thirty. It's about time.

"But you don't want to marry her?" I guess.

He snorts again, and I'm about to jerk on the steering wheel and end this goddamn pained conversation for the both of us right fucking now. I am over this shit. I honestly don't care what my brother does with his dick, but we have a job to do right now, and I need his head in the game.

"I like her," he says, letting out a sigh. "She's nice and all." He pauses before he continues. "But I want what's owed to me. That is not her."

I hum, understanding finally washing over me at his words—*what's owed to me*.

A virgin of his choosing.

Bound to him.

Promised to him.

Possessed *by* him.

His prize for dedicating his life to his family. I can understand my brother turning down that deal for the one he is owed. Especially if he truly was fucking her just to pass the time. He's not really one to have dozens of one-night stands. He typically will keep someone around for a few months before he scrapes her off and finds another.

I just didn't think this one was a plaything. He's been with her for over six months. I assumed it was serious. Coleman doesn't really talk about his feelings, so I can only go off his actions.

Apparently, I assumed wrong.

CHAPTER
TWO

PARKER

IT HELPED.

I didn't think it actually would or that she had necessarily done much, but it did help. I am almost excited to go back and talk to her again. But not that excited. I can definitely wait. I have a whole week to prepare, and I'm wondering if it's almost too long of a break.

I'm not sure I'll be able to work up the courage again.

But I'm going to try and remember this feeling so that I can remind myself it was a good thing, a good day, and she's a good counselor.

Dr. Hamilton's office is also a short distance from my condo, which is really nice. I can actually walk. Although I won't want to in the summer, this afternoon it's not too bad. The warm breeze feels nice as I move through the city streets and head toward my building.

The café next door is packed full of people, and I glance at my watch to check the time since it's usually pretty empty. I'm surprised to find that it's five, which means everyone is getting one last shot of energy before they commute home.

Taking half a day off work is not something I would typically do, but I was so stressed out and worried about this appointment that I knew I couldn't concentrate at work, so I took half of a personal day.

Typically, crowds don't bother me, although I do enjoy the space of an empty room. I'm feeling a bit down myself and would love a drink. Slipping into the back of the line, I wait my turn. As I wait, I can't help but think about my counseling session. I hope I don't have that dream tonight.

It almost seems as if when you talk about something, you're speaking it into existence, and in this case, it's the form of that same nightmare over and over again. Chewing on my bottom lip, I tug at the dry skin there with my teeth, and since I can't find any, I scrape my teeth across my lip over and over until I create some.

When I taste the metallic tang of blood, only then do I stop.

"Can I help you?" a spunky voice asks.

Lifting my head, I realize I've moved forward, and I'm next in line, without a single recollection of it happening. Closing the distance between me and the barista, I smile and give her my order.

Venti iced vanilla latte with almond milk and an extra shot.

It's the exact same every time. I don't want to try the brand-new anything. I don't want to try the seasonal anything. I just want my drink. It's comforting. It doesn't change. It doesn't disappoint. It is perfection every single time.

I'm sure this is part of my anxiety issues: needing the routine, needing the exact same drink every single time I order one, only eating at certain restaurants, and when I do, the exact same meal every time.

Trying something new for me is not only rare but exhausting. Anytime I have to go out to dinner with friends and they choose somewhere I've never been before, I usually study the menu for a whole day or two before I go and I try to find something that I can handle.

I'm just neurotic about it. I would love to be able to take chances… which is why I'm seeing the doctor to begin with.

I want to be normal… or at least a *little* normal.

Once I've ordered, I pay and step to the side to wait for my order. The baristas are busy moving around the machines, whipping up drinks as fast as they can. I watch in amazement as my mind wanders, which it tends to do often.

I've always been told by my friends and my aunt and uncle that I live in my head. I'm in the clouds, and I am too much of a dreamer. They don't realize that being in my head is not necessarily a dream or a fun place to be. It's not like I'm having a party up here with my thoughts.

"Parker," the barista calls out.

I'm thankful to be broken out of my thoughts. Smiling, I take a step forward and move toward the counter. Thanking the barista, I wrap my fingers around the cup and turn around to make my way outside and next door to my home.

It doesn't take me long to get into the building, ride up the elevator, and safely lock myself inside of my condo. I won't have to leave again until Monday morning for work. Friday afternoon with no weekend plans means that I can lie in bed and read for hours.

With a heavy sigh, I strip out of my clothes, not bothering to close the curtains. There's no need to when you're as high up as I am in the building. The glass is mirrored, too, so nobody can see inside.

In just my bra and panties, I sip on my iced latte and sink

down in the chair. The counselor's sofa is nice, but it doesn't beat my chair. It's an oversized adult leather-clad beanbag chair. It's soft and so comfortable that I don't think I'll ever get rid of it. It's where I think and relax and drink coffee or water, depending on the time of day.

Sitting cross-legged, I bring my coffee to my lips and take a long drink, then I reach into the side of the chair and grab hold of my book. It's a romance, naturally. Although, it's definitely a lot spicier than the bodice rippers that I used to sneak and read as a teenager.

The one thing that my aunt did not do was watch me closely around her very vast collection of romance books. It's a good thing, too, because she never actually taught me about the birds and the bees, but those books were educational.

Very educational.

Smiling to myself, I open the book, but I don't start reading it. Sinking my teeth in my bottom lip, I scrape them across and think about the fact that I am silly as all hell. I'm a virgin. I've never even been kissed, and I'm telling myself that I know everything about sex. I'm such an idiot.

I find the chapter where I left off and begin to read all about the couple who seem to be bound and determined to stay away from one another, even though that is the absolute last thing either of them wants.

Within seconds, I am lost in the story. The words begin to shift, turning into characters, and a movie plays before me. It happens this way every time I read. I don't watch much television.

I don't need to.

Not when I have this.

WELLS

THE MAN SOBS BEFORE ME. He's on his knees, snot and tears streaming down his face. It's a pathetic sight, really. I've done this more than a few times in my life, and it always causes me to cringe. I can't get over these men and how fucking pathetic they are.

Coleman clears his throat behind me, and I know he is trying not to laugh. We're not supposed to show any real emotion at all, even if it is laughter. We are forever meant to be emotionless and stoic in every way possible.

"What have you done wrong?" I ask.

Coleman is just here as backup and only because we happened to be in a meeting with Dad, then I had to see Mom before this. So, he's joining me on this little job. Plus, he's driving me around this afternoon. I quite like it.

"I stole from Henry Hamilton," he whimpers.

"You did," I agree. "And why did you do this?"

He shakes his head, tipping it backward slightly as he looks up at me. "Because I didn't think he would find out."

Our family business is real estate. It's what we know, what we've always known. We buy commercial properties, we rent them out, we sell them. It's what we do. On the surface, we deal with sellers, investors, and with banks. Beneath the surface, we deal with sellers, investors, and bankers.

This man is a banker.

Though he isn't dead yet, he's as good as.

"And who did you give this money to?" I ask.

He shakes his head. "Nobody. I used it for my kids' college."

Leaning forward, I tilt my head to the side and lift my hand to run my palm across my jaw and lips. He's full of shit, a liar, and using his kids in his lie, which makes him a goddamn piece of shit at the same time.

"Your houses in Mexico and Florida prove otherwise," I

murmur. "Did you think I would not have had you looked into before I came here?"

"My family," he blurts out. "I have a daughter. Do you want her?"

I snort, though my face shows zero expression. I can barely keep a straight face that this man would willingly offer his daughter as a lamb to the slaughter. A fucking piece of shit. Shaking my head slowly, I clear my throat.

"No, and if I did, I would not need your permission to take her."

Coleman clears his throat again, which is his signal for me to hurry up because he's hungry. He knows that tonight we're to go to a family dinner.

Although, I'm surprised that he's in a hurry for that because he usually despises them, and since he's in deep shit with Dad, he's probably going to have to hear about that for a while. A thought that makes me smile.

Family dinners.

They're a requirement, however, not by my father, but my mother.

We always do as Mother asks because our mother is the true director when it comes to the home and her boys. Jerking my chin in a single nod, I lean forward, producing my knife. Normally, I would do something much cleaner in this circumstance, but the cleanup crew has been bored recently, so I'm going to give them a job to complete.

I lift my knife and press it against the center of his throat. "Maybe I'll fuck her anyway. I could always use new ass to tap. I'll make sure to let her know that her daddy sent me."

Pressing the knife harder into his throat, I watch as he begins to bleed. "This is for your betrayal."

Pressing the knife even farther into his neck, I watch as the blood begins to flow from his throat before it sprays all over me. I should not like looking into his eyes and watching the light drain out of them.

I should not enjoy it as much as I do, but I've been doing this for ten years, and every time, I like it a little more. I'm probably some kind of psycho or something, but I don't care. I have a feeling this means I'm losing my humanity. I'm probably going to be a monster soon if I'm not already.

I'm pretty sure I am a monster made by the family, created, harvested, and fed day after day, month after month, and year after year.

"Cleanup crew has been called," Coleman states.

I drop the knife and leave it beside his body. They'll get rid of the weapon as well as the body. Taking a step backward, I shake my head once, getting rid of thoughts of inhumanity, the family, and everything that flows through my mind on a regular basis and look over at him.

"You ready for Mom's takeout?" I ask.

He chuckles. "Yeah. Where do you think she ordered from this week?"

Together, we walk out of the office. It's a Saturday night, and the whole building is empty. The meeting wasn't set, at least not with me. They don't happen often, but meetings on Saturdays aren't as rare as one would think, especially when you're meeting with clients and investors from all over the world.

This was supposed to be a meeting between the banker and his favorite client, Titus Atticus, a faux name that I give for a very real person in history, one that I'm sure nobody else recalls. A real estate investor from ancient Rome. I find it fitting.

"Pasta," I call out as I take the handkerchief from my pocket and wipe the blood from my face.

It's not enough. I'm going to need to shower and change my clothes. We move through the office, and I head toward the executive bathroom, knowing there will be a shower. Coleman calls out that he'll grab my bag from the car, which has a change of clothes inside.

Moments later, I'm freshly showered, my bloodied suit with the body as the cleaners arrive. We leave, knowing that they will have everything perfect and the surveillance tapes erased within the hour. My father is nothing but meticulous when he has his cleanup crew trained.

"I think we're going to have Chinese," Coleman murmurs as he starts the car's engine.

"Why's that?" I ask.

He shifts the car into *Reverse* and backs out of his parking spot before he clears his throat and moves forward. "I don't know. Call it a hunch."

Leaning back in the seat, I close my eyes for a moment and instantly, my vision is filled with an image of *her*. Haunting green eyes, innocent and yet not. I can't get her out of my head. I want to see her again.

I want to fuck her.

I will have her.

THREE

WELLS

PASTA WAS A GOOD GUESS. CHINESE WAS BETTER, BUT WE HAVE neither for dinner tonight. My mother picked up Greek, which is surprising, but I'm not complaining because it's one of my favorites. I couldn't even begin to pronounce any of the food I love, but online ordering comes in clutch with that shit.

In my mind, I would like to think that we are cultured because we have money, but there are some things you cannot buy. Fortunately, we have enough money that nobody mentions the fact that we are not cultured at all.

Sitting down in my place, I take the napkin and place it on my lap. Once a week, since we've been teenagers, my mother demands we be home for dinner. It didn't matter what sport we played, what date we had planned, or what job we were working for the family. It was nonnegotiable and still is.

"To family," my dad announces as he lifts his glass.

"Family," we all repeat in unison and take a drink of wine.

Red wine.

Always.

"Tell me something about your day," my mother says as soon as the toast and drink are finished.

She asks this every week. When we were kids, she asked this every night at the dinner table. No phones are allowed, no television, just the five of us conversing and always something productive.

Stabbing some lamb with my fork, I bring it to my lips, then shove it into my mouth so I don't have to speak first. Coleman growls under his breath, knowing that by default, he will have to go first because he's the oldest.

I feel his foot slam into my shin, and I snort but smile as I continue to chew. Only at my mother's table do we turn into children again. It's almost comical. Every week, it's the same shit over and over.

"I broke it off with that girl I was seeing," Coleman states.

I hadn't known that he actually broke things off with her. I knew he was pissed that Dad wanted him to marry her, but I didn't think he'd already done it. Shifting my attention to our dad, I watch as his eyes narrow, but only slightly.

"Are you upset about it?" Mom asks.

Shrugging his shoulder, Coleman reaches for his wineglass and brings it to his lips before taking a sip. "I'm not. She was not anyone I saw a future with," he replies, his gaze cutting to Dad's. I see Dad's eye twitch.

Coleman is so fucking fucked when Dad gets him away from Mom. He's going to beat the absolute shit out of him. Clearing my throat, I shift in my seat slightly. I should probably try and save him from this conversation, but I'm enjoying it far too much.

"You'd been seeing her for months, correct?" Mom asks.

"Drop it," Dad growls.

My gaze flicks back and forth between Mom, Dad, and Coleman, loving every fucking second of this shit. It's nice that it's not me in the hot seat because, typically, it is. I'm always fucking shit up, always causing problems, and as the middle child, it's expected, if not anticipated.

"Hendrick, you've been quiet, and I haven't seen much of you lately. Care to explain? Is it work that keeps you so busy?" she asks, shifting her attention from Coleman to the youngest brother, Hendrick, glossing over me, and I'm happy as fuck about it.

I almost laugh because, as a leader, Hendrick is busy with work but not as busy as he probably could be. He's still just twenty-two, and he has discovered that his good looks, money, and earned cockiness can get pussy thrown at him. I remember being the same way at his age. Hell, I'm still that way.

"Just been busy," Hendrick mutters. "Working and stuff."

Coleman snorts at the word *stuff*. I don't blame him. I swallow my food, ready to stab another piece, when my mom shifts her questioning to me. "Wells?" she asks.

Exhaling a breath, I lift my gaze to meet hers. She doesn't say anything. She's got some salad on her fork, her gaze never leaving mine, her brow arched as she waits. I'm sure she thinks she's somehow figured something out about me. Perhaps she thinks she's unlocked some sort of secret.

I have no idea.

It's my mom, and while she hasn't used us as experiments, it's clear she uses her tips and tricks on us without even trying. She's always been kind and considerate. Has never been cruel or intentionally done anything to mess with our heads, but when this is your job, you know how to speak to people to get information out of them, and she is a master.

"Who was that girl in your office today?" I ask.

I may as well just be honest and open. My mom doesn't beat around the bush in any way, so being indirect does not always work.

"You know I cannot discuss patients with you," she says.

Lifting my fork, I give her a smile before I stab another piece of lamb. "I know, but you will because you love me. Plus, you know that what happens at the family table stays at the family table."

"It does, but this is different," she murmurs.

"Brenda," my dad warns.

My mom shakes her head, lifting her wineglass to her lips. "Rules are rules. My ethics are not something I am willing to compromise for someone you wish to have a dalliance with."

I chuckle at her word—*dalliance*. I love her. She's the best and always keeping us boys, now men, on our toes. Like using completely outdated words that have no damn reason being used in a daily conversation, but she always finds a way.

I don't respond to her, knowing she'll give me the information I want later, and if she doesn't, I'll just find a way into her office to figure it out myself. It's not like it's difficult. Along with using unreasonable verbiage on a regular basis, my mother always keeps everything written down on paper, including all of her session notes.

"All right, then," I murmur, but I haven't let it go, and she knows this.

The rest of the evening, our conversation turns trivial, and by the time our food is finished and cleaned up, everything that seemed strained in the beginning vanishes. We are now a family, as always. Joking, laughing, and then we stand and make our way into the kitchen.

Me and my brothers get to work on the dishes, a chore that has been ours since we were kids. We make quick work of them with my parents sitting at the bar watching us, the conversation flowing throughout the room.

I'm not sure what it means. If there is anything better. But I do know there are people on this Earth who would kill for this. I would kill for the people in this room. And I can't wait until we fill this place with even more laughter in the future.

Someday.

Perhaps sooner rather than later.

PARKER

DAY two of not leaving this condo, and I should probably feel as if the walls are closing in on me, but I don't. In fact, I could stay here for probably a year before I felt like I needed to venture out into the world.

And this is why I seek counseling and not just online counseling anymore. I could stay in my place and never leave. I would be perfectly content to do it, too. Not seeing another human sounds almost like a version of heaven.

So, I made the appointment, and it took me an entire month, but I made it to her office, and I even spoke with her. But now I need a few days to decompress. It's not that I'm afraid of being out in the world, but I know I could easily stay away from the world and be happy.

I am afraid of what could happen in the future.

The very near future.

My phone buzzes on the small table next to my adult beanbag chair, a chair that I'm sure has an imprint of my butt on it by now. Reaching over, I glance at the caller ID and let out a sigh. It's my friend Allison.

I think about ignoring the call. I even set the phone down, trying to forget it's there. But it buzzes against the table, so I decide to pick it up and answer it.

I don't know why, but this feels important. Allison is a texter, and to have her call me just sends alarm bells throughout my entire body. She'll send me a million long-winded paragraphs before she'll call. This must be important.

I slide my thumb across the screen, then lift it to my ear. As I open my mouth to say hello, I am cut off before I can say anything. She lets out a wail so loud that I have to pull the phone away from my ear for a moment.

When she's finished, I place it back and ask her what's going on. I'm thinking that something happened to one of her parents, maybe a sibling. My heart races in my chest at the thought of some devastating accident or illness.

But then she lets out another wail before she speaks. When she does, she hiccups three times before any words come out. "Well," she exhales, "I lost my job this afternoon."

I don't know why I ask her *how* because I'm pretty sure I already know, but I do anyway.

"How?"

"Well," she snaps, "the boss's wife found out, and shit hit the fan. So, the bitch gave him an ultimatum. Me or her. I wasn't holding my breath for him to choose me or anything, but he answered far too fucking quickly for my personal taste."

I can tell she's annoyed and angry, but I know it's because of how quickly he made the decision. She felt like nothing when he'd been telling her something different for months. And even if she won't admit it, she had wanted it to be her. She wanted to be chosen.

"Shit," I hiss.

Allison has been having an affair with her very married boss for months. She's a secretary to the president of a bank. The affair lasted for a whole year, and I can't believe in all that time, she stayed quiet enough that it took the wife this long to find out.

Every chance I got, I told her to break it off with him, walk away and forget he existed, but I think she loved being the other woman. I think she enjoyed the game, the cat-and-mouse chase, the feeling of being in charge.

The control.

That is something I can understand, which is probably why I never truly pushed the issue, even though I didn't agree with any of it at all. She's an adult. She can make her own decisions. Plus, it's not like I'm really someone who can say anything. I've never even been kissed.

"Let's go out tonight," she says, snapping out of her funk, which tells me she wasn't really in love. She's just mad that her playtime was interrupted. Honestly, I don't know why I'm friends with her.

Allison and I knew each other before either of us knew that boys were cute. We've been best friends since the fourth grade. We played Barbies together, although hers were always dating boys, having sex, and pole dancing, while mine were driving around in the Porsche, the one where the lights really turned on.

It was amazing.

Everything about Barbie was amazing, and I miss the way it made me feel.

We left home and went to college together, where we were roommates, and we're still best friends.

"Where do you want to go?" I ask, shaking thoughts of Barbie away as new anxious images of crowded clubs fill my head. I know that's where she'll want to go because that's always what she chooses when she needs to let off steam.

"A club, duh. Except, I found a new one that I want to try."

"I'm not sure..." My words trail off, but Allison lets out a growl, and I snap my lips closed.

"You're going," she states. "I'll be there in two hours, and we'll have fun, I promise." I almost laugh at her. I've heard that promise before, and not once has it lived up to the hype.

There is no bar, no club around Dallas that I haven't been to with her. It's always some sweaty club with cheap drinks and creeps who come up behind you and shove their crotch against your ass cheek in a failed attempt to dance.

"Okay," I sigh. "I'll do it, but just know it's under protest."

"See you in a couple hours," she quips before she ends the call.

Tossing the phone back onto the table, I lean back in my chair with a heavy sigh. Going out to a club is the last thing I want to do, especially after the stressful therapy session. Well, the session wasn't stressful. Getting and staying there was my issue.

However, I support my friends. Always. They're the only family I have right now. Well, since I was a little girl. My aunt and uncle don't really count. They made sure I was fed and clothed, but that's about as far as they went. I haven't even heard from either of them since the day I packed my things and went away to college… a whole two hours from *home*.

Friends are my only family, and thankfully, they're very understanding because I am not an easy friend to have. I prefer solitude. I never like to go places. It's like pulling teeth to get me to go anywhere, but I would do absolutely anything for any of them.

CHAPTER
FOUR

WELLS

"Boys," my father barks as soon as dinner is finished and we've relaxed by the gas fireplace, drinking more wine and chatting among one other. The relaxation hour is now finished.

It is time for business.

My mother sighs and lifts her hand, waving us away. "Fine. Go with your father. My time with you is complete. I'm going to go upstairs, finish my bottle of wine, and take a nice long bath," she murmurs.

She stands, reaching to the side table, and wraps her fingers around the neck of the bottle as she picks it up. I watch her for a moment as she moves through the formal living room. She stops and looks over her shoulder at me.

Her eyes find mine, and she holds my gaze before she lets out a heavy sigh. She's had enough to drink now that her lips are a little looser than they were a few hours ago when I asked about the girl in her office.

I almost ask again about her but decide against it. I'll stick with my original plan of breaking into her office and stealing what I want from her planner. It's illegal, an invasion of privacy, and an asshole move, but I don't really give a shit. That feeling of guilt and morality left my soul a long time ago.

"Wells," my mother calls out.

She gives me a wide smile, one that I know means she's had a bit too much to drink. I almost laugh. Unlike some people, my mother is a fun drunk. She's usually not someone who does silly things, except when she's had too much to drink.

"Mom?" I ask when she doesn't speak right away.

Her lips curve up into a smirk. "I don't know her well, but I just wanted to say she's my patient, and of course, that means she has her own set of issues, but it's nothing I would ever be too concerned with."

Then she turns her back to me and continues on her way, up the stairs and toward her waiting warm bath, likely a book, and her wine. My father barks my name from his office, and I know he's impatiently waiting for me.

Hurrying toward the room, not wishing to be further on his bad side, I close the door behind me and make my way to the sofa before sinking down onto the leather seat. In my father's home, in his office, we all have our places. This is my seat; Coleman's is in the other corner of the sofa, and Hendrick leans against the wall.

"Dead men do not pay," my dad announces.

I know exactly what he's referring to, and I knew this would come up. I am not surprised, and I already have a response at the ready. He's not wrong—they do not pay what they owe.

However…

"Dead men can sign over their vacation homes that are worth the same amount they owe us, though," I state.

"Before they die, of course," Coleman murmurs.

"Of course," I agree.

Our dad leans back in his chair, his gaze flicking between us, then he lets out a sigh. "You two believe you've thought of everything, don't you?" he asks. "But have you thought about the wife, the kids? Do you think they'll believe he just signed everything over to you? Plus, doesn't that look like the family had something to do with his death?"

I would laugh, except I don't because that would be gloating, and gloating was beaten out of me when I was about fourteen years old. Being cocky is one thing. Gloating is another. The latter is forbidden. For an organization that is all about illegal activities, we have a lot of fucking rules.

"It's already been filed with the county and country where the properties are located. The documents have been notarized," I say.

There is a moment of silence in which my dad places his elbows on the table, his eyes searching mine. "You have done your due diligence. I appreciate that," he murmurs.

I know there is a *but* coming. I can tell by his tone. So, instead of trying to explain myself, I wait for the *but* to come. And he does not disappoint. He stands and walks over to his window, and I know he is going to make a big fucking deal about this shit. I look at Coleman and roll my eyes.

He snorts right before our dad turns around, his gaze flicking between us. Hendrick is out of the equation, mainly because he was likely fucking some random bitch while this shit was going down. Plus, he's the baby and only a leader. He doesn't have the same kind of responsibilities or bullshit that we have to deal with.

Sometimes, I wish I could go back to being a leader. It

was enough responsibility, but not too much. I liked it. The power felt good, but I knew I didn't have too much on my shoulders. Now, it seems if I fart the wrong way, my dad is up my ass to correct it.

"But," he continues, "I wish you would have consulted with me. Next time, I expect to have a conversation before anything permanent or irreversible is done, yes?"

Without even a blink, without even a thought, all three of us say in unison, "Yes, Director."

This is who we are, our father's well-trained machines. "You're good boys," he murmurs. "Now, the next issue at hand," he states. "Marriage."

I watch as Dad makes his way back to his desk to sit down before he clears his throat and arches a brow in Coleman's direction. I almost laugh, glad to have this conversation not include me again.

Coleman groans, but Dad's gaze snaps to his. "And *you* are fucking pissing me off about that."

There is only a moment of silence before Coleman stands to his feet. He walks over to the desk and places his hands on the wooden top. I watch him, wondering what the fuck he's thinking.

Nobody charges toward our father, not in anger, not in excitement, not in anything, and this man is doing it boldly, although we're not in mixed company, so maybe that's what has him so brave. It's just the four of us men, no other family around to witness.

"I do not want her. She's been used, tainted. I want the virgin, the prize that is owed to me that I earned."

Our dad smirks. He tilts his head to the side as if he finds this not only funny but also interesting. I find it humorous, though likely not for the same reason that he does. So, instead of laughing, I decide to watch and take notes because once Coleman is married off, I know he'll be looking to me next.

"Seems as though you're a man after my own heart. So, you do not love this one. I made a very good case for you with the father," he murmurs.

"I do not want her for my wife—for *mine*."

"Then you will not have her, but you will choose a wife. It is time. You will be thirty in six months' time."

"And when I'm thirty?" Coleman asks.

Dad laughs softly. "You'll be declared an executive. It's time. Fifteen years in the family earns you something, and you've more than paid your dues and earned your place. You've passed all the tests and the levels."

Executive.

Five years.

I have five years until I am in Coleman's position. Which means I'll need to find a wife, settle, and then I can be an executive. I'm not sure how I feel about that. I should be excited, but part of me is anxious at the same time.

I want that, though. To be an executive. To have a wife that is mine, a woman to call my own, who is wholly and solely for myself and only myself. I don't care what kind of person that makes me sound like. The fuck of it is I am likely that exact person anyway.

I am part of the family, a high-ranking member, and I was promised a virgin wife to call my own. And much like Coleman, I expect that. There will be no other way around it. I am owed what I am owed, and I plan on cashing in when the time comes.

Happily.

PARKER

ALLISON'S KNOCK on my door is unmistakable. I know it's her as sure as I know that I don't want to go. Smoothing my palms down the front of my dress, I grab my purse and let out a heavy sigh. I shouldn't be so annoyed, but I wanted to stay in my chair and not move all weekend.

Making my way toward the door, I hear my heels click against the marble flooring and reach for the doorknob. I still can't believe I have this condo. It's so fancy, too fancy for me, but I love everything about it, and it's paid off.

Twisting the handle, I open the door and plaster on a smile. Allison rolls her eyes. "This isn't torture. We're going to have fun," she states.

She can read me in seconds, which should be annoying as hell, but it's not. At least not usually. Tonight's not going to be fun, and it might be actual torture. I know it is. There's no other way around it. I don't want to go to some club where people are going to be dancing, touching, bumping, and grinding... *everywhere.*

"Let's just go," I mutter.

Allison rolls her eyes again. I reach for my purse on the side table, then move through the door and into the hall. Turning, I lock my door behind me.

My building is extremely safe, and half of the people who live here don't even lock their doors, but considering my anxiety and nightmares about someone watching over me while I sleep, I always lock my door. Always.

"Tell me about your appointment today. Did you go into the building?"

Nodding once, I sink my teeth into my bottom lip and scrape it across to find some dead skin, but there is nothing. I think about telling her absolutely nothing, but I know that if I ignore the question, she'll just continue to ask me over and over.

There's no ignoring Allison.

"I made it into her office. I told her about the dream." I say the words, and all seems good.

I'm sure I should go into detail about the session. She no doubt wants to hear it all, but I'm not going to say a word. It's true that Allison knows all the same information as I do. She has been over more than once to pick me up off the floor after sinking down in a fit of rage, emotional crying, or whatever the case may be. She's always been just a second away.

I realize I'm not a good friend to her. Not like she is to me. I stop in my tracks. We're just a few steps from the exit, but I turn to Allison. Slowly, she faces me, her gaze searching my own as I whisper.

"I'm a terrible friend," I exhale. "I'm always focused on my own neuroses, and I've yet to ask about your man situation, about your life right now." Allison reaches for my hand, squeezing It gently.

"There is nothing to apologize for. Do you think I don't know exactly who you are? Don't you think that if I had an emergency, I know I could call you and you would drop everything to help me?"

My lips curve into a small smile. "You know I would," I reply.

She squeezes my hand once more, then releases it as she takes a single step forward. "I know you would. And that's why you're here right now. Because you know I need this, and you're the only person I want to go out with tonight."

Even though this is not what I want to do at all, whatsoever. I would rather be sitting in my comfy chair, in my underwear, reading a spicy romance novel. But I am here with Allison, my best friend, dressed and ready for an evening that I want nothing to do with.

Together, we continue out of the building and toward her car, which is waiting at the curb. Something causes my steps to falter. Stopping at the passenger side of the door, I look down the sidewalk in each direction, expecting to find someone there watching me, but there is nobody.

I look over my shoulder to glance back at the building. Again, nobody. I can't shake the feeling, though. Someone's eyes are on me. I know what it feels like to be watched, that sensation I had as a little girl, waking up to see someone watching me. It's not something you can easily shake off or forget about.

And I feel it right now.

Opening the door to her car, I try to ignore the feeling, the way the hairs on the back of my neck stand at attention and my spine tingles, but I can't. Either someone is watching me, or I'm about to get struck by lightning, and since there isn't a cloud in the sky, I'm going with someone watching me.

"Are you coming?" Allison calls out.

My entire body jerks once, then I give her a smile and shake off the thoughts I was focusing on. Sinking down into the seat of her car, I close the door and glance around again, hoping to find someone walking down the street or something, but again, there's nothing.

"Let's go."

"You good?" she asks.

Nodding once, I smile. "Yeah," I lie.

CHAPTER
FIVE

WELLS

"You breaking into Mom's office tonight to get that girl's number?" Hendrick asks as soon as we step outside the house.

Coleman chuckles beside me, but I can tell he's lost in his own thoughts. Dad is going to send him a dossier of women to look at. I'm not sure if that's what I want for myself. It's a list of women who are basically available for purchase. There's something that doesn't sit right with me about that.

Not that I'm some man with a moral high ground. I'm not. I just want the fear in their eyes to be about what my cock is going to do to their virgin snatch, not if I'm going to kill them when I'm done with them.

Although, that wouldn't be bad either if I were being honest. Fear can be a great fucking turn-on, but I don't think I would want the woman who I am supposed to share my life with, the woman who is going to have my kids, to be physically fucking horrified by me. So, maybe I'll try to find my own virgin to keep.

Maybe it'll be this girl.

Maybe not.

Probably not.

"You wanna help me?" I ask, shifting my attention over to Hendrick.

He grins. "I do this; we go out tonight?"

"Coleman, you in?" I ask.

Coleman is a few steps ahead of us. He turns his head, his eyes finding mine. I can tell he isn't thrilled about dumping his piece of ass. It's not that he scraped her off. It's because Dad tried to make him marry her. I think that's what's bothering him the most in this situation.

My brother is very much a Hamilton. He doesn't like being told what to do… ever. Even if it's what he does *want* to do, he will bow the fuck up and not do it out of stubborn spite. If you ever want a Hamilton to do something, try to force him to do the opposite.

"Let's do it. I need a fucking drink after the day I had, anyway."

Hendrick smirks, and I shake my head. I shouldn't think this sounds like a great fucking time, breaking into Mom's office, then going out drinking with my brothers, but it is. "Meet at the office, then we'll go to my place and leave for the club in one car?"

Coleman clears his throat. "I don't plan on going home tonight, so I'll take my own ride."

"Same," Hendrick says.

Chuckling, I realize it sounds like a great fucking plan. "Sounds good. See you at Mom's."

Without another word, the three of us climb into our cars and take off toward the downtown Dallas area. Pulling up to Mom's office building, I park against the curb of the back alleyway, knowing there aren't any street cameras there, but there are building ones.

Hendrick and Coleman are close behind me, and we all three exit our vehicles, then walk up to the building.

"You got Mom's building camera info?" Coleman asks, turning to look at Hendrick.

Hendrick is a nerd, always has been, but it's worked out in our favor because he's been able to do a lot of shit that we couldn't even pretend to be able to do. That includes jamming surveillance and security camera systems.

"Jammed," Hendrick states as he shoves his phone into his pocket.

Coleman shoves a key into the back door, but before he opens it, he looks back at Hendrick. "Alarm?"

"Do you think this is amateur hour?" he asks. "I did that before I fucked with the security computer system."

Coleman turns the key, opens the door, and together, the three of us walk into the building. Luckily, this isn't one of the buildings that has or needs twenty-four-seven security. My mom's office is upstairs, but the rest of the offices are much like hers—psychologists, real estate offices, things like that.

Coleman locks the door behind us, and we move toward the staircase to make our way up to her floor. Thankfully, she's not all the way at the top, so it doesn't take us long to climb the staircase. Moving down her hallway, we stop in front of her doorway, and I watch as Coleman lifts a key, slips it inside of the lock, and turns it to unlock the office door itself. He has a master key to all the offices, and Mom's is no exception. A perk of the family owning the building.

Stepping into the room, I flip the light on. "Mom will have it written down in her calendar," I state.

"Just make sure you don't move anything. She'd know if someone moved a paper clip a millimeter," Coleman mutters.

I would laugh, except he's right. My mom is a perfectionist when it comes to her office space and her appearance. I don't know that it bleeds over into any other part of her life, but work, clothes, and makeup are always on point.

As I walk toward her desk, my eyes scan the top before I touch anything. Her appointment book is sitting right on top. Without moving anything but the pages, I open it and flip to today, finding the time I was here.

Parker Nichols.

My lips curve up into a grin. "Parker Nichols," I murmur loud enough for my brothers to hear.

Taking my phone out of my pocket, I take a picture of the entry, although I don't think I'll forget that name. It's different and intriguing. I won't forget it.

Hendrick is at the filing cabinet, and he tugs it open before he begins to riffle through it. "Found her notes."

Closing the book, I turn my head to look over to my brother. He's holding up the notebook on Parker. "Want to know how fucked up she is?" he asks.

"Go for it," I say, but I probably shouldn't.

These are her personal things, thoughts, feelings, and my mom's notes. Things that only my mother is supposed to know. It's like reading a diary entry or some shit. However, that doesn't stop Hendrick. He clears his throat and begins.

"Parker Nichols suffers from anxiety due to her trauma as a small child. She awoke to a man standing over her when she was asleep. He was dressed in a dark suit. He did not harm her, but she believes he is the person who killed her parents, as after he left, she said it was discovered that her parents had been killed. Although she believes this man was involved, he did not scare her."

Coleman grunts, then Hendrick continues, "Mom scribbled some shit down at the bottom in the corner, but it's just a name and a question mark."

"What's that?" I ask.

"It says, *Henry?*"

Henry. "Like, as in Dad?" Coleman asks.

"I don't know. I'm assuming. That's weird, though, right?" I ask.

"Maybe..." Coleman's voice trails off. Then he lifts his head, his eyes finding mine. "Anything else you need?" he asks.

"Nope," I say, popping the *p*. "Let's roll."

We leave the office, lock everything up tight, and once we're driving away from the building, Hendrick unjams everything he jammed when we arrived. We all run home to change and shower before heading to the club, but I use my time to look up Parker Nichols, and I discover that she only lives a few blocks from me.

The temptation is too great. I must see her.

Now.

PARKER

THAT FEELING of being watched washes over me yet again. I don't know if I should be scared or comforted. I'm in public at this club, so I don't feel scared... *yet*. But it's strange. I haven't felt this in years. *Why now?*

"You good?" Allison asks as she shoves a glass into my hand.

I don't bother even looking at the contents. I know it's water. I don't drink much. Not that I think there is anything wrong with alcohol. I just don't like to drink it very often. Although maybe I should tonight because I can't shake that feeling, and I'm getting a little annoyed with it all.

I'm pretty sure it's anxiety.

I mean, at this point, everything wrong with me is probably some form of anxiety.

That meeting with the psychologist got me all stirred up, and I'm even feeling a little shaky. I wonder if that's the reason I have that sensation of being watched, that it's all in my head. My anxiety taking control and taking over. I wonder if I should call Doctor Hamilton about this. My thoughts quickly vanish when I realize I've been lost in my head, and Allison's been waiting for an answer.

"I'm good," I lie.

She smiles and shakes her head once. "You aren't," she whispers. "But you will be. I can feel it."

Lifting the glass of water to my lips, I take a drink. Together, we move toward an empty pub table. Placing my glass down, I let out a sigh, giving Allison my biggest fake smile. She knows that it's fake, too, but she has the decency not to say anything, probably because she's wearing one herself.

"Do you want to talk about it more?" I'm trying to change the subject and take the focus off me.

She shakes her head. "What's there to tell?" she asks. "I was fucking a married man and got caught. I knew it was a possibility. I knew it could happen. And I did it where I worked. My boss. Which makes it a million times worse because now I'm jobless."

"But?" I ask.

She shrugs a shoulder. "I needed it to happen. He had this hold on me. I don't know how I let it happen. I didn't love him. I mean, I loved fucking him, but I didn't love him as a person. He's nobody I would want to be with. He's a cheater."

Picking up my glass, I take another sip and try not to laugh. I know she liked him. Even if she didn't love him, she liked him a lot.

"So, what happens now?" I ask.

There is a moment of silence. The bass from the music bumps in the room. I can feel it throughout my entire body. Placing my hand against the center of my chest, I feel it pounding. *Thump, thump, thump.*

Over and over.

It beats in my eardrums, and I wonder why people like this. All it does is cause me to feel like I want to run. Hard and fast. I'm here for Allison, though, so I don't do that. Instead, I attempt to give her all my attention.

Allison shrugs a shoulder, then looks down into her martini glass before she lifts her attention to meet mine. "I'm going to figure it out. That's not the only job in the world, but tonight, I want to drink a little, dance a lot, and have some fun."

She lifts the glass to her lips, swallows the contents whole, and reaches for my wrist, tugging me behind her as she moves toward the floor. I hate the dance floor. I hate the random men who dance with me.

I hate it all, but for Allison, I will do it… just tonight.

CHAPTER
SIX

WELLS

SHE STEPS OUT OF HER CONDO BUILDING WITH ANOTHER woman around her age. They're both dressed for a night out on the town. She's gorgeous. Even if I think her dress is a little short to go out without a man on her arm. She almost looks like a different person from earlier, all dressed and made up. But her eyes... They're the same.

Parker stops at the car door, looking left, then right. She senses my eyes on her. She's aware. That's good. I don't want a fucking oblivious bitch. Her friend says something to her, and I watch as her spine straightens, then she sinks down into the front seat and closes the door, glancing around again right before the car takes off.

Keeping a close eye on the car, I take in the license plate, then text the number to Hendrick before I shift my car into *Drive* and follow it. A few moments later, Hendrick calls me. I'm only a few blocks over, parking at the garage across from one of the more decent clubs in town. Not exclusive, but it's not necessarily easy to get into either.

I watch as the two breeze right inside without even waiting in the mile-long line, mainly because they are both hot as sin. My phone rings. Sliding my thumb across the screen, I clear my throat before I say Hendrick's name.

"Owner is a drop-dead gorgeous blonde named Allison. She works at a bank, in the office part. Secretary to the president. Been fucking him for a few years. Guy's married. She got fired today. I'm going to go ahead and assume that the wife found out."

"I don't want to know how you got all of that information in just seconds," I mutter.

He chuckles. "Where are we meeting? I need to go to a club and get laid. Dinner with Mom and Dad always fucks me up."

I don't ask him why. I know it's because he's the baby, and he feels as if he can't live up to me and Coleman's shadows or some shit. But he doesn't see it yet, doesn't realize that he is without a doubt the smartest member of the family right now, especially when it comes to this tech shit. Computers, research, intel in general. He will, though. He will come into himself. He's just young. Soon, he'll realize how much value he has.

"We're going to Club Nova," I reply.

He clears his throat. "Why there?" he asks.

Though, I can tell he already knows. He's probably got a tracker on me or some shit. I wouldn't put it past him at all. Actually, I wouldn't put it past my fucking dad. Mainly because I don't put shit past Dad.

"You know why," I grind out.

"I got dibs on the blonde," he says with a chuckle.

"May have to fight Coleman for her," I say.

He growls, but he doesn't say anything. He ends the call,

and I stay in my car, waiting for them to show up. Hendrick must call Coleman because less than five minutes later, I see both of their cars pulling into the parking lot and parking on either side of mine.

I chose, and always choose, the farthest spot away to give me plenty of room and ambiguity. They do the same, taught to us by our father, by the family. When they turn their engines off, I open my door and unfold from the car.

The three of us adjust the jackets of our suits, and together, we make our way toward the door. One foot in front of the other, past the line of mediocre people waiting to enter. They won't gain entrance. It is not for them. They'd be better off going to a sports bar or something.

"Your name on the list?" the bouncer asks as we approach him.

Coleman takes a step forward, his eyes boring into the bouncer's. "Do we look like we need our names anywhere or that we'd even give you our names?" he asks.

The bouncer flicks his gaze to each of us, then, without saying a word, shifts to the side and allows us to pass through. Wordlessly, we walk through the club. I don't look for Parker, even though that is all I want to do. Instead, we make our way to the bar and order drinks.

Women and men both watch us as we move across the floor. We're on everyone's radar. It's not lost on me that not only do my brothers and I exude a sense of power and masculinity along with an air of mystery that most people are drawn to, but we are also not bad looking.

The people who have been hovering around the bar move away as soon as we arrive. There's something about the men we are. It's as if they know without a doubt that we could kill them all in about five seconds if we wanted to. Not that we would, but it doesn't take away from the fact that we very well *could*.

"Help you?" the bartender asks.

"Three Pappy Van Winkles, neat," I call out, ordering three whiskeys for me and my brothers.

The bartender jerks his chin before he turns his back to us and begins to prepare our drinks. Turning around, I face the dance floor, hoping to catch a glimpse of her. I know she'll stand out to me. Those big green eyes of hers are unmistakable.

"You know what you're looking for?" Coleman asks, turning, he hands me a glass of whiskey.

I take a drink as I scan the room, then I find her. A blonde and a brunette. The blonde wearing a bright-red dress that screams for attention. The brunette wearing a simple black dress that is a little shorter and tighter than I would prefer she go out in alone, although I know I technically have zero fucking say about that... yet.

"That's them," I say over the thumping bass of the music.

Hendrick whistles, and before I can tell them anything else, he's gone. I watch as he moves toward the women. There is a light that shines in the middle of the dance floor, and it's almost as if it highlights just the two women.

"I'd peg you for wanting the blonde," Coleman states.

Turning from the women, I look at him. He's watching them with a disinterested gaze. It's almost as if he is staring in their direction but doesn't see them. He doesn't see anything, and I know he's still thinking about the woman he broke it off with and Dad's demands. Plus, the woman he's going to choose. He's got a lot to think about. Picking the wrong woman could be a fucking nightmare.

"Something about the brunette's eyes," I mutter.

"If you want her, then you better get over there because the hungry animals have started circling."

Shifting my attention back to the dance floor, I see exactly what Coleman is talking about. There are four hungry wolves, and they all have eyes on my woman. She's tempting. Her body sways to the music like a gazelle, enticing the beasts to a feast.

Except they won't get her. They are nothing but hyenas.

I am the lion.

And I always catch my prey.

PARKER

ALLISON DRAGS me onto the dance floor, and the music shifts as soon as we step onto the polished concrete floor. It moves from quick and upbeat to a sultry tone. I'm not sure what to do since I don't want to sexy dance with myself... or anyone, really.

I watch as a guy with short, dark hair brushes past me and heads straight toward Allison. He's tall and broad. His arms and legs are lanky, though, like maybe he's still in his early twenties. I don't know what I'm even thinking because *I'm* in my early twenties.

They begin to dance, and it's hot. I can only see his back, but her eyes find me as she straddles his thigh and she widens them. Her lips part, and she smiles.

Oh, she likes him.

That's good.

That is why we're here.

Maybe I'll be able to leave early if she's already found what she is looking for.

I start to move off the floor, mainly because I'm not sexy dancing by myself, and I don't want a random guy to shove his junk between my ass cheeks, so I'm going to sit down at our little pub table and maybe read on my phone app.

Taking one step backward, I feel a hard wall behind me.

Then, two hands grip my hips, and warmth slides from my ears down my neck.

"Dance with me."

It isn't a question. It's a demand, and it's sexy as sin. I'm not someone who dances with random men, but I want to with this one. Sliding my tongue along my bottom lip, I start to turn around, but his fingers grip my hips tighter.

"No faces, just dancing."

Why is that sexy?

I'm not sure, but it is. For the first time in my entire life, I throw a little caution to the wind and I dance with a stranger. He's behind me. His torso presses against my back, his hands never leaving my hips, and inwardly, I beg for him to touch me, somewhere, anywhere.

He doesn't.

The music stays sexy and sultry, each song after the next. Closing my eyes, I lean my head back against his chest and turn my face into his neck. Inhaling like a total creep, I smell him, and he *smells* amazing.

His scent is a mix of spicy, rich alcohol, like whiskey, and an oak barrel with spices. I don't know; it's hard to pinpoint it exactly, but it's perfect and masculine. It's not overpowering—it's sensual and sexy. It's in control, just the way he is.

I don't know how I got all of that from a few words, his hands gripping my hips, and his scent, but I did. I'm not sure how long we dance. It goes on for song after song after song. Then I feel a hand touch my shoulder, and I turn my head to look over and see Allison and her guy standing beside me.

"I'm going to head out. Are you good to get home?" she asks. "If not, he said he'd take you home." She jerks her thumb toward the very handsome tall stranger beside her. My eyes widen. I flick my attention from her to him, then back to her.

"She'll get home just fine," the voice behind me growls.

Alarm bells start to ring. I open my mouth to tell Allison to not go anywhere with some guy she just met, but no words come out. Allison lifts her hand and waves before she hooks her arm in his, and together, they disappear into the crowd.

I try to take a step away from the brick wall that still has me held tightly to his body, but I can't go anywhere. His fingers tense against my hips, and I feel his breath against my ear again. "I'll make sure you get home safe, cupcake."

Cupcake?

I don't think anyone has ever, not ever, called me any kind of nickname.

Opening my mouth, I start to ask him how he's going to make sure that I get home safely because there is no way in hell I'm going to go home with him. But before I can say a single word, he begins to whisper in my ear.

"A driver will be waiting for you outside after one more dance."

One of his hands finally, *finally* leaves my hip and slides up the center of my body, between my breasts and against my chest, before his fingers wrap around the front of my throat. At the same time, his lips touch the shell of my ear. A shiver of desire slides down my spine.

I've never felt this way before.

Yearning. Craving. Longing.

I want this man to touch me—*everywhere*.

I need to run, but I can't move. I'm frozen in place.

CHAPTER
SEVEN

WELLS

ONE MORE DANCE.

Then, the car will be waiting outside for her, which will be Coleman in the driver's seat. I'm hoping he will be able to get some information out of her that I cannot find online, in bank statements, or going through her phone. Although, Hendrick seems to be a wealth of unattainable knowledge.

When the song ends, I release her tender throat. I could have killed her in seconds. She allowed me to wrap my fingers around her neck, such a vulnerability, and I'm not sure she realized exactly what she was giving me, but I aim to take it.

And take.

And take.

Until there is nothing left.

Then I'll be done with her and ready for my bride.

"The car will be out front," I rasp. "Until next time, cupcake."

Walking away from her, I slip into the crowd. I make sure I'm hidden, although she has no idea what I look like. I watch as she spins around and tries to find me. Frantically, her eyes search the crowd in hopes of finding the man she's danced with all night long.

"Give her a ride home, act like you're an Uber?" I ask, even though it's not a question. "She'll recognize my voice."

"I don't understand. Why don't you just do what Hendrick did with the friend?" Coleman asks.

My lips curve up into a grin. "It's much more fun this way, brother."

Coleman rolls his eyes to the ceiling, giving me a smirk before he jogs away and out of the club. Shifting my attention back to Parker, I watch as she looks around for another moment, then her shoulders drop, and she heads for the door.

I don't take my eyes off her. I watch as she slips out the door, then look at my phone and wait until Coleman texts me. A few moments later, my phone buzzes with a new text.

> BROTHER 1: The package is safe. Meet at my place in thirty.

> SEE YOU THEN.

Leaving the club, I jog toward my own car and reach for the door just as my phone rings. Looking at the caller ID, I frown at the sight of my father's name flashing on the screen. I slide my thumb across, lift the phone to my ear, and sink down in the front seat of the car, locking the door behind me.

"Dad?" I ask.

"I need you at the house. Coleman, too. Business."

I wonder if, somehow, he found out that we broke into Mom's office, but wouldn't he ask for Hendrick, too? I shake my head, clearing my throat.

"I'm on my way. What's this about?"

He hums, and I know I fucked up. You never, not ever, ask a man of the family what a meeting is going to be about or any type of business over the phone. I know that. I learned that when I was fifteen, and yet I still asked.

I open my mouth in an attempt to save myself, knowing I couldn't even if I had something quick-witted to bark out when my dad speaks.

"I am going to ignore that since this isn't a normal request. This is important business. I'll see you soon."

I start the car, shift it into *Reverse,* and call Coleman. It rings a few times. When he doesn't answer, I grunt, knowing he's probably still getting Parker home safely. Heading toward my parents', I hope Coleman calls me back before I get there.

It doesn't take long, only seconds, for him to call me back. I'm not even on the interstate yet. "Could you not wait for my call?" he barks.

"I could wait, but this isn't about that. Dad called. He wants us at the house."

There is a moment of silence. He doesn't say anything immediately. Instead, he growls as he drives. "What does he want?" Coleman snaps.

"Business is all I know, and it's just us."

"Only managers. This cannot be good."

I agree. It can't be. But we already got our asses handed to us over the way we handled shit earlier today. I can't imagine that our dad would give us another tongue-lashing so soon. I inhale a deep breath and let it out slowly.

"Just meet me there."

Ending the call, I drive straight toward my parents' house.

As soon as I pull into their circular drive, I'm not surprised to see that the only light on is in my father's office. My mom has probably had her bath, her wine, and read a page or two of a book and is completely passed out.

Staying in my car, I wait for Coleman to pull up next to me, but while I wait, I search for Parker Nichols online. It only takes me a moment, a second, until her name pops up with her social media pages.

Clicking on Instagram, I smirk that the whole thing is public. She doesn't have anything that really shows anything personal, though. There are artfully taken photos of coffee, books, skylines, sunsets, and sunrises.

She likes to read, and she enjoys pretty things. I can respect that, and it only makes her more intriguing to me. What she doesn't have are photos of friends, expensive jewelry, clothes, or vacations.

Frowning, I begin to delve deeper into her world as I continue to wait for Coleman. Something pops up, deep in the recesses of the internet, several pages into my search. A newspaper article. It's an archive, so it's not recent, but I notice the names, and it causes me pause.

DALLAS INVESTOR HUSBAND AND HEIRESS WIFE SLAIN WHILE DAUGHTER ASLEEP IN BED.

PARKER AND MELANIE NICHOLS MURDERED IN THEIR BED WHILE SIX-YEAR-OLD DAUGHTER PARKER NICHOLS WAS ASLEEP JUST MERE FEET AWAY DOWN THE HALL.

Parker was named for her father, but that isn't what catches my eye. Investor and heiress. Murdered in their beds. This sounds like it could very well be the family.

My heart begins to race as the implications of that, of this budding situationship with Parker, begin to grow. If she were to find out that the family had any ties to this, it could really fuck up the whole thing.

Maybe my mom was onto something when she wrote my dad's name at the bottom of her notes. Holy fucking shit. This could be family related.

A knock on my window causes me to jump, and I look over to see Coleman's smiling face staring at me from outside. Rolling my eyes, I open the door as he takes a step backward. I unfold from the car, clear my throat, and stand.

"She enjoys reading. She seems sweet. I'm not sure you should pursue this whole thing."

"Pursue?" He arches a brow, but he doesn't say anything. "I'm not pursuing shit. I am taking her."

"Wells," he murmurs.

Shaking my head once, I turn toward the house and start to move toward the door. I'm not sure what awaits us on the other side. Turning, I look back over my shoulder at my brother. "Don't worry about me, brother. I don't know what will become of me and Parker, but she intrigues me."

PARKER

STRIPPING OUT OF MY DRESS, I kick my high heels off and head toward the shower. The house is silent, but I can still feel the music pulsing throughout my entire body. My blood feels like it's pumping, my heart slamming with each beat.

I feel almost as if I'm high... if I knew what feeling high was like.

Reaching for the handle, I twist it to hot and wait for the shower to warm. It doesn't take long. When I feel the steam in the room, I shift the water temperature to the middle of the dial and step under the spray as it cools off.

I close my eyes and let the water wash over my face, my hair, and down my entire body. As I do, I imagine that the water is the stranger's hands. His fingers move over my body. I sink my teeth into my bottom lip and scrape the skin as my fingers slip between my thighs.

I don't really do this often, but I can't help myself. I've never felt this way before. I've never been so hot and bothered by anyone. Swirling my fingers around my clit, I whimper as the warmth of the water, the pressure of my fingertips consumes me.

My thighs tremble as I continue. It doesn't take me long. Considering I'm the only person who has ever touched my body, I know exactly what I want and how I want it. Closing my eyes, I rest my back against the tile as I lift one foot and place it on the bench.

Thrusting my hips forward, I can't stop, I can't help myself, I have to find my release. Gliding two fingers inside of myself, I press my palm against my clit and continue to thrust forward. The friction is delicious, and then I come.

It's hard and fast.

But even as I find my breaths coming out in pants, I still feel... empty.

I finish the shower by quickly washing my hair, then turn off the water and reach for my fluffy, light-blue towels. I wrap one around my hair and the other around my body as I move toward my bedroom.

The window shades are open, and I don't bother closing them as I drop the towel and walk over to my dresser. Opening the drawer to the right, I grab hold of my favorite silk night shorts and camisole. They're light blue. They even match the towels.

Blue is my favorite color. It always has been. I don't know if that's because my mother's eyes were blue, and her engagement ring was a blue sapphire encrusted with diamonds. I wear it on my right third finger.

Blue is and always will be special to me.

Reaching for the comb on top of the dresser, I run it through my wet hair as I stare at my reflection in the mirror. I don't know who this girl is. My face is pale, but my cheeks are flushed. I can't get this man off my mind. I can't think of anything but him. I don't know what he looks like, what color his eyes are, what color his hair is. I can only guess his height, which, if I had to make an estimate, would probably be around six foot three inches.

I don't know anything about him other than the way he smells and how his hands feel on my body. All of which I really loved about him. Oh, and I know the way his voice sounds. Deep, rugged, sexy, and rough.

Once I'm finished combing out my hair, I walk over to the bed and tug the comforter and top sheet down. I slip between the sheets and let out a sigh at the feeling of the European flax linen as it glides across my skin.

I don't spend much money on my clothes, shoes, or bags. But I do spend more than I should on organic linen sheets and other home essentials and food. I love to be comfortable, and I'm what some might call a little crunchy. I love organic and natural fibers and foods. I love to feel healthy in mind, body, and soul.

Clothes, shoes, and bags don't bring me peace. So, there is nothing that I have in my closet that means anything to me. I don't spend my money there, and honestly, I try not to spend my money too quickly anyway. I know it will run out if I go wild. I'm extremely conservative when it comes to that, well, aside from food and housewares.

Reaching for my e-reader, I swipe my thumb across the screen and find my latest book. I let out a heavy sigh as I begin to read. It doesn't take me long to forget the sexy guy at the club, because I get lost in the world of the book.

Until my phone buzzes with a notification. Turning my head, I stare at the notification for a moment, afraid that the phone may actually jump off the table. Smiling, I shake my head and pick it up.

There is a text message from Allison.

> ALLISON: Things were amazing. Hendrick was out of this world. Just wanted to let you know that I'm safe. Call you tomorrow. We'll do coffee.

> Glad all is well... and well... amazing! Let me know what time, and I'm there.

Setting the phone down, I chew on my bottom lip. I don't want to do anything tomorrow except lounge in my underwear and read. But I'll go to coffee with my friend, because that's what she needs, even if it's everything opposite of what I want.

I'm trying to be a good friend to her. She's always been such a good one for me. I place my e-reader down on the nightstand and turn the lamp beside the bed off. Shifting down onto the pillow, I lie on my side and close my eyes.

I don't know what will happen tomorrow, but I did something different today. I did something out of my comfort zone, and I survived. Not only that, I liked it, and I would even go as far as to say that I had fun.

This was a win.

CHAPTER
EIGHT

WELLS

I'M SURPRISED TO SEE MY UNCLE DEAN, AN EXECUTIVE, SITTING in my father's home office as soon as Coleman and I walk into the room. Arching a brow, I glance between them, then settle my gaze on my father.

"It seems we have an issue," my uncle announces.

Coleman and I don't speak. We wait for whatever the issue could be. I have no idea what could have happened between dinner and now, but I am waiting to find out. When my uncle speaks again, it's not what I expect at all. In fact, it's almost comical.

"One of the buildings we were buying has fallen through. The sellers have suddenly canceled the escrow with no reason."

There is a moment of silence, and my uncle's gaze flicks to my dad, then back to mine, then Coleman's, but he doesn't speak. He's completely silent as I wait for him to finish whatever the fuck he's got on his mind.

A seller canceling an escrow doesn't happen very often, especially when it's a commercial piece like this one. And even more, when we are the buyers. But it isn't unheard of either. So, I'm unsure as to why this calls for a middle-of-the-night meeting.

"Was it her father?" Coleman asks.

Shifting my gaze to Coleman's, I open my mouth to ask him what the fuck he means. The girl he was fucking, her father was an associate, but I didn't think he had any kind of real power. Our father is the one with power in this business.

"It was," Uncle Dean states.

"What the fuck?" I ask.

My dad stands, placing his palms on his wooden desk. It's clean, not a paper clip in sight. He's much like my mother when it comes to his space, and I wonder if this is why they make such a great team. It seems as though they have a lot in common when it comes down to it, even if their daily activities aren't in exact sync all of the time.

"The girl your brother has been casually fucking for six months; she thought it was going somewhere. So, when he broke it off suddenly, she ran to her father crying. Her father is an associate of ours, but not just that, he was selling us a building. It was a fucking steal, and we were going to make bank on it. Now we don't have a goddamn thing," Dad growls.

"How was I supposed to know?" Coleman barks. "I didn't want to marry her. I broke it off. Now I'm going to marry someone who was promised to me. You act as if I'm not owed the wife I desire."

Uncle Dean stands, and I'm surprised. He usually doesn't try to step on Dad's toes, especially when it comes to business and the family, but there is something else happening here, and I'm confused.

I open my mouth to ask but snap it closed, deciding it isn't really my place to ask questions. I'm not in charge of anything when it comes to real decision-making in the family or the business. I'm a manager, and I have responsibilities, but this is completely different.

"We need that deal," Uncle Dean states.

Turning my attention to my dad, I tilt my head to the side. "Why do we need that deal?" I ask. "What is the big thing here that I'm missing?"

"It's a good deal," my dad mutters.

"No, that's not it. I've seen good deals come and go, and none of them have sparked a middle-of-the-night meeting. None of them required contracting marriages between a member of the family. So, you're going to have to do better than that."

Wrong. Thing. To. Say.

My father moves so fast that my heart slams against my chest at the simple shift of his arm. He lifts his hand, grabs hold of my shirt, and yanks my whole body forward. I didn't think I was standing close enough to his desk for him to reach, but it's almost as if he has an elastic arm.

My body is pulled across the desk, my hips and waist pressing against the edge. My face is inches from my father's, and I can hear his breaths. He growls, then he speaks, just loud enough for me to hear.

"I do not have to do *shit*, boy," he grinds out. "I am the director. You are nothing without me. I will not be talked to in that way. Not here, not anywhere, not fucking ever. Do you understand me?"

He sounds animalistic, and I know I fucked up. So, instead of talking back to him, I keep my damn mouth shut.

He lifts his other hand, flattening his palm, then slaps it across my face before he releases me.

I fall down on the desk, my chest slamming against the wood. This will be as far as the beating goes for my insolence. However, if I do it again, even in private, there will be more awaiting me.

"Stand," my father growls.

Placing my palms against the warmth of his wooden desk, I push myself up to stand, straighten my shoulders, and take a few steps backward, my eyes flicking down to the shiny wooden top of the desk.

"The reason this is such an issue is that we already have a tenant for this building. Contracts have been signed, and we will be held in breach of contract if this does not continue through. That breach will be with the government, and I want this deal. This will give us a sense of security that we cannot simply buy."

I don't know why he didn't lead with that shit. It would have saved us all the dramatics and me being slapped like a bitch. But it doesn't matter, and I'm not about to question it, either.

"What do you need from us?" Coleman murmurs.

"I need you to ensure that he decides to go through with the deal. However that gets done, it doesn't matter. I am trusting you boys to handle it without police or death."

So, threats.

I like that.

Coleman dips his chin, taking a step backward. I do the same and turn away from my father's desk, moving toward the door when he calls out my name. Instead of just looking over my shoulder, I turn completely around and lift my head, my eyes finding his.

"Wells, you're a good boy."

Dipping my chin, I turn from him and make my way out

of the office just before I hear my uncle and father's voices in a low murmur. I don't know what they're saying. It doesn't matter because it doesn't concern me.

With the mission on our minds, we make our way out of the house and toward our cars. Coleman stops beside my driver's door and waits for me. He lifts his eyes, his gaze searching mine, and I can tell he feels sorry for me being slapped like a bitch, but he has the good sense not to mention it.

"Do we pay your ex a visit or her father?" I ask.

"She stays at home most nights," he chuckles.

"Both, then."

"Both."

PARKER

STRETCHING, I wonder if last night was a dream, then I realize it wasn't. I sink my teeth into my bottom lip and wonder if I should call Allison, but then realize that it's eight in the morning. There is no way at all whatsoever that she's awake yet.

Pushing myself up, I scoot back and rest my back against the headboard. The sun is shining brightly into my room, something that has become a habit of mine, leaving the curtains open so I can be woken by the sun.

I think I started doing it after my parents died. The anxiety that fills me at being in a dark place is just a little too consuming. So, open windows, moonlight that turns to sunshine, it's something I don't think I could do without now. I can't imagine sleeping in the dark, even though I have automatic blackout curtains on every window in my condo.

Throwing my legs over the side of the bed, I stretch again before I stand. The floor is warm, the wood being the absolute best choice when I was choosing materials during the remodel after I purchased the condo a few years ago.

I make my way to the bathroom to take care of business, wash my hands and face, put some moisturizer on, brush my hair, and then put it up in a messy bun before I head out of the bathroom and toward the kitchen.

I wonder if I should go down to the café for coffee but then decide against it because I don't want to get dressed quite yet. Plus, if Allison calls, we'll just go down there together.

Walking over to my Keurig, I grab a pod from the drawer beneath it and pop it in. I always leave a coffee cup beneath the machine now. I can't count the number of times I've been so exhausted from lack of sleep the night before and started the damn thing with no cup.

With a heavy sigh, I move through the kitchen, gathering creamer from the fridge and collagen powder from the pantry and setting up my little station. I do this pretty much every morning. I don't know if the collagen powder really does anything, but I'm not taking any chances of not using it either.

Once my drink is made, I walk out onto the small balcony that looks out over the city. Sinking down on the chair, I bring my legs up, holding my mug in front of my shins, and rest my chin on my knees.

It's calm.

Serene even.

It's also a bit stifling, but I don't mind the heat and humidity. I'm used to it. This is and always has been home for me. The sounds of the city are below me, but it's not chaotic the way people would think. It's calming.

At least, it is to me.

Lifting my head, I bring the mug to my lips and test the temperature of the drink. Perfect. Not too hot, not too cold, exactly the way I love it. Closing my eyes, I let out a sigh and just breathe, taking in the moment.

Until I feel it again.

My eyes pop open, and I glance around. I look down at the street, but everyone there is walking by and not paying attention to me. Lifting my gaze, I take in the buildings around me, but there would be no way to know if someone was watching me because they all have one-way mirror windows the way I do in my building.

I don't know who is watching me or where they are, but I can feel their eyes on me. Again, it doesn't necessarily scare me, but it's unnerving. I don't want to be watched. I don't want anyone to stalk me. But if someone is going to do it... at least I don't feel scared out of my brain... *yet*.

My cell phone rings inside the house, and I jump, holding my coffee out. I let out a sigh of relief when it doesn't spill all over me. Turning slightly, I set it down on the table and stand before I hurry inside to answer the call.

It's Allison.

I pick the phone up, slide my finger across the screen, then hold the device to my ear. "Meet me for brunch ASAP," she shouts before I can even offer her a greeting.

She doesn't sound hurt or scared but excited. "Is this a good brunch?" I ask.

"The best," she says with a squeal. "Moxies in thirty."

I love Moxies, so I'm not mad about the demand to meet there. Their brunch is amazing, and I'm more than willing to leave my condo for that. Even though I was really hoping I wouldn't have to today. But Allison sounds way too excited to wait on this, so I hurry and change, then rush to my car.

CHAPTER
NINE

WELLS

I'm sure that renting the apartment across from her condo for two months was the wrong move. However, I don't care. It was likely even more of a mistake to buy special-grade binoculars to see through the one-way-mirrored windows so that I could look straight into her place—into her bedroom.

When she sleeps, she looks even more innocent than she did in my mom's office. I'm not sure how that's possible, but it is. She looks like breakable porcelain.

Except, I'm not a good man, and I want to break her into a million pieces.

I want to fuck her until tears stream down her face. I want to watch her skin turn a purplish hue while I choke her. I want to watch her come undone, fall apart, and beg for me to do it again and again.

I want her to need me with every breath she takes.

And she will.

I watch her sit on her balcony, her chin resting on her knees, a cup of coffee in her hand. I wonder if she'd let me fuck her on that table for the world to see... though I won't give her a choice.

Her choices will no longer be hers to make.

When she is mine, so is every single fucking thought in her pretty little head.

Mine.

I've never owned anyone before.

It's been said since I was fifteen that a woman would be mine to have, to own, to keep, but I've never given much thought to it. I'm sure it's completely fucked up that I want to try with her. Play with her. But I do.

Parker Nichols will be mine.

I will break her.

She stands, placing her coffee on the table, her nipples at attention before she turns and rushes back into the condo. My cock stands at attention at the sight of her ass bouncing as she hurries inside.

My phone rings just as I'm about to unzip my pants, and I let out a frustrated growl. Sliding my phone across the screen, I growl into the phone.

"What?"

Coleman chuckles on the other end of the line. "You okay?" he asks. He knows where I am. That I'm watching her.

"I'm good. What the fuck are you doing calling me?" I ask.

"They'll be home in twenty minutes. They always have lunch together on Sundays."

I snort. "Weird. They're like us."

Coleman doesn't respond. Instead, he clears his throat. "You ready for this?" he asks.

"To scare the shit out of some people, to threaten, and maybe have a little fun? I was goddamn born ready."

"Will your girl be able to be left alone long enough for you to do this?"

"You worry about yourself and your fucking *girl*, yeah?"

He lets out a chuckle. "Get your ass to my place." He ends the call, and I check on Parker one more time before I leave.

She is taking off her skimpy pajamas, and I let out a groan at the sight of her full tits. I don't want to leave here yet. I want to watch her a little longer. With one hand, I unbuckle and unzip my pants. Shoving them down my hips, I free myself.

Spitting on my hand, I watch as she shimmies out of her bottoms, leaving herself completely bare for my eyes. Wrapping my palm around my cock, I start to stroke it up and down while imagining that it's her lips wrapped around me instead of my own hand.

She walks around the room in her glorious nakedness. I can't stop watching her. My hand moves, squeezing and releasing as I jack myself to the sight of her. It shouldn't be this sexy, watching her as she unknowingly moves around her room, but it's hot as fuck.

I groan as I come, and she steps into the bathroom.

"Fuck," I hiss to myself. "Fuck."

Quickly, I clean myself up and slide my phone into my pocket as I grab my keys by the front door and lock up behind me. Leaving the building, I head down to my car and straight to Coleman.

It doesn't take me long to get to his place. I know Parker has a job, but I also know that when her parents died, she got a hefty trust fund, the bulk of which her selfish aunt and uncle were unable to get their hands on.

Her condo is paid for in cash, her assets heavily diversified, and her paycheck she spends on her monthly bills, being conservative enough that she's able to continue saving, even in this economy.

That says something about her. She's young, but she isn't stupid or selfish. In fact, she's light-years ahead of even men when it comes to finances, and I like that.

There's something about watching her, about learning everything I can about her before I actually *fuck* her that is a goddamn turn-on.

The foreplay is out of this fucking world.

Even if she doesn't realize that's what's happening, which is even fucking hotter, and I hope to keep it this way for a while. She has no goddamn clue in the world that I'm here, jacking off to the sight of her naked body.

That I watch her.

That I crave her.

That I plan on taking her for myself.

Soon.

As I drive toward Coleman's, I can't help but let the anticipation of this woman, of taking her once and for all, consume me. I know it will take some time, but I don't think I have ever been this excited about something in my life aside from joining the family. I also don't think I've ever been this patient.

Usually, I take what I want when I want it.

Waiting for anything has never even been a thought in my head, except when it comes to Parker. Waiting for her is a fun little game I crave, and I'm quite enjoying myself.

Coleman's place comes into view, and I pull up to the street, where I see him leaning against the wall, waiting for me. He pushes off and makes his way toward me. Opening the passenger door, he sinks down into the seat, clearing his throat as he slams the door.

"Took you long enough."

"Had to take care of something," I grunt.

"Whacking off while you watch your little doll?" he asks.

Instead of answering him, I lift my hand and flip him the

bird. He lets out a bark of laughter as I ease the car into traffic. Instead of trying to get more information out of me or fucking around, he gives me directions to the house.

It's in Preston Hollow, which is not the slums by any means. In fact, we ride up to a house that's worth at least five million dollars. I shift my gaze over to Coleman. "How exactly does this man associate with Dad?"

"Commercial real estate," Coleman murmurs.

"Not living here. Explain further," I demand.

Coleman turns to me, his eyes darkening, and I know he's getting ready to tell me something that either I won't want to hear or that I'm not supposed to know.

It doesn't matter.

He's going to tell me because I should fucking know what the hell is going on here. This isn't just about a building that the government is going to lease from us. This is more.

"He sells IDs, flawless IDs."

"And?" I ask.

"Ones that get certified by the government and validated."

"How?" I ask. Although, I still don't think that's all he's doing. This house alone is worth millions.

"That agency that's going to be renting from us?" Coleman asks although I know it's not anything he wants me to respond to. I wait for him to continue. "Passport Agency Department."

"He buys fucking valid passports from the government and sells them on the sly?" I ask. "Holy fuck."

"Holy fuck is right," Coleman mutters. "Dad wants in on this shit. Being able to travel anywhere in the world without being detected, tracked, or traced? There is an appeal, not just for him but for the entire family and anyone he deems worthy."

Coleman is right. If shit went down and we needed to get out of the country, if we needed to completely disappear, we could do that. Sure, there is always facial recognition shit, but if we're able to get out quickly and then disappear before those warnings are sent anywhere that has those systems, we would all be golden.

"Well then, let's scare the shit out of these people. I want my passport," I say, my lips curving up into a grin.

Coleman chuckles and nods his head once. "Yeah, let's."

PARKER

LATE BRUNCH with Allison turns into dinner as she gushes about the hot guy she took to her bed last night. Or as she calls him… *her stud*. That grosses me out to think about, but she has zero shame when it comes to sex.

I wish I could be like her, and maybe I could if I'd ever done the deed, but since I haven't, I'm still pretty reserved when it comes to talking about it… reading about it is a different animal. I *love* reading about it.

"I can't believe I've monopolized this whole thing," she says as she reaches for her umpteenth cocktail and brings it to her lips, sucking the last of the contents before she continues. "So, tell me, did you kiss the hot guy you were dancing with?"

Shaking my head, I wrap my fingers around the cold glass of water. It's wet with sweat, and I lift it to my lips, taking a drink as drops fall onto the white tablecloth. Setting it back down on the wet ring it's already made, I stall for a few breaths before I answer.

"No, we just danced. I don't know his name. I didn't even see his face," I say.

Her eyes widen, then her lips slowly curve up into a grin. "I saw his face," she says on a whisper. "And believe me, you would not be disappointed. He was delicious. He was at least five years older than us, maybe more. He was dark-haired, dark-eyed, tanned skin. Tattoos. Hot. But wearing clothes that easily cost a thousand dollars. A watch that costs at least three."

I'm not sure if her explanation of him excites me or scares the absolute shit out of me. It's clear to me just by the few words she's said that this man is extremely out of my league. It's better he doesn't know my name or anything about me.

I don't think I need to see him again.

"So, do you think you're going to see Hendrick again?" I ask, trying to change the subject.

She hums, her eyes go all glossy, and I sink my teeth into my bottom lip as I watch her get all dreamy about this guy. Allison hasn't been dreamy over anyone other than her ex-boss in years. I'm excited for her, even if it doesn't work out. At least it showed her that there are other men in the world and not just married ones.

"I think so. He said he'd call, but he could have just been saying that."

"He could have, or he could like you."

She hums, then shrugs a shoulder. "It doesn't matter, not really. What I should be focusing on is getting another job."

She's not wrong. A job would be important. "Are you going to do something totally different?" I ask.

I watch as she slides her tongue across her bottom lip. She only does that when she's getting ready to tell me something she's super excited about. I lean forward, my lips parting in awe as I wait for whatever it is she's about to say.

"I was able to save a ton of money, like, enough to pay my bills and rent for six months. Plus, he bought me a ton of expensive gifts, and I kept every one of them mint and in their original boxes. I can sell them for more than what he spent, which will give me some working capital."

"What are you telling me?" I ask.

"I'm ready to open my sex shop."

Blinking, I stare at her for a moment. I'm not even sure what she's talking about, and she acts like I should know everything about this grand plan of hers. I've never heard her mention this in all the years I've known her.

"Allison?" I ask.

"I've always wanted to open an upscale lingerie and sex toy shop. It's been a dream of mine, and now I think it's time. All I need is a loan for rent and to buy the products, which I think I can get. And then an actual space."

I'm not sure what to say, but instead of discouraging her idea, I decide I need to support it because I have a feeling if Allison is in charge, she's going to be wildly successful. Anything and everything that Allison does, she brings something to the table that nobody else has, and I am, without a doubt, certain she has thought this through.

At least, I hope she has.

"Well, go over your plan with me," I offer with a smile.

CHAPTER
TEN

PARKER

THE WEEK HAS BEEN BORING. *WORK. WORK. WORK.* AND nothing else much, aside from several texts from Allison, who is working hard on getting a loan and finding a building for her new venture. I love my job. I really do.

It's as nerdy as I am.

I'm a market research analyst for an investment company. I do all the research and reports to project where money should be invested in the long term and what will make the most profit. I love it, mainly because I can work alone in my office.

Just me and my research.

It's what I love. It's where I am comfortable. Alone with numbers. My anxiety vanishes the moment I power on my computer and begin to research, take notes, type them out, and gather the data I need.

But I know that the anxiety will return. When it's time to

head home. When it's time to see Doctor Hamilton again. When I have to walk into that office building of hers, go up the stairs, into the room, and talk about my life.

Sucking in a breath, I hold it for a moment before I let it out slowly. The clock ticks as I work. Usually, it wouldn't matter, but today, I have to see the doctor, and my heart races faster and harder with each minute that passes until it reaches five o'clock.

Once my alarm rings, announcing it is indeed time to clock out, I begin to move, almost as if I'm a zombie and am just going through the motions as I close my computer down. I have a big project I need to finish by Monday, so instead of leaving my computer here, I pack it up in my laptop bag and throw the strap over my shoulder.

Gathering my purse and everything else I need, I slip out of my office and head for the elevator banks. Nobody else is here. The building is quiet and empty. On Friday afternoons, it always vacates before five. It seems as if people go to lunch and just never come back.

I did that last week, but I didn't just leave. I actually requested the time off because I am nothing, if not a habitual rule follower.

Moving through the building, I realize I haven't felt that sensation of being watched at all today. Although, I haven't left my office either, except to use the bathroom and refill my water bottle.

But even as I walked to work, then around the building, nothing. I wonder if it was all just a fluke. Or maybe I've been focusing my attention on work and haven't had time to even think about it.

I sink my teeth into my bottom lip as my mind wanders to something else I've been avoiding thinking about... well, some*one* else. The stranger from Club Nova. The way Allison described him hasn't disappeared yet. I don't know what he was doing with me, and then he didn't ask me any questions, didn't try to get my number, didn't even let me see his face.

It's all so bizarre... and enthralling all at the same time.

Moving down the streets of Dallas, heading straight toward Doctor Hamilton's office, I feel as if I'm lost in a daze. This man, this stranger, he made me feel things I've never felt before. I've never touched myself thinking of a real man in my life.

Usually, if I do that at all, it's after a spicy scene in my book, and I imagine the characters like a movie, playing out their desires right there in my mind. But I've never imagined a man who I know, not that I know him. I didn't even see his face.

I am a mess.

As I approach the doctor's office, I realize I haven't been thinking, and the crippling anxiety hasn't, well... taken me down. Tugging the front door open, I take a step into the lobby and wait for the pain and panic to seize my lungs.

Nothing happens.

In fact, I'm able to breathe even as I walk toward the elevator bank, except as I extend my arm and touch the up button, the sensation of being watched washes over me. My spine straightens and the hairs on the back of my neck stand at attention.

Turning my head, I look over my shoulder to check if anyone is there... The lobby is empty. Frowning, I shift my attention back to the elevator as it dings. I step into the car, turn around, and look again, trying to find the eyes that are indeed on me.

They aren't there.

There is nobody.

The doors close, and the elevator climbs. That sensation of my lungs squeezing happens with each ascending floor. I thought my mind was busy enough that I could avoid all of this, but I was wrong.

When the doors open, the bell ringing sounds like an alarm. My feet move, even though I don't tell them to. It feels as if I'm thrust forward, not of my own accord. I stumble, then right myself and my bags as I stand in front of the office door.

Lifting my hand, I wrap my fingers around the knob and gently turn it. My breathing sounds like wheezing at this point, but I make myself go inside, forcing myself to find the lobby couch. There is no secretary. She's probably already gone home for the night.

Once my butt hits the sofa, I wring my hands together in my lap, telling myself to breathe, whispering the word over and over. Until I hear a man's voice whisper instead of my own.

"You're going to be fine, cupcake."

My eyes pop open, and I expect to see whoever said that standing in front of me, but there is nobody there. Turning my head, I look at the door, but it's closed.

"Parker?" a voice calls out.

Turning, I look to see Doctor Hamilton standing at her doorway. "Why don't you come inside?"

I start to ask her if there was a man here, if he walked through this room, but I decide against it mainly because I don't want her to think I'm completely crazy. A little wacky is one thing, but completely and totally gone?

No thank you, not yet, at least.

Standing, I give her my most sincere smile and dip my chin as I walk into the room past her. Making my way straight toward the leathery sofa, I sink down and take my purse and laptop bag off my shoulder, placing them beside my feet on the floor.

"It's good to see you again, Parker. It appears as though it was a bit easier for you to come in here today?"

Her question is innocent enough, even observant. But it isn't exactly the truth, either. I open my mouth and begin to speak but decide against it. At least not yet. Nodding once, I clear my throat and shift in my seat slightly, uncomfortably.

"Tell me, how was your weekend and week?"

That was all I needed. I can't keep my mouth shut. Everything, everything spills out of me. Every little detail, except pleasuring myself in the shower. I don't tell her any of that, not a single moment of it, but everything else I blather on about as if she were Allison. A friend. And not a psychologist.

WELLS

SHE'S BEAUTIFUL.

I'm not sure why, but seeing her close to a panic attack, close to a break, is fucking breathtaking. I couldn't help but say something as I walked past her in my mom's office building. I knew she had an appointment today, and I had to see her up close. I had to know that it wasn't my mind playing tricks on me, that she was truly as beautiful as I'd seen from a distance.

And she is.

Breathtaking.

And mine.

Soon, I will have her all to myself. I'll be able to bring that anxiety, that fear, into the bedroom, and she'll look at me that way instead of at nothingness. I can tell she's alone in more ways than one. I can see it not only by watching her but in her eyes. Haunted loneliness, a sweet creature begging to be controlled.

And she will beg.

I want her to beg me to hurt her.

Beg me to bruise her.

Beg me to fuck her.

Leaving my mom's office, I make my way toward my own. We have some paperwork to complete, a lot of it actually, considering the new building for the passport office is back on the table. The associate and his daughter will be in shortly to finalize the resurrection of the sale.

Another thing that was left unsaid by Dad was the fact that the daughter isn't just a daughter; she is also half-vested in his company. Now I'm wondering if Coleman won't be forced to marry her anyway. This union would be a good one, especially if it keeps the daughter and daddy happy.

Parking in my spot, I gather my shit and unfold from the car. I glance around the parking garage and smirk at the sight of Coleman's car already here. This meeting is going to be long and will probably include dinner and drinks, which is why we planned it after business hours. Not that anyone in the office would bat an eyelash at drinks and food during any kind of meeting.

But you never know in this kind of situation, especially with it being for illegal purposes, what will happen. So, we learned a long time ago not to hold them while the office was staffed.

I walk into the building and take the elevator to the top. The conference room is at the top level of the building. It overlooks the entire downtown area, and it's one of the favorite locations. The elevator car rises slowly.

And as it does, I can't help but think of Parker.

She didn't seem so lost today, maybe a little out of it, but she appeared as though she was a little more relaxed. I'd like to think that I had something to do with that, but I haven't even kissed her yet... but I will.

The doors to the elevator car open, and I step out into the

hall. It's quiet in here, but there is murmuring at the end of the walkway, and I know I'm likely the last person to arrive. I'm not late. Regardless, I'm sure my father will look at me with disapproval for being the last to enter.

I reach for the door to the conference room, push it open, and take a step inside. Uncle Dean, Dad, Coleman, Shiloh, and her father, Ray Randolph, are sitting in their seats, waiting.

"There he is," my father announces, which lets me know he's displeased with me.

He'll get over it, or he'll punish me. Either way, I can't control it at this point. Dipping my chin, I murmur an apology for my tardiness. Ray speaks before anyone else can, and I can see why Coleman doesn't want to be part of this group.

"Your dad is full of shit. You aren't late at all," Ray announces, his voice booming and bouncing off the windows around us.

I know I'm not late. I know my dad still isn't happy with me being the last person to walk into the room, but I do know I'm not late. I don't need this loudmouth to tell me shit. But instead of saying that, I dip my chin toward my father with a silent acknowledgment and sign of respect before I sink down into my usual chair.

"Let's get started with these papers. The food should be here soon, and we can enjoy the rest of the evening."

"I don't think I'm ready to sign these. I don't like the way this came about," Shiloh states.

Coleman levels her with a glare and leans forward, his gaze focused on hers and never leaving as he speaks. Although he doesn't actually talk to her, it's clear that his intentions are for her to understand what he's about to say. Even if it isn't directly *to* her... it is definitely *for* her.

"Ray," he begins, "this deal will go forward. One way or

another, it will happen. There is nothing else that can be done about it. Your agreement was made, and if this is not done, blood will be shed."

Ray gulps, his gaze flicking to Shiloh, then back to Coleman. But it's Shiloh who speaks. "You don't get to threaten us," she announces, although her voice wavers a bit.

She is not as badass as she thinks she is, and it's almost sad. But when I truly take her in, I observe her and see she's in love with my brother. This is to get him back. This is to make him pay.

This is all to force him to pay attention to her... to see her as a woman of worth.

"It is not a threat, Shiloh. It is a promise."

I watch as they have a complete stare-down with one another, then Shiloh roughly grabs a pen next to her and scribbles her name on the contract.

"Fuck you, Coleman Hamilton."

Coleman's lips curve up into a grin, and I know he's going to reply to that. "Already did, babe," he purrs and then winks. Uncle Dean clears his throat and shifts in his seat uncomfortably. I watch him, wondering what the fuck his issue is, but I don't ask.

"Drinks," Dad barks before the conversation turns ugly and everything gets canceled all over again.

CHAPTER
ELEVEN

PARKER

I'm not sure why, but after only two sessions with Doctor Hamilton, I feel almost reborn. I know I'm nowhere near *fixed*. There is a lot of work for me to do. But I am feeling better than I ever have with virtual sessions. I don't know if it's seeing her in person or who she is. I have a feeling it's more just because she's so awesome.

As I make my way home, the sun sets, and I am mesmerized by the watercolor-painted sky. I think about the breathing exercises the doctor gave me and the assignment. She wants me to write in a journal every day.

She wants me to write about my past. Before my parents died, the night they were taken. Then, after my parents were gone. Then college, then adulthood, and now. Although college to adulthood to now encompasses only a couple of years, that part shouldn't be too hard. It's not like I've really done much.

Just thinking about journaling all those things, bringing up those past feelings and the current ones, causes my heart to jump inside my chest. Stopping in the middle of the sidewalk, I pinch my eyes closed and try to breathe. I try to slow my racing heart.

Once I feel a bit better, I open my eyes and continue walking home. It takes a little longer than usual because of the whole heartbeat thing. It happens two more times, and I chalk it up to my anxiety rising and rapidly falling this evening.

Walking into my building, I take the elevator to my floor and slip into my condo, locking myself inside for the night. I have plenty of work on my laptop and apparently a lot of journaling to do... and breathing.

I can't forget the breathing.

Doctor Hamilton also said that she wanted me to do something new this weekend. But she only mentioned that, so I've told myself I will only do that if I have time... and spoiler alert, I will not have time.

I set my computer bag down on my coffee table, make my way toward the kitchen, and rummage around for something to eat. I haven't been to the store. Chewing on my bottom lip, I let out a sigh and reach for a piece of uncured salami and a block of extra sharp white cheddar cheese.

I shouldn't eat just salami and cheese for dinner, so I scrounge around until I have an orange bell pepper and a cluster of grapes. Now it's a charcuterie, so it's not some make-do thrown-together mess. It's fancy.

Walking over to my chair, I decide that work can wait until tomorrow. I'm going to read and eat snacks tonight. I strip out of my work clothes, sink down in the chair, and place the plate on my knees as I open the reading app and settle into my book.

I'm not sure how long I read. No doubt it's hours. I've

finished my snacks and the water I walked into the kitchen to grab, though I don't remember anything because I was engrossed in my book. Lost to the world that I've delved deep inside and not willing to get out of, not even to walk around my condo and get a water.

But I'm brought out of that world in an instant when a new text message appears on my phone. I almost drop the thing into my lap. Usually, I like to read on my e-reader, but I didn't feel like going into the bedroom to get it today, and I'd forgotten that I wasn't on it, so the text itself scared the shit out of me, but then I read the words, and my heart races.

> UNKNOWN: YOU ARE SEXY AS SIN SITTING IN THAT CHAIR, INNOCENTLY READING... EXCEPT YOU'RE NOT READING ANYTHING THAT IS INNOCENT, ARE YOU?

If my anxiety has calmed down, it is no longer that way. It is officially through the roof. Turning my head, I look over my shoulder and expect to see someone watching me from the balcony, but there is nobody there.

There are some buildings across the street, but I know that even if someone were looking out of the window and straight toward my place, they wouldn't be able to see inside this room. That was something I double- and triple-checked on when I bought my condo. I didn't want anyone to be able to see inside if I had my curtains up.

I didn't want anyone watching me... I don't want anyone watching me... ever.

> Who is this?

I demand.

I see those three typing bubbles pop up and hold my

breath as I wait for this stranger, this person, to give me something, anything that will tell me this is a really bad joke. I swear if this is Allison, I might never talk to her again. But then I realize that it wouldn't be Allison because she knows my history and would never do this to me.

> UNKNOWN: FACE THE WINDOW AND TOUCH YOURSELF FOR ME.

My heart slams against my chest.

> You have the wrong number.

> UNKNOWN: NO, I DON'T... PARKER NICHOLS.

I stand up quickly. My heart jumps to my throat, and I spin around to look out the window. Someone knows my name, has my number, is watching me, and I can't stop them. I knew that sensation was real, that someone had been stalking me. I just didn't know who, and I didn't know it was quite like this.

My phone buzzes in my hand again. I sink my teeth into my bottom lip, scrape them across, and tug on a piece of skin on my lip as I try to decide if I can look at that incoming message. My curiosity wins over anything else.

Flicking my gaze down, I look at the text thread as I hold my breath. There's a picture. When I touch the image, it blows up so I can see it all. I gasp at the sight, almost dropping my phone. It's my very first ever dick pic.

I know that if he can see me, he is probably laughing at my shocked expression, but I've never seen one like his before. Biting the inside of my cheek, I try to keep my smile from appearing, but I know that I fail when the next text chimes.

> UNKNOWN: YOU'RE BEAUTIFUL. MY
> COCK ACHES FOR YOU.

Doctor Hamilton told me to do something I'd never done before. So, I go against everything inside of me that is screaming to block this entire conversation, and I respond. This is so dangerous. I know it is, and I should be calling the police instead of texting him back.

> I can't say the same because I don't know what you look like. Who are you? Please tell me.

There is nothingness, a moment of me just staring at my phone, thinking about going back to the dick pic and studying it for a while longer. I don't get the chance because an incoming text moves it up in the thread even further.

> UNKNOWN: YOU'LL KNOW SOON
> ENOUGH, CUPCAKE.

My entire body seizes. Every single part of me. *Cupcake.* It's him. The guy from the club.

Oh.

My.

God.

WELLS

WITH MY FINGERS wrapped around my cock, I watch her through the binoculars. She's just realized that the man texting her is the same one who danced with her at Club Nova. Fuck me, but the look of shock on her face almost makes me come.

I want her to look at me that exact way when I sink my

cock inside of her. Moving my hand up and down my dick, I continue to watch her as she moves her thumbs over the screen of her phone.

> CUPCAKE: Do I get to meet you since you already know my name?

I've saved her as *Cupcake* in my contacts, knowing that if anyone ever gets my phone, well, first of all, I will have to be dead. Secondly, they don't need to know her real name. I'll never put that in my phone or anywhere where someone who means me and my family harm could find it.

> SOON.

I'm not sure what I expect her to do, but it's not what she actually does. I almost drop my binoculars when she begins to undress. She doesn't look at me. She doesn't know where I am, but she does focus her attention straight ahead, maybe even looking at her reflection in the glass of her windows, and that is hotter than if she were looking into my eyes.

When she's completely naked, I watch as she slides her fingers between her legs. Holy fucking shit. I don't think I've ever been this excited in my entire life. I'm not typically someone who gets excited about sex.

Don't get me wrong. I love sex. But I've been doing this since I was fifteen, with paid professionals and with one-night stands. I'm not a relationship person like Coleman. I like a different flavor each time, and it's not always out of excitement. It's usually out of physical necessity.

This is different.

Parker is different.

My hand moves up and down on my cock, stroking myself to the rhythm her fingers create between her legs. I can see the way they're moving, her hips thrusting forward as she closes her eyes and parts her lips.

Fuck me.

Goddamn, I wish I could fuck her right now. I would completely fucking consume her. I would own her, bruise her, choke her, fuck her, and ruin her for anyone else. When her eyes pop open, I know she's come.

Only then do I let myself. Then, I type out a message for her. I'm not sure when I'm going to actually come to her. I need to rein in my control so I don't kill her. I feel like I probably would if she were here with me right this minute.

THAT WAS BEAUTIFUL.

CUPCAKE: I WISH I COULD SEE YOUR FACE.

SOON.

Cleaning up, I shove my phone into my pocket and watch her until she gathers herself and goes to bed. I watch her a little longer until she falls asleep, then I watch for a few more moments before I leave and head to my own place.

I'm not sure when I will reveal myself. I'm having far too much fun this way. However, it'll have to happen soon because my dick is starting to get raw as much as I'm whacking off lately. I'm not used to that shit at all.

My phone buzzes in my pocket, and I reach inside, tossing the binoculars down on the table beside me. It's Coleman. Sliding my thumb across the screen, I let out a chuckle as I greet him. I know he's probably good and piss drunk by now after that meeting with Shiloh and her father.

"Come over," he demands.

"Why?" I ask.

"Because I don't want to be alone."

I almost make fun of him, but I decide I need to do that in person so he doesn't get completely fucking butthurt. Clearing my throat, I tell him I'll be there in just a few minutes. He snorts, telling me he'll see me after I'm done perving on the girl. I would flip him off if he could see me.

Ending the call, I lift the binoculars to my eyes again and watch her for another moment. She's already showered and in bed. She turns to her side, faces the window, lifts her hand, presses it to her lips, and blows me a kiss.

Fuck me. This girl is sweet as shit. I'm going to completely fuck her up and screw her over, and I can't help myself. Smirking, I watch as she closes her eyes, a small smile playing on her lips, then she falls asleep.

Reluctantly, I leave the apartment and Parker behind.

CHAPTER

TWELVE

WELLS

COLEMAN IS SITTING IN HIS HOME LIBRARY, BOOKS surrounding him, a glass of whiskey in his hand, a frown on his face. Flopping down in the chair across from him, I reach over to the table next to him that has a glass and the decanter. Pouring myself a drink, I lean back in my seat and bring it to my lips.

"You are pissed off. What happened?"

"Pissed off?" he asks. "Not even close."

Arching a brow, I take another sip of my drink and watch him for a long moment. He doesn't elaborate, and I think about telling him to buck the fuck up and be a man, but I decide against it. He's obviously going through something, and he called me here to help him with it or at least drink with him about it.

"So, what is it?" I ask.

He shrugs a shoulder, bringing his drink to his lips. "Shiloh."

"You love her?" I say.

He shakes his head. "I meant it when I said that I didn't. But she tried to fuck me over more than once."

"Coleman?" I ask.

He clears his throat, leans forward, and rests his forearms on his thighs as he watches me for a silent moment.

"When this deal closes, she's done."

I don't speak, mainly because I'm not sure exactly what he's telling me. If I had to guess, it would be that he's going to kill her, but I know Coleman better than that. Mainly because that sounds like some shit I would do, not him.

"She's going to push a marriage, and I don't want her. She's already made it very clear that she's willing to use manipulation tactics to get what she wants, and I want absolutely fucking nothing to do with that shit."

"So you're going to kill her?"

He shrugs a shoulder. "You're going to help me."

"Me?" I ask. "I'm already on thin fucking ice with Dad. There is no way in hell he's going to be okay with this. He'll strip me of my title."

Coleman lifts his glass to his lips, taking another drink, and as I look him in the eyes, I realize he's fucking drunk. Not just a little drunk, but he is already trashed.

"Do you care?" he asks. "If Dad gets pissed off for a minute, do you care? This is for the good of the family. Do you think that Shiloh won't find a way to fuck me over, fuck the family over a different way? She is a spoiled little rich girl and is used to always getting what she wants."

"All this because you don't want to marry her?" I ask. "Seems a bit extreme."

He lets out a bark of laughter. "I won't marry her. But this doesn't have to do with that. It's more along the lines of her trying to bring business into it and try to squash a deal that was already in the works."

I agree with him. It was a bullshit move, and honestly, if it were anyone else, we probably would have orders to kill them. Bringing my glass to my lips, I empty the contents and hiss as it burns going down my throat.

"Do you have a woman for your wife in mind?" I ask.

He looks at his empty glass, then sets it down on the table, picks up the decanter and pours himself some more. All of this he does in silence, but before he picks up his glass again, I watch as he stands and turns from me.

With a sway, my brother walks over to his desk and reaches for an envelope. He picks it up, holding it for a moment, then turns and faces me. Without a word, he flings the envelope toward me. With zero effort, it lands in my lap.

I know what it is. This is his choice, or rather, his options to choose from. Slowly, I lift the flap of the envelope and reach inside. I can feel papers that have been stapled together as if they're in packets.

Pulling them out, I clear my throat as I look at the top one. "Is this your choice?" I ask.

Coleman moves back to his seat, sinking down in the cushion before he reaches for his glass. He takes a drink, gulping the contents as he closes his eyes. I wait for him to tell me if this is her, but while I wait, I read her dossier.

She's nineteen, a little young, but she's the oldest of five siblings. She wants a family of her own, she's pretty, and she enjoys music, movies, and quiet nights at home. I take everything that's written here with a grain of salt.

Mainly because these are all written out to be the most enticing to a man of the family. She is meant to appear to be a homebody who won't fuck around on her husband, an innocent virgin, and potentially a good housewife.

"The third one is my choice."

His words surprise me. Lifting my head, I look at him, my brows snapping together. "The third?"

He dips his chin. "The third."

Riffling through the packets, I pull out the third one and see her. She's blonde, beautiful, and, again, young. They're all young, though. She's twenty-one, she's in her last year of college and is an *A* student majoring in accounting. She's the second oldest child of four. Her brother is studying to be a doctor, her younger sister finishing high school this year.

"She's pretty," I murmur.

"Her father came from money. Opened a casino and resort in Vegas. Economy has been shit. They aren't doing too well."

"So, he's in debt enough to sell his daughter off?"

Coleman shrugs his shoulder. "Basically, that's the long and short of it."

I think about the situation, and really, it's a pretty good one. She comes from money. It won't be a complete shock to enter our world. She'll know when to talk, when to keep quiet, and what is expected of her, generally speaking.

However, I don't know how anyone can just accept being sold off to pay their family's debts. Especially someone who does come from money and is finishing college with a degree in something that she can actually make a good living doing.

Sinking my teeth into the corner of my bottom lip, I think about the girl who stares back at me. She's young, beautiful, smart, and about to become my brother's wife. Not just his wife, though. She will be his possession.

"But you want Shiloh gone before you take your vows with this one," I murmur.

"I'm giving Dad my answer tomorrow. I want the wedding to happen in three months. This deal with Shiloh and Ray closes in fifteen days."

My lips twitch into a smirk. "And on day sixteen, Shiloh mysteriously dies."

"Exactly."

"Okay, but if you truly want my help, this must be an accident. There's no other way around it. I'm not going to have Dad ride my ass about it."

Coleman smiles. It's one of his victorious ones. He shakes his head a couple of times, then throws back the rest of his drink, slamming the glass down on the table with a loud thud that seems to bounce off the walls around us.

"We have fifteen days to come up with a plan."

"Then we will," I agree. "One that will be flawless and leave us without an ounce of suspicion."

PARKER

I DEBATE CALLING Allison to tell her about my secret text message rendezvous, but I decide against it. I'm not sure what I would tell her, and I'm a little embarrassed that I threw caution to the wind like that.

Instead, I take the bound book of plain paper out of my nightstand, something I've had for about a year and never even cracked open, and I journal.

Instead of writing about my childhood, I choose to write about this stranger. I'm pretty positive that nothing about this is healthy in any way, shape, or form, but at the same time, I can't help it. Because for whatever reason, I feel like this could be exactly what I need. It seems safer than anything else in this big, scary world.

As I write, I think about that fact. To me, a stalker seems safer than someone at a club or even a little café. What does that say about me? About my life? And more importantly, about my future?

What happens when he makes himself known to me? Will he expect us to have a relationship? Will I have to tell him that I'm a virgin and that I am definitely not that sexpot who touched herself in front of that window?

My body heats with embarrassment just thinking about the moment. I loved it. I felt so sensual. Sexy. Like I could be someone's lover and not just nerdy, anxiety-filled Parker Nichols. There was something that just clicked inside of my head. I did it, and I loved it all.

There is a moment of silence where I stare at the journal, seeing absolutely nothing. Reaching for my bottle of water, I lift it to my lips and take a drink, trying to shake myself out of the memories of last night.

I need to finish my journaling, then I need to work on my reports for my job. I can't get this unknown man out of my head, though. He found my number after he danced with me at the club. How? And who is he to be able to get my cell phone number like that? Not just my name but my number, too.

Instead of hyperfocusing on this situation, I decide to finish my journaling then switch to my report for work. I need to keep my mind busy, and this is the only way I can get completely lost.

When I finish my bottle of water, I make my way to the kitchen and pull another bottle from the fridge, then prepare a small snack of salami, cheese, and grapes again. I don't know why, but that is the best combination ever.

Walking over to my favorite chair, I set my plate and a new bottle of water on the small side table, then walk to the coffee table and grab my computer bag. Glancing over at my phone that sits on the coffee table next to my journal, I decide to grab that, too.

What if he texts me again?

I want to be available, even though I know it's the exact

wrong thing to think, but I can't help myself. It's what goes through my mind. I want to hear from him. I want to read the messages he sends. I want to try to figure out who he is.

Maybe he's someone who I work with.

Maybe he's someone who I know.

Maybe he's a complete stranger.

The possibilities are endless, and that is intriguing.

I'm not sure how long I work. I seem to get completely lost in the numbers, in my research. And what feels like hours later, my eyes move over to my phone to check the notifications to see if anything has come through.

Nothing.

Going back to work, I continue at the same pace for what feels like only minutes. Checking my phone again, I find no notifications, but it's also three in the morning, so I decide it's time for me to get some sleep. My eyes are blurry, and all the numbers are starting to merge into one big jumble inside my mind.

Saving all my work, I close down my computer and put my plate in the dishwasher, throw my empty bottle of water away, and head to bed. As soon as my head hits the pillow, my eyes close, and I wonder where my mystery man is.

Then I hope that I dream of him.

Maybe my subconscious knows who he is and will show me his face as I sleep. It's a nice thought, even if it probably won't happen. Letting out a heavy exhale, I drift off into dreamland.

CHAPTER
THIRTEEN

WELLS

THROUGH THE BINOCULARS, I WATCH HER SLEEPING IN HER bed. The time is coming. I can only look for so long before I need to do something about it, and that time is almost here. But not quite yet.

Setting my binoculars down, I grab my phone and keys before I leave the empty apartment. I move through the building and head across the street to Parker's. There is a woman standing at the door, her eyes wide as she watches me approach.

She's pretty, and if I didn't have my sights set on Parker, I might take her around the corner to the alley and fuck her. But I'm on a mission, I'm focused, and my attention right now is all for Parker.

Without a single word, I jerk my chin toward the door. Wordlessly, she lifts her key card and unlocks the main entrance for me, but before I can pass by, she places her palm on my chest. Her gaze lifts to mine.

"If you want to see me, I'm in number fifteen."

I dip my chin but don't respond to her. I have no interest in seeing her or visiting her... ever. I'll be going to condo number one hundred twelve and only condo number one hundred twelve. Moving into the building, I head toward the elevator bank and slip inside when the doors open.

I reach out to touch the number-ten button for Parker's floor, watching as the car rises. I smile as soon as it dings and the doors open, showing the hallway to her floor. There are only seventy condos in this building on sixteen floors, and Parker's floor only has three.

Moving down the hallway, I stop in front of her door. I was a little busy this afternoon getting a copy of her key made. It is so wrong of me to do, and yet... I am still doing it, and shamelessly at that.

Shoving my hand into my pocket, I take out the key, then slowly slip it into the dead bolt, turning it before I push the button on the door handle and open the door.

Quietly, I close the door behind me, making sure not to make a sound. It's four in the morning, and I should probably be asleep, but I'm still a little drunk and a bit high thinking about the plan my brother and I devised for Shiloh.

Also, we have a meeting with the family tomorrow, so I won't be able to watch Parker because my mother also demanded that we join her for dinner. It's been a busy week, and we didn't visit on our normal night, so she is going to ensure that dinner is had before the week is done, which means Sunday night.

I prefer Sunday nights anyway. It seems like a good way to end the week. Dinner with the family. And in a few months, we'll have a new face at the table. I'm not sure why that causes me to smile. It's not that I'm going to have much to do with her, as she'll be Coleman's wife, but I suppose it's because things are changing. I enjoy change, unlike some people.

I silently move through her condo. I should probably be impressed by how nice it is. I know it's worth several million dollars because my girl's parents were not slouches. She comes from money, and she has taken care of her generational wealth very well.

Before I approach her bedroom, which is my final destination, I notice something on the living room table. It's a notebook. Frowning, I move toward it. I want to know what is written inside. I don't know why, but it calls to me.

Sinking down on her couch, I reach for the book and open it to the first page. It's dated for yesterday. The cursive writing is flowy and feminine. My eyes scan the words, and as they register, I realize she's writing about me.

It's a journal.

A journal I shouldn't read.

But I do because morals and shit don't mean much to me.

When I'm finished, I realize she wants me. But not just that. She is a virgin. Which I suspected, but now I have confirmation. Biting the inside of my cheek, I can't help but think about what that means.

I could take her.

Even if I fucked her before we were married, she'd be mine. If it works between us, I could own her. The thought causes my spine to tingle. Closing the journal, I set it back down on the table before I rise.

I'm not sure I truly want to keep her, but the thought is intriguing, to say the least. It's probably just because Coleman is getting ready to settle down with his wife. He's chosen a woman. He's made a decision, and I'm thinking about mine, which will be coming up sooner rather than later.

Shaking my head, I decide this is a moot point. I need to forget about it all. Who knows where I will be or what I'll want in the next five years when it's time for me to choose my wife? Chuckling, I want to slap myself upside my own fucking head at the fact that I'm even thinking about any of this shit.

As I walk into Parker's bedroom, I pause at the sight of her. She's sleeping, her hands tucked beneath her cheek. She's lost to a dreamworld, but I can't just stand over her. I can't just watch her. I have to touch her.

I need to taste her.

Carefully, I wrap my fingers around the top sheet that covers her body and gently glide it down until I expose her silky pajama set and her bare legs. *Fuck me*. Reaching for the waist of her shorts, I slowly slide them down and toss them to the floor.

She's not wearing panties.

She moves, rolling onto her back with a whimper. I freeze, watching her, wondering if she's going to wake up. She lets out a sigh, but she doesn't open her eyes or do anything else that would make me think she's woken up.

What I'm doing is so fucking wrong, but it is going to feel so fucking right for her. Wrapping my hands around the insides of her thighs, I gently guide her legs apart. Then, before she wakes up, I bury my face in her pussy.

Fuck.

Me.

She smells amazing.

I flatten my tongue to taste all of her, and I can't hold back the moan that escapes my throat. I've never tasted anything like this before in my life. It's magnificent. I swirl my tongue around her clit, then drive it back inside of her cunt.

There is nothing else for me. I am fucking done. This

woman is going to have an addictive hold on me that will be like nothing else. Because even though I'm tasting her in this moment, at the same time, I can't wait to do it again.

PARKER

I'M HAVING the weirdest and best dream of my entire life. I can't even open my eyes because I don't want it to be over. Lifting my hips, I let out a moan as the warmth spreads from my pussy to the rest of my body.

It's amazing, beyond amazing.

I don't think I've ever felt anything like this... ever.

I also don't want to wake up. I want this to last forever and ever. Until the end of time. But when my belly tightens and my entire body seizes, my eyes open and I sit up, trying to catch my breath.

I look down. It feels like I peed myself, but when I see a man... a dark-haired man between my legs, I open my mouth to scream.

Ohmigod. Ohmigod. Ohmigod.

There is a man between my legs. His mouth was between my legs. For the first time in my entire life, a man had his mouth between my legs. A man I've never seen before. A stranger.

Ohmigod!

He lifts his hand, covering my mouth before my scream can escape my throat. "Shh," he hisses. It's too dark. I can't see his face, just his dark hair and dark clothes. "I won't hurt you, cupcake..."

His voice lingers like maybe he's waiting to say *yet*. But he doesn't. When the single word *cupcake* reaches my ears, it's as if my body relaxes instantly. Inhaling deeply, I force myself to calm, and his scent washes over me.

I remember it.

I remember him.

He releases me, and when his lips curve up into a smile, I can see his white teeth, the whites of his eyes, and not much else. Slowly, he releases his hand from my mouth and stands from the end of the bed.

He's tall. Much taller than me. I have a million questions, and yet none of them leave my mouth. But he is not at a loss for words. He clears his throat, lifting his hand to his mouth, and I watch as he wipes it across his face.

I wish I could see more than just the shadows of his body moving. I wish I could see his features better.

I wish for a lot of things.

"What's your name?" I finally am able to ask, though only on a whisper.

He chuckles. "Wells." He reaches out, extends his index finger, then slides it across the bottom of my foot.

It's with this move that I realize my legs are spread wide open and I'm naked from the waist down. Closing them quickly, I try to reach for the comforter and bring it up to cover myself. The move causes Wells to laugh softly.

Wells.

I've never heard of such a name before, but that doesn't mean anything. Wells. I like it, or maybe I only like it because I want to like him. I shouldn't. I know this is the weirdest thing ever, but I really want this to be something... I want it to be everything.

"How?" I ask.

"Doesn't matter," he grunts.

"What happens now?"

He hums, but he doesn't say anything immediately. Instead, he moves closer to me. I suck in a breath, holding it when he sinks down on the side of the bed. He reaches out, cupping my cheek as he faces me. I don't know if he can see my face, but I still can't make out his.

"I'll be back, cupcake."

Lifting my hand, I wrap my fingers around his wrist and squeeze him gently. "Why me?" I ask.

He hums, leaning forward, and I feel his lips brush mine. "Because you are mine."

Then he stands, turns, and walks away without another word. I listen, hearing his shoes against the flooring of my condo, the door opens, then closes, and I hear the dead bolt lock into place.

He has a key to my home?

How?

I touch my lips right where his brushed against mine. That was my first kiss. I move my hand from my lips and slip it between my legs. There is wetness there. It's a mixture of his saliva and me... my release.

No... his mouth between my legs. *That* was my first kiss.

Ohmigod.

FOURTEEN

PARKER

I DON'T SLEEP THE REST OF THE NIGHT, NOT THAT THERE'S that much night left. I glance at my clock after Wells leaves, then clean up and put my shorts back on. It's after five in the morning. I only slept for an hour, but I'm way too spun up to even attempt to fall back asleep. My heart is racing, my body is hot and tingly.

Slipping my tongue out, I slide it across my lips, wetting them because they feel dry. I am still sitting in the middle of my bed, my legs crossed as I stare ahead at nothingness and just try to breathe. I am completely and totally in shock over what happened.

I turn my head to find my phone sitting on the night-stand. I think about calling Allison, but I know she's probably not awake yet.

Then I wonder if she's with Hendrick.

She was pretty into him, and when Allison gets that into

someone, she'll do whatever it takes to *have* them. To consume them. And since she's done with her boss, or rather he's done with her, she'll want someone else to fill her nights, especially since she's not working yet.

Bringing my knees up to my chest, I rest my cheek on them as I stare out the window at the building across from me. I think about Wells and wonder how he found me, got access to my secure building, got a key to my condo, and then just walked inside like he owned the place.

It should not be sexy and exciting. It should scare the hell out of me. But it doesn't. It's sensual and sexy. It's the most dangerous thing I've ever done in my entire life, and it doesn't give me anxiety.

I did something new. And I liked it—a lot.

No way should I be breathing easy right now. I should be hyperventilating, crying, unable to breathe, unable to think clearly. But I've never felt so free, so clear, so calm in my life. Am I feeling this way all because of this man? And if I am, how is that possible?

I scrape my teeth across my bottom lip before I throw my legs over the side of the bed and stand, nabbing my phone off the nightstand before I leave the room to sink down into my chair in the living room and open the Safari app on my phone.

I'm not sure what I'm going to search for, but it's going to be this person. I try typing *Wells, Dallas, Texas,* into the search bar. All it does is bring up banks, companies, and people with the last name Wells. He said it was his first name, so none of those fits, plus none of the people pictured are tall, sexy, dark-haired, white-teethed men.

So, they're out.

Chewing on the corner of my cheek, I pinch a piece of skin with my teeth and roll it back and forth as I try to think of something else to search for to find him. I can think of absolutely nothing. Letting out a frustrated sigh, I almost toss my phone onto the rug in front of me when it buzzes in my hand with an incoming message.

Sucking in a breath, I slide my thumb across the screen. It's a new message from him.

UNKNOWN: I CAN'T GET YOUR TASTE OFF MY TONGUE. DELICIOUS.

Lifting my hand to my cheek, I cup it and feel the heat there. This man, this stranger, this stalker, he knows the way I taste. My first kiss was... down there. I don't understand why that is hot. It shouldn't be. I should be disgusted and embarrassed... What if something is wrong with me?

What if I'm a freak?

With my hand on my cheek, I stare at my phone, but I don't see anything as I think about the possibility that I have something wrong with me. What if my anxiety is because I'm really some kind of weirdo?

UNKNOWN: PARKER.

I blink my eyes to adjust so I can read the notification. No longer am I unable to see. It's as if that single text has caused everything to realign. I wait for something else to come through, but it's clear he wants me to respond to his previous message. The way he's sent just my name causes a chill to slide down my spine.

It's demanding.

And I don't know if I like that or not, but I'm leaning toward liking it. Because even though I don't quite understand how or why, I like everything about this man. Pressing my lips together, I roll them a few times, then start to type something back, delete it, then start again.

Why do I like the thought of that so much?

SEND.

And I do.

The three little dots appear as he types a message back. Holding my breath, I wait for the message to appear. I know it's going to cause my lungs to seize, as all his texts have done so since he started sending them to me last night.

UNKNOWN: BECAUSE YOU'RE MINE.

My breath hitches.

I do like the sound of that.

I am his, and I didn't even know it. Then I wonder if I've always been his. Maybe that's why nobody else ever appealed to me, why nothing has ever happened with anyone, why it's seemed as if I was alone in the world until this moment. I'm totally overthinking all of this, and I know it, but I can't help myself.

Will I get to see you again, maybe in the daylight?

UNKNOWN: YES.

His one-word answer causes my heart to squeeze. *Yes.* But when? I wait, and wait, to see if he's going to say when, but he doesn't. I bite the inside of my cheek as I hold my breath for a moment, then let it out slowly as I begin to type my own one word.

A simple question.

When?

The moments tick by. I think about standing from the

chair, showering, and getting dressed for the day, but something causes me to pause. To wait. And I do wait. Minute after minute, until I let out a sigh of relief at the sight of that bubble, of those three little dots, then a short message comes through, and my hopes are instantly dashed.

It feels as if I'm on a roller coaster of emotions right now, and I've only known this man's name for a few hours.

> UNKNOWN: I'LL COME TO YOU IN THE
> NIGHT FOR NOW.

The only thought that flashes through my mind is that he's somehow ashamed of me. My heart cracks at the thought. But then, why wouldn't he be ashamed of me? I'm plain, a loner, a nerd, and a *virgin*.

There is no way that a man like him wants to be seen anywhere near a woman like me. I should take the little bit of attention and affection he's willing to show me in secret and just shut up and be happy about it.

> Okay.

I don't know what else to say. *Okay* seems to be all I can type. Setting the phone down on the little table next to the chair, I decide I need to take a moment for myself. Standing, I leave the device where it is and make my way toward the shower.

I need to let the hot water wash over my skin. I need to think about this. And I need to maybe contemplate calling the police because none of this is normal. Then, I need to journal it and perhaps have an emergency meeting with Doctor Hamilton.

Yes, that's what I should be doing.

Scheduling an emergency counseling session.

WELLS

CUPCAKE: Okay.

I DO NOT like the way she texted that. It's clear to me there is an issue with me not committing to when or where we'll meet again. I have no doubt that she is desiring a time line, but at the same time, she cannot have that from me, at least not yet.

Mainly because I'm not sure exactly where I want any of this to go with her. If I take her out in public, that is a whole different scenario. I like this, the secrecy, the anonymity of this whole thing.

Watching her, sneaking into her place, touching her, tasting her. It's fucking out of this goddamn world. She stands from the little chair she seems to favor and walks into the bedroom. Shifting my focus on said bedroom, I watch as she strips out of her sexy pajamas and makes her way naked into the bathroom.

My phone buzzes with a new text alert. Sliding my thumb across my screen, I look down at the message. It's from Dad. Frowning, I snort at the fact that my dad is texting me about anything. He usually calls and/or demands I come to his office so he can deliver his orders. He never texts me... ever.

DIRECTOR: COME TO THE HOUSE EARLY.
YOU'RE DRIVING ME TO THE CLUB.

The club.

It's where we gather for our family meetings before we have dinner with our mother. My father has never, not ever, asked me to take him there. This is new and odd at the same time. I'm not exactly sure how to take any of this and wonder if I fucked up somewhere.

I WILL BE THERE.

DIRECTOR: GOOD.

Rolling my eyes to the ceiling, I grab hold of the binoculars again and try to find Parker. She's just stepping out of the bathroom, the towel wrapped around her body. I watch as she opens said towel, drops it to the floor, then moves toward the dresser.

She reaches out to open the drawer and gathers her underthings. I can't stop staring at her tits. They sway with her movements, and I imagine sucking on them, licking them, tasting them. Soon. When she begins to dress, only then do I place my binoculars down.

I can't help but think about this thing with her and what it means for the future. I'm not sure what will happen between us, but I admit that I like the fact she's a virgin. That she's mine for the taking. Possibly for the keeping. But on the other hand, that sounds far too permanent. I'm not sure I'm ready for an eternal commitment of any kind.

My phone rings, and this time, it's Coleman calling me. Sliding my thumb across the screen, I stand and stretch as I greet him.

"Hello?"

"Seems as though Shiloh isn't going to even last the fifteen days."

I don't respond to him immediately. I'm sure that whatever it is he has on his mind, he's going to tell me exactly what he means. I stare straight ahead at the mirrored one-way glass that I know hides Parker from the view of the naked eye.

When Coleman doesn't say anything else immediately, I take it that he's either thinking or he wants me to ask him what the fuck he's talking about. I can tell this whole situation is bothering him, but at the same time, this is his shit show, not mine.

"What the fuck happened now? And hurry because apparently, I'm picking Dad up and taking him to the club."

"The fuck?" he asks.

"Tell me about it."

Coleman growls. As the oldest of the three of us brothers, he should be the one who is called any time Dad needs anything, especially when it comes to work. I don't know what is going on or why he would ask me to take him to the club, but it's not like I can tell our dad anything other than what he wants to hear—which is always *yes, sir*.

"Shiloh came to my place and attempted to seduce me. She said that she knows what she wants, and it's for us to build an empire together."

Laughing, I clear my throat and grab my keys as I leave the apartment. I lock the door behind me, shove them into my pocket, and head toward my car. I don't have to pick up Dad immediately, but I need to shower and change before I do. Maybe eat something, too. I honestly can't remember the last time I ate other than Parker's pussy.

"She has no fucking clue. She thinks she knows something, though," I murmur.

"Oh, she thinks she knows a hell of a lot, except she doesn't know shit. That woman thinks because she and her father have dipped a toe into the underbelly of society, that she's fully aware of the way my life operates. She thinks she can manipulate and strong-arm me. I want her gone."

"*Coleman*," I warn.

I make a tsking noise as my tongue hits my teeth a few times. "This isn't even personal anymore. Now, it's the principle."

"Then I'll take care of it," I say because, at the end of the day, my brother is all that matters—family is all that matters.

112

A life for a life.

And this bitch is fucking with our livelihoods, which is the same fucking thing, in my opinion, as taking a life. My father doesn't feel the same way, but I am indeed not my father.

Anything that is done to hurt the family in any way, financially or physically, I consider taking out a threat against our lives, and that is something that is not and never will be tolerated.

My father only considers physical threats and actions. I add in money as well because, at the end of the day, if they take money from us, if they fuck up any big deals, manipulate and play, then they're trying to fuck up our lives, and that is just not acceptable.

Ever.

"Wait until the deal is done. I can wait the fifteen days, but when it posts, I want her gone."

"Then she is gone."

CHAPTER
FIFTEEN

WELLS

"Your brother is a loose cannon, but that's not why I asked you to pick me up," my father murmurs.

I open my mouth, then close it and press my lips together, rolling them once before I release them. I'm not sure if I'm supposed to reply to him about this or not. But I decide to stay quiet. He's got something on his mind, and I'm going to let him get it all out.

"This is about you. We need to discuss your future."

"Future?" I ask, gripping the steering wheel tightly. I can hear it crack beneath my grip, but I don't release it.

I don't want to discuss a goddamn thing with him about my future. About me in general. I'm happy doing my job for the family. I'm good with all I have going on right now. Especially with my budding situation with Parker. I do not need my father fucking with things before they've even started with her.

"Your brother has chosen his prize. You are the same rank as he is. Have you thought about choosing a woman for yourself as well?" he asks.

I have.

The past few weeks, I've done nothing but think about a wife, a future, and the woman who I might want to have for myself. I don't want to tell him that, though, at least not yet. There is still a lot about Parker that I don't know. I'm not even sure if she would be a good fit or if I would want to keep her for life. It's not a decision to be taken lightly.

"I won't be thirty for another five years," I say instead of answering his question.

He hums but doesn't say anything immediately. Continuing toward the club, I bite the inside of my cheek as I attempt to focus on the road. I can almost hear the wheels inside of my dad's head spinning.

It's clear that he's got some kind of reason for asking me this, and it's not because he wants to see me settled down or wants grandkids. I wait him out. I know he'll say whatever it is. He wouldn't have called me here to drive him alone if he hadn't planned on it.

"I've gathered a set of dossiers for you while I was getting Coleman's together. However, they're younger. So they wouldn't be ready for a few years. Which would make it just about right for you."

"Why?" I ask. The thought of looking at pictures of underage girls to choose a wife makes me feel all kinds of fucking wrong.

"Why?"

I hum, deciding to make him answer me. And he does. "Some associates have daughters coming up and have asked if there was any way we could permanently combine our assets in a way that would not be broken."

"I see," I murmur. "So, since that didn't quite work out

with Coleman and now everyone is walking a thin line, you want to seal a deal with me and some girl early so it doesn't happen again."

My dad chuckles as he shrugs his shoulders. That's exactly what he's thinking. "I'm not signing anything," I say. "Not until I know what I want. I've given my life to the family, but marrying someone for the family's financial gain or whatever the reasoning is, is not part of my deal."

He doesn't say anything right away, mainly because he can't. We finish the car ride in silence, and I pull into my spot at the club, shifting the car into *Park*. My dad reaches out and grabs hold of my bicep.

Turning my head, I look over to him. He's got a very serious, almost grave expression on his face as he speaks. "Sometimes," he begins, "sometimes, even though it is not exactly what we had envisioned for our future, it ends up being exactly what we needed."

I open my mouth to respond, but he holds up his hand and shakes his head once. "I am not asking you to give me an answer immediately. I'm just offering this as a viable option. It would alleviate a lot of issues Coleman had with that woman. It would make your life and the family's a lot easier."

And at the end of the day, the last sentence is what this is about. It would make the family's life easier, meaning my father's. Clearing my throat, I reach for the handle to open the car door. My father releases my arm but continues to hold my gaze with his.

"I'm sure it would make things easier, and I'll think about it. But I'm with Coleman. I want what I was promised."

My dad shakes his head twice, then levels me with his gaze again.

"You were promised a virgin bride of your own, a woman to own. A woman who was yours. And only yours. You will still get that. There were no other stipulations to the offer,

Wells. All four of the girls in the folder are virgins, and the fathers have signed affidavits that they will stay that way, or the contract will be null and void. And as long as the contracts are met, one will be yours as soon as the ring is slipped on her finger."

I hate this.

Mainly because my dad has thought of everything, and technically, he is not wrong. Pushing the car door open, I unfold from the vehicle and stand before I turn back toward the car and bend slightly to where my dad is still sitting in the passenger seat, watching me.

"I will think about it. I will read them."

He dips his chin but doesn't say anything else, and the conversation is finished. Together, we walk into the club, and he moves toward the uncles while I move toward my brothers. Coleman grunts as soon as I approach.

"It was about me choosing a wife," I mutter.

"Fuck," he hisses.

"A wife whose family will be a good asset to ours."

"Fuck," he repeats.

That about sums it up.

Fuck.

There's just no other way around it at this point.

Fuck.

We're unable to talk about it further, although I don't know what else needs to or could be said about the situation. It is what it is. I have four teenage girls' pictures to look at and try to imagine what they'll look like in five years and if, in five years, I'll want to marry one and keep her for myself.

No pressure.

"We have a lot to discuss this evening and some decisions to make," my father announces.

Everybody stops talking and gathers around the table. We have spots designated by our rank. Coleman and I sit together, although one of our cousins is between us because he's twenty-eight and has been a manager for a year longer than I have.

"Let us begin," my father calls out, and the meeting officially starts.

PARKER

I'M NOT sure what I expected for the day, but sitting around feeling extremely anxious and guilty was not at all what I thought it would be like. Not even work can take my mind off my emotions.

With my phone in my hand, I have Doctor Hamilton's after-hours number ready to go, but I can't seem to touch the call icon. Staring at it, I wonder what the hell I'm going to tell her? A stranger broke into my place, put his mouth on me, made me come, and now I'm upset about it, but at the time, I was exhilarated.

My condo buzzer sounds, and I jump, my phone flying out of my hand and landing on the rug beside my feet. Standing, I walk over to the buzzer and frown at the sight of Allison standing at the front of the building, holding two packages in her hands.

Touching the button, I start to speak, but Allison is faster.

"It's Allison," she calls out as if I don't have a camera and screen to see her.

"Come on up," I murmur, touching the button to open the door for her. I watch as she tugs it open and slips inside the building.

She's going to know something is wrong with me the instant she sees my face. I run my fingers through my hair like a comb and whimper when they get caught in the tangles. It doesn't take her long to reach my floor. Looking through the peephole, I watch as she steps off the elevator and moves toward my door.

I inhale a deep breath and hold it for a moment, then plaster on a fake smile, twist the knob, and tug the door open. She stops in front of me, her eyes finding mine and narrowing for a brief moment.

"You need to talk. Thank God because I need to talk, too. I brought dinner. I know you never eat on the weekends, so here I am."

Stepping to the side, I allow her to walk past, and she does. But Allison doesn't just walk, she breezes. She's confident and sexy, even in her slouchy wide-leg jeans and oversized, off-the-shoulder, thin gray sweatshirt.

"I am a wreck," I whisper.

She hums as she moves through my kitchen. "I found out that I can't get a loan," she cries out.

I know she isn't trying to say that whatever she's going through is worse than what I am going through. She's instead commiserating. She lets out a sigh as she takes two plates out of the cabinet and sets them down on the countertop as she begins to riffle through the bags, taking boxes out.

"You never have wine, but I brought some mainly because I need it. Want to join me tonight?" she asks.

I think about her question. Normally, I would decline. But I think a glass of wine might help calm me down a bit tonight. I'm just way too spun up. Then I'm going to have to vocally admit what happened, how much I liked it, how I'm anticipating him coming back, and at the same time, how absolutely anxiety-filled it makes me.

"Wine me," I say.

Allison laughs softly, then she takes out two wineglasses. "It must be legit if you're agreeing to wine."

"Not just agreeing," I say. "It's a need."

"Shit, maybe you should go first."

She thrusts a plate of food toward me, and I wrap my fingers around it, holding it against my belly. Turning from her, I walk over to the breakfast nook table and sink down in my usual chair.

Allison walks over with her plate, sets it down, then comes back with two glasses filled to the top with red wine. Standing up, I hurry over to the drawer and grab a couple of forks, then return to the table.

I reach for the glass of wine in front of me and bring it to my lips, taking a healthy drink before I place the glass back down. I stab a piece of lettuce from my salad, bring it to my lips, and lift my gaze, looking across the table. Allison stares at me.

"What?" I ask.

"I think you need to talk to me," she says.

I watch as she lifts her glass to her lips and sits back in her chair, her gaze focused on mine and only mine. She is here to listen to me, and I shouldn't even have said anything because she came here to talk to me about her problems and not listen to mine.

I open my mouth, and the words flow out. They spill, and I don't stop until the whole story is complete. Allison's eyes are wide, her lips are parted, and she stares at me in what I can only describe as shock and awe.

She had not been expecting any of what I had to say. I know she is stunned that I'm not scared to death, that I haven't called the police or fled the condo altogether, especially after the childhood I had.

"Well," she begins when I've finished. "It's the hot guy from the club. So, there's that."

"What does that mean?" I ask.

She shrugs a shoulder. "He was superhot. That's all I got. I don't know how to respond to this, and the fact that you're into it is honestly kind of freaking me out."

"It's freaking me out, too," I whisper. "I really don't know what to do, but I want him."

Allison leans forward, placing her forearms on the table, and sinks her teeth into her bottom lip before she speaks.

"Parker," she whispers, "you want him because he's the first man who's ever shown interest in you like that. But that doesn't mean it's good for you in any way."

My spine straightens. I could tell her all the ways every single man she's hooked up with was wrong for her, but I don't. Instead, I dip my chin in a single nod. Allison knows more about me than anyone else in this world. She also has never been anything other than kind to me, so I know that her words are more about concern than anything else. But I would be a liar if I said they didn't hurt.

They do.

CHAPTER
SIXTEEN

PARKER

ALLISON AND I ARE TWO BOTTLES DEEP INTO WINE AND HAVE moved from the breakfast nook table to the living room. I'm sitting in my chair, where I'm the most comfortable, and she's on the sofa, her body turned to face me, her feet in the cushions.

"Then the guy tells me that my debt-to-income ratio is not suitable. He also said that my idea was... *not sustainable or a good fit for them in this economy.* So, I'm fucked, and I better get my ass to a nine-to-five again."

Sinking my teeth into my bottom lip, I scrape it across my skin and let out a heavy sigh. "Let me loan you the money," I blurt out.

Allison gasps. It's loud and causes me to jump slightly. Shifting my gaze to meet hers, I hold my breath for a moment and watch her. She shakes her head a couple of times, then lifts her glass to her lips and empties the contents.

"That's not why I came here, Parker. That's not why I told you," she says, her voice coming out in a whisper. "I will still get my dream, but I can wait for a few more years. They said I'm too much of a risk, and honestly, I probably am. I have an idea, and I've done some research, but beyond that, I don't have anything else."

Reaching out, I touch her hand. "Allison, I have the money. It doesn't do anything for me but sit there. I hardly even touch it. I can help you. Plus, I wouldn't be giving you anything. It would be a loan."

"I know." She lets out a heavy sigh. "But no."

I'm not sure how I should feel about this. I'm offering my friend something, but she won't let me help her. I want to. I have nobody in my life except Allison. If there is anyone in this world who I want to be happy, it's her.

"Please think about it," I plead. "Let me help you."

She shakes her head a couple of times, then reaches for the half-empty third bottle of wine on the table and pours herself another glass. I haven't poured myself any wine in a while. I'm on my second glass, and that's more than enough for me.

"Enough about me. Seriously, my shit is stupid. I'm going to go and find another secretary job, save my money, and I'll be good. But you," she announces, lifting her hand and extending a finger toward me, "you need real help."

"I do?" I ask.

Her lips curve up into a grin. "Yeah, you do. What if this guy comes to your bed tonight? Are you going to let him fuck you? Because that's what it will be. A fuck. It won't be anything sexy and loving."

Her words are brash and harsh, but they are the truth. I'm under no illusion that this man loves me. I just learned his name, and it's obvious this isn't a relationship of any kind between us. Lifting my glass to my lips, I take a drink, finishing it before I speak.

"I'm twenty-three years old," I say. "I've never been kissed. I think at this point, love isn't going to happen."

"But do you want to do this with a stranger? And I'm sorry, but he could be really creepy, Parker. I mean, sure, he's hot, and you know me, I have no issue with a good one-night stand, but this scares me for you."

I open my mouth but close it quickly, mainly because I don't know how to answer her. I don't know how to respond. What I should say and what I want to say are two different things. So, instead of saying either, I just shrug a shoulder.

Then, I finally organize my thoughts and my words before I speak. "I want to just say that for the first time in my life, I'm going to let the cards fall where they may. I feel so much pressure and anxiety that it seems like there is no hope for me. I want more."

Allison's eyes soften, and I can read the pity in her gaze. I hate it, but I know it is what it is at the same time. I haven't gotten the help I needed when I needed it. I should have been in counseling from the time I was six years old. Even if my aunt and uncle wouldn't have paid for it or allowed it, then I should have gone when I turned eighteen.

But I didn't.

And now I'm a twenty-three-year-old who has never been kissed and has a crush on her stalker who has already made it clear that he's going to be coming into my condo in the middle of the night to fuck me... and I'm excited about it.

"I just want you to be happy," she whispers.

Allison eventually leaves, swaying as she goes, but I can tell she wants to stay. My anxiety is better. I don't want to call Doctor Hamilton right now. But at the same time, I feel like a gigantic failure. I know Allison didn't mean to make me feel that way, but it's what happens when I truly sit down and think about my life.

Closing down the condo, I lock the doors and clean up the kitchen and living room from the evening with Allison. Then I take a long hot shower and walk through the bedroom naked before I make my way to the dresser.

I have sexy underthings. Even when I know nobody will see them, I still like having silk things to wear to bed. But this feels different. This feels like I'm dressing for somebody else, not just myself, and now I'm not sure what exactly I should be choosing.

I scrape my teeth across my lip, finding a piece of skin to rip off before I reach for the raspberry-colored silk nightie with matching panties. Once I'm dressed, I brush out my hair and slip into bed.

Turning the lights off, I stare at the dark ceiling and wonder if he's going to come here tonight. I'll never get any sleep. I'm going to lie here and wait for him to open my front door. I don't know what to do or how to even think at this point.

Inhaling a deep breath, I hold it and slowly let it out. My anxiety feels like it's completely rearing its ugly head. The wine is wearing off, and now my heart is slamming against my chest as I think about what's to come.

Maybe Allison was right. This is creepy. There are so many things wrong with all of this, and yet, when I think about him being here, about his mouth between my legs, and the way I felt—it felt so right.

Rolling onto my side, I close my eyes and try to force myself to sleep. Nothing happens except my eyes move from side to side beneath my lids. I'm not sure when, but I must fall asleep because the next thing I know, I feel soft lips at my neck and suck in a deep breath.

Opening my eyes, I find that I'm shifted to my back and there is a man on top of me. But it's not just any man. It's him. It's Wells. I lift my hands and wrap them around his arms. He's dressed. Sucking in a breath, I look into his eyes.

"Wells?" I ask, even though I know exactly who it is.

"Parker," he rasps.

"I'm scared," I whisper.

He hums, his lips touching mine, and I can taste spicy hard liquor on his mouth. My entire body melts in an instant. Holy shit. My first kiss and it's beautiful. So beautiful. I know Allison was worried, and so was I, but with his lips on mine, that worry melts completely away.

WELLS

"Nothing to be scared about, cupcake."

My voice is rough. I'm trying not to be too loud, but I want to roar with ownership. Mainly because she is mine. And now I'm going to claim her. That is what this is—me claiming her. I don't want to think about my dad, about the family, about marriage. All I want to do is fuck this woman right here beneath me.

Claim her.

Own her.

"Wells," she exhales. Her voice is soft, sleepy, and sexy. "Are you going to fuck me now?"

Sliding my palm beneath her head, I tangle my fingers in her hair as I look down into her eyes. It's too dark to see what color they are, but I know they're a beautiful emerald-green color that makes my cock ache with the need to see them looking up at me when she's on her knees.

Leaning down, I touch my lips to hers in a barely there kiss, a brush of the lips, before I murmur against her mouth.

"Yeah, baby. I'm gonna fuck you now. Then I'm going to fuck you later. Then tomorrow morning, I'm going to fuck you again. Might go on like that for a good long while."

Her entire body breaks out in goose bumps to the point where it actually shivers. Slamming my mouth down against hers, I slip my tongue inside of her and swirl, tasting her. A moan travels up my throat, and she swallows it.

Nibbling on her bottom lip, I break the kiss then move my mouth to her jaw, kissing down her neck, licking and sucking my way to the hollow of her throat. She lifts her hands, her fingers wrapping around my biceps, her nails digging into me through my shirt.

Her hands tremble as she slides them from my biceps to my chest. Pushing up, I look into her pretty face and wish, not for the first time, that the lights were on so I could see all of her, every fucking inch of her sweet body... every expression on her face.

Her fingers begin to unbutton my shirt slowly, inefficiently. I'm about to rip it the fuck off when she finally finishes. Her hands curiously explore my chest and slide up to my shoulders, pushing my shirt off and down my arms.

"Life for a life," she reads slowly.

"Yeah," I grunt. "It's my family motto."

I say those words and end it right there. Because I'm not going to go into any of it. I'm not going to tell her about my family, my life or my work, not until it's necessary, and right now, the only thing that's necessary is my dick inside of her tight cunt.

Rolling onto my back, I take her with me so that she's straddling me. I grip the outsides of her thighs, then slide my hands up to her hips, only pausing a moment before I shift her nightgown up and over her head, throwing it somewhere in the room behind her.

In frustration, I reach over and turn the bedside light on.

Parker gasps, covering her breasts from view. My lips curve up into a grin as I look up at her, but her face is wearing an expression of awe, and I realize this is the first time she's seen me in the light.

The first time she's seen my face.

I watch as she sinks her teeth into her bottom lip, then scrapes them back and forth, her telltale sign for not only anxiousness but also something she does when she's deep in thought. I don't say a word. Sliding my hands up her waist, I wrap my fingers around her wrists and gently tug them away from her tits. "Wells," she whispers.

"You're beautiful, Parker. Up close, breathtaking."

She inhales a deep breath, letting it out shakily, and I watch her, tearing my attention from her tits to her face as I hold her hands by her hips. I focus my gaze on hers.

"You're beautiful, Parker. Every inch of you."

I release her hands to let my fingertips slowly graze the side of her waist, and I watch as her muscles twitch the entire time, then I cup her tits. Sliding my thumbs across her hard nipples. It's my turn to sink my teeth into my bottom lip as I stare at her.

Parker wraps her fingers around my wrists and whimpers. "I've... this is all new."

"I know," I rasp. "I'll try to be as gentle as I possibly can."

A lie.

Gentleness is not in any fiber of my being. Not at all whatsoever. But for Parker, I'll try. At least tonight. Using my thumbs and fingers, I pinch her nipples and tug on them, careful not to be too rough. She gasps, her head falling backward slightly, her neck exposed and sexy as fuck.

I do it a second time, which earns me a moan.

Then she straightens her head, and her eyes find mine. "Why me?" she asks.

It seems to be out of the blue, but I know she's likely been thinking those two words over and over in her head since I left her last. I wish she didn't have these cute-as-fuck silky panties on.

Her pussy is screaming... or maybe it's my cock that's aching. Either way, I want to be inside of her. If this isn't a testament to my control, I'm not sure what is. Picking her up, I lay her back on the bed, my hips fitted between hers.

I grip her panties and tug them, shredding them in my hands before I touch my mouth to hers. Breaking the kiss, I move down her body, my mouth at her center, and inhale her there before I taste her. Just a taste because that's not what tonight is about.

I move off the bed, climbing off to the side. Standing, I look down at her and smirk at the sight of her pussy on display. Fuck. When she starts to close her legs, I reach out and wrap my fingers around the inside of her knee, stopping her.

"I want to see you. Open," I order.

CHAPTER
SEVENTEEN

PARKER

Opening my legs, I stare at him. He's beautiful. I'm not sure how a man like this even saw me. Sinking my teeth into my bottom lip, I stare at him, holding my breath as he tosses his shirt away.

Then he reaches for his belt. I stare at his tattoos. The ink all over his body is black, and there is too much for me to focus on. I am in awe of him in general. He's got muscle stacked on muscle. His arms are as big as my head. His abs look like they've been carved out of stone.

His short, clipped beard and his slicked-back dark hair, along with his cocoa-colored eyes, have me completely and totally frozen, frozen with my legs open. I don't understand how I've turned into this wordless being who follows orders, but here I am.

I watch as he tugs his belt off, then he unbuttons and unzips his pants, shoving them down his legs and leaving him in just his tight, stretchy boxer briefs. Pushing up to my elbows, I watch him as he hooks his thumbs into the waist of his underwear and tugs them down his legs.

I suck in a breath and hold it as I watch him. He wraps his fingers around his length. It's huge. Well, I have nothing to compare it to, but to me it looks gigantic, much larger than his dick pic. Then I realize it has to go inside of me, and my entire body clenches.

"Parker," he purrs.

This beautiful man is going to put that gigantic thing inside of me.

Nope.

I start to scoot off the bed, but he doesn't allow me. Instead, he moves forward, his hand touching the center of my chest. He's wearing a smirk as if he knows exactly what I'm thinking, and maybe he does.

"Show me what you're going to give me," he growls.

God, I want to give him everything.

Every *little* thing.

Spreading my legs, I place my feet on the side railing of the bed. My breathing comes out in quick pants as I watch him. He is smiling a wicked smile. I'm not sure what's going to happen next, but judging by the way he's watching me, he knows exactly what's coming.

And whatever it is, it's going to ruin me.

Wells moves close to me, his hips between mine, and then I feel his... *thing* against my center. I pinch my eyes closed, waiting for him to do whatever it is he's about to do, anticipating the pain of it all. I hold my breath.

When nothing happens, I open one eye as I watch him. He is focused on me, his cocoa eyes sparkling with mischief. Then his thumb presses against my clit and he begins to rub it in circles.

"Wells," I exhale.

He hums, his thumb continuing to move in circles over and over. Jerking my hips, I lift them slightly as my body climbs toward a climax. I feel heat building from the inside out. My belly squeezes and then twists.

I can't believe this is happening. That this is real. I'm about to have sex for the first time with a man who has been essentially stalking me. A complete stranger. And I can't wait. I'm excited.

I want this.

I want him.

I'm so close I'm ready to fall over the edge and succumb to my orgasm when I feel an intrusion between my legs. It isn't slow. One swift thrust, and he's completely inside of me. His hand is still between my legs, his thumb drawing circles against my clit, and I'm not sure whether I should moan or cry out in pain.

I suck in a deep breath, holding it as tears fill my eyes, but I don't allow them to fall. Instead, I blink them away. His eyes are on mine, his thumb working between my legs, and he's buried deep inside of me, his entire body still as he allows me to adjust to his invasion.

I'm not sure there's any adjusting to him inside of me. It feels like I'm being ripped apart into a million different pieces. The way his thumb touches my clit, circling it rhythmically, makes me close my eyes. I hold my breath. My muscles are tight, and I try not to whimper, but I fail.

"Breathe through it," he grinds out.

Pressing my lips together, I inhale deeply through my nose and slowly let it out of my mouth. Wells shifts his body weight to one hand, the hand between my legs leaving me, and I instantly wish it could come back. Then I feel his fingers wrap around the back of my knee, hitching my leg up and tugging it around his hip.

I cry out. My center feels as if it's been ripped in two at

the shift. He growls, definitely not feeling the same way as me. He lets out another growl, then a moan, and my whole body jerks beneath his.

"Open your eyes, Parker."

I don't.

His hand wraps around the front of my throat, and he squeezes. With a gasp, I open my eyes. My lips are parted, and I try to breathe, but I can't. He's squeezing too tightly.

"Keep them open, yeah?"

I try to nod, but his hold on me is too tight. He shifts his hand, his fingers still very much applying pressure to my throat. His thumb slides across my bottom lip, then he shifts his head closer and touches his lips to mine before he releases his grasp on my neck. But he doesn't completely remove his hand. He keeps his fingers there as a reminder.

His hips move, pulling almost completely out of me before he slides back inside. I don't know what it's supposed to feel like, but it hurts. If he notices me wince, he doesn't seem to be bothered. He does it again.

By the third roll of his hips, it doesn't feel like I'm going to be ripped completely apart.

Then he slides his thumb across my jawline and stops at the underside of my chin, applying pressure there as he forces my head back slightly. "You're perfect," he rasps as his hips begin to move harder and faster.

My breath hitches.

He starts to move so hard that it sends shots of pain throughout my entire body. It hurts, and I want to tell him to stop, but at the same time, I don't want him to. I am so confused. I don't understand what's happening right now. I know I should want him to stop because it hurts, but I don't want him to stop because that hurt also feels different.

"Wells," I whimper.

He doesn't speak. His fingers tighten again, and his

mouth touches mine while he moves hard and fast. I can't breathe, I can't move, I can't do anything except feel—everything. When my belly tingles, when it tightens and twists, I know I am close to an orgasm, and I'm more confused than ever.

It doesn't just roll through me. It slams into me. It consumes me. Opening my mouth, I try to scream, but nothing comes out, mainly because his fingers tighten again, cutting off my airway. Then he stills above me. My eyes are focused on his, and his on me, and he roars as I feel his cum empty inside of me.

Ohmigod. Ohmigod. Ohmigod.

That.

Just.

Happened.

WELLS

MY BREATHING COMES out in pants as I release my grip on Parker's neck. Rolling onto my back, I stare at the ceiling and let out a heavy exhale before I reach over and gather her in my arms. Usually, I fuck and leave. Mainly because I don't really fuck women who I give two shits about. I use them for their bodies; they use me for mine, and it's a win-win.

But this is different.

Parker is different.

Neither of us says anything for a moment, and I know this is the time to speak to her. She doesn't know me, doesn't know a goddamn thing about me, and I just took her virginity. I didn't know they made virgin college graduates anymore, but here she fucking is.

Gliding my fingers through her hair, I tug on it gently so that she'll look up at me. She does, her emerald gaze finding my own. She's wearing a frown, and I'm sure she's over-thinking everything that just happened.

"Talk to me," I demand.

She lets out a heavy exhale, her teeth sinking into her bottom lip and scraping backward before she speaks.

"I liked that, and I don't think I should have because a lot of it hurt."

Searching her gaze with my own, I clear my throat before I speak, trying to ensure that my words come out the right way. The way that I intend them, not in a way that she can mistake them.

"Sometimes, that act is soft and sweet, others hurried and hard. Then there are times when it is so intense that it consumes your entire being."

"That was the intense one, right?"

I hum, tugging on her hair again. There is a moment of silence where we just stare at one another. Fuck, I could tell her so many things that would terrify her. She would scream and run from me in a moment if she knew any detail of my life.

But she's mine.

"Yeah, cupcake. That was intense. In fact, that's probably all you'll get from me."

She places her hand at the center of my chest, then moves her palm to my chest tattoo and extends her finger as she begins to trace my family's motto, the words *A Life for a Life*. Always a fucking life for a life, and just that alone would send her running straight to the police, fleeing for her life.

"I thought as much," she murmurs.

Her finger continues to trace the black ink on my body, her eyes following the movement, then she pauses and lifts her gaze to meet mine. She sinks her teeth into her bottom lip again but doesn't scrape it across. Instead, she releases it and begins to speak again.

"Will you come back again? Or is this just for tonight?"

Lifting my hand, I wrap my fingers around her wrist and roll her onto her back. Thrusting her arm back over her head, I press it hard against the mattress. She spreads her legs, allowing my hips between hers. I watch as she winces from the sensitivity as my pelvis rests against her tender cunt.

Dipping my head, I touch my mouth to hers in a hard kiss. I lift my head to rest my forehead against hers as I let out an exhale. "That," I say, "will happen over and over and over again. It was not just one night."

"Wells," she breathes.

Shifting slightly, I run my nose alongside hers after I brush my lips across her own. "I'm not a nice man," I confess.

"I'm not that great myself," she murmurs.

I almost laugh in her face but decide against it. "Sleep, cupcake."

Pushing off her again, I make sure to pull her against my side and keep her there. In fact, I'm not sure I will ever let her go now that I have her. Watching her from across the street has definitely lost its luster now that I've been inside of her.

Now that I've claimed her for myself.

CHAPTER
EIGHTEEN

PARKER

Something warm, wet, and delicious touches my shoulder, causing me to wake. Turning my head, I look over said wet and warm shoulder to see that it's my coffee-eyed, bearded, tattooed beast behind me.

"Good morning, cupcake," he rasps.

"Morning," I breathe.

His hand slides from my waist to my belly, and he applies pressure there, holding me against his front. That's when I feel his hard length nestled between the cheeks of my ass. I'm not sure if I should like that, but I do.

I like it a lot.

His hand on my belly slowly slides down and cups between my legs. I whimper at the sensitivity there. It aches, and I have no doubt there is a bit of swelling and it's feverish there. But that doesn't stop him.

It doesn't stop Wells.

I'm not sure if anything *could* stop him. This man, without a doubt, goes for what he wants and expects to get it, no matter what it is... and he does. He got me, and I'm lying here wondering how the hell I let any of this happen.

Gently, almost as if they are feathery, his fingers stroke between my legs. So light that if I weren't concentrating or as sore as I am, I probably wouldn't even feel it. Lifting my hand, I wrap my fingers around the back of his neck, feeling his hair between them.

I still feel like this is some kind of dream. Nothing about this seems to be real. His lips touch the side of my neck where it meets my shoulder. A shiver breaks out over my skin. This is almost too sweet, the complete opposite of last night.

"I'm going to fuck you," he murmurs against my neck, his tongue snaking out to taste me there. And I think that's all he's going to say, but it isn't. He continues, and when he does, my breath hitches from his words alone. "I'm going to fuck you on your stomach. Take this cunt again. Own you, Parker. You're mine now."

Nobody has ever talked to me like that before, not ever in my life. And I don't know why, but I like it. Then again, just since knowing he exists, I like everything there is to like about this man. And I don't think I should.

He seems all kinds of dangerous and scary.

He's not safe at all. He is nothing like the man I should want for myself, and yet, maybe he's everything I need at the same time. Not just because he's sexy, dangerous, and knows what I need to orgasm, but maybe because he has that air about him. He's in control.

He knows who he is. What he wants. How to get that. While I am a floundering fish with no idea about anything at all.

His fingers continue to move between my legs a little

faster, and he consumes me completely all over again. There is nothing in this room except him and me. Our breathing and the blood rushing through my ears are the only things I can hear. The rest of the world has completely vanished.

I keep waiting for him to do what he promised and flip me onto my belly, but at the same time, I'm quite enjoying this position and his hand between my legs as I climb closer and closer toward my release.

The pain ebbs and all I can feel is need. The need to find my release. Pleasure flows through me as I arch my back, pressing my ass against his hard length, causing him to groan in a sexy, sleepy way. I didn't think he could be sexier, but he really is.

"You do that, and I'll fuck you there, too, cupcake."

I'm not sure why, but that sounds amazing. And I have never even contemplated it, but I've read enough books to know that there can be pleasure in that. His teeth tug on the lobe of my ear before he whispers.

"Not today. But eventually, and you will like it."

A chill slides throughout my entire body as he lets out a soft chuckle. He doesn't stop there, though. He continues to whisper against the shell of my ear, and it sends me over the edge. Just his words, his whispers, everything is too much for me to even attempt to hold back my orgasm.

"Come for me, cupcake. Show me just how good my girl can be. I want to feel your cum on my fingers."

I grip the back of his neck, my nails digging into his skin as I cry out with my release. I don't even get a second to come down from my high. He does as promised and flips me onto my stomach.

Reaching forward, I grab hold of the sheets, gripping them in my fingers, and hold on. I'm not sure what's going to happen. I understand the mechanics, but still, I am nervous about what he's going to do exactly.

His knees are between mine, and he grips my hips. I expect him to haul me backward, but he doesn't. He reaches for one of my knees, bending it and shifting it wide as if he's positioning a doll for his viewing pleasure.

"Lift up on one elbow," he gently demands.

I do, sinking my teeth into my cheek, wondering what is going to come next. He moves around behind me, shifting his weight around, and he sinks one knee into the mattress beside my straight leg while keeping the other between my thighs, straddling my straight leg.

"Wells?" I ask softly, looking over my shoulder back at him.

He smirks down at me, his fingers wrapped around his hard length. "Grab my arm with your other hand," he instructs.

Wrapping my fingers around his bicep, I am forced to arch my back a bit more. I'm not sure about this position. Until I feel him slide inside of me. I gasp. His hands are flat on the mattress beside my waist as he begins to move in and out of me slowly.

"Fuck, you feel so good, cupcake."

His words come out on a growl, and I can't help but whimper. It's the only thing that comes out. My breasts sway with each thrust of his hips. They feel heavy and achy. But me... I feel beautiful. Wells dips his chin, moving his head down so that his mouth is just below my earlobe, and he kisses me there.

"Turn your head. I want to see your face when I come inside your tight cunt."

His words are naughty.

So naughty.

Turning my head, I open my eyes and focus on his coffee-colored gaze. His lips curve up into a grin, and his gaze connects to mine. His focus is on mine. It does not shift or

142

break. His hips continue to move, and I feel myself climbing toward my release again.

It seems impossible to come again after just having done so, but I can feel my belly tighten, tingle, and flip as he moves inside of me. Pushing back, I meet his thrusts as I continue to climb toward the edge and then fall over.

When I come, it's with a sound that I can only think of as a guttural scream. It comes from deep inside of me, and it consumes my entire being. Wells's mouth touches mine. His hips move harder and faster, all rhythm completely gone before he buries himself deep inside of me. I think he's going to split me in half before he rips his mouth from mine and lets out a roar that shakes my walls.

Holy.

Shit.

WELLS

I PROBABLY SHOULDN'T HAVE FUCKED her this morning in that position or that hard, but I did. And I would have regrets, except I don't. I don't regret one fucking second of it. I feel fucking fantastic.

Parker collapses boneless below me, and I slip from her body. There is dried blood on her sheets from last night, and I would lie and say that I'm a bit sorry about that, but again, I'm not. Leaving her in bed, I walk over to her bathroom on shaky legs and reach for the handle of her bathtub faucet, turn it and start the water,

Testing, I make sure that it's not too hot because I am, without a doubt, certain that her pussy is going to hurt when it touches this water. As the tub fills, I turn to make my way back into the bedroom.

I lean against the doorjamb with my shoulder as I watch

her in bed. She's naked, her leg still cocked to the side, her pussy leaking my cum. Her ass fucking beautiful and her face soft and sweet as she attempts to catch her breath.

"Bath is running," I announce.

She opens her eyes, her lips curving up into a small smile. "Are you joining me?"

I should leave right now. I've already stayed longer than I ever have with any other woman. A bath is a form of intimacy that I don't think I'm capable of. But when she looks at me from across the room this way, I want to give her everything.

"Wells," she calls out.

Her voice takes me out of my head, and I push off the jamb and make my way toward her. Reaching out for her, I climb into the bed and roll her onto her back before I slip my hands beneath her and pick her up.

"Wells," she cries, wrapping her arms around my neck. "I'm too heavy."

Tipping my chin down slightly, I search her eyes with my own for a brief moment, then shake my head once with a grin playing on my lips.

"Cupcake, nothing about you is too heavy."

I walk into the bathroom and gently set her down in the warm water of the tub. I almost join her, but I decide against it. It's too much for me right now. I've been watching her for weeks, but I don't know her, and that step is far too much. Something I've never done before. I can't do it, not right now.

"You're not joining?" she asks.

Instead of telling her the truth and risk finding disappointment on her face, I decide to lie. "Breakfast, cupcake. We gotta fuckin' eat," I say, giving her a wink. "You relax, and I'll get food."

Her eyes widen, and an expression akin to horror crosses

her face. I almost laugh at her but don't want to piss her off. She opens her mouth, then closes it again before she scrunches her nose.

Cute as fuck.

That's what she is right now, thoroughly fucked, and with her messy hair and wrinkled nose, absolutely cute as shit.

"I hardly have any food here," she confesses.

My eyes widen in surprise, and my brows lift. "You don't? Million-dollar condo, couple-hundred-dollar sheets on that bed, and you don't have food?"

She lets out a laugh, shaking her head. "I make girl dinners, Wells."

"What the actual fuck does that mean?" I ask, crossing my arms over my chest.

She shifts in the tub, the water sloshing around slightly as she turns to face me a bit more. "It means I eat snacks. Charcuterie-type food. I'm not going to cook a full meal for one person, plus I don't know how."

"You don't know how?" I ask. "To do what?"

"Cook."

Blinking a few times, I tilt my head to the side and smirk as I watch her. She can't cook. I open my mouth to ask her how she has lived on her own through college and has a career, yet she can't cook, but I don't get the chance because she offers me the information instead.

"My parents died when I was little. I was raised by my aunt and uncle, but they weren't really the kind of people who cared to teach me those things. Then college. I lived in the dorms and didn't have to worry about it. Cooking hasn't really been a priority."

I should feel like an ass, but I already knew all that shit about her life. I take a step backward, my arms falling to my sides. "Then I'll order something," I state.

"Okay," she exhales.

Turning around, I walk out of the bathroom and leave her alone. Searching for my clothes on the floor, I pull on my pants, zipping them only. I tug on my shirt but don't button it as I make my way into the kitchen.

With my phone in hand, I glance down at the screen to see if I have any missed notifications. There is just a text from Coleman, and I expect it to be about Shiloh, but it's not. Instead, it's for me.

> BROTHER 1: HOPE YOU GOT IN THERE. IT'S TIME FOR US TO GET TO WORK. THIS BITCH IS PLAYING... STILL.

Fuck.

> WE NEED THIS DEAL TO GO THROUGH FIRST.

> BROTHER 1: SHE WENT TO MY NEW BRIDE'S HOUSE.

My eyes widen as I read the words. Fuck. That is not good at all. Not only is it not good, but it is also not acceptable—in the fucking slightest. I bite my bottom lip as I inhale deeply through my nose, then I let it out of my mouth slowly.

> THEN I WILL TAKE CARE OF IT TONIGHT.

> BROTHER 1: WE.

Then we it will be.

> MEET AT MY NEW APARTMENT AT ELEVEN.

> BROTHER 1: YOUR STALKER PAD.

NOT STALKING IF I GOT THE PRIZE.

Coleman doesn't respond with anything except an eye-roll emoji. I don't bother texting anything else, and instead, I decide to order lunch for me and Parker. I had planned to order breakfast, but glancing at the time, I realize it's almost noon, so lunch it is. I choose my favorite restaurant and get some Greek along with Baklava for dessert.

CHAPTER
NINETEEN

PARKER

I'M NOT SURE HOW LONG I STAY IN THE BATH, BUT WHEN THE water turns cold, I decide it's time for me to get out. I reach for the towel on the floor beside me, then touch the release on the tub's plug and listen to it begin to drain for a moment.

I glance down at the drain and watch as the water swirls and creates a little tornado before I force myself to stand and wrap the towel around me.

Wells was correct when he said that I spent a lot of money on things but didn't have any food, and it's comical because I think that all of the time about myself. He just voiced exactly what I've thought a million times.

Walking over to the vanity, I start to gather my toothbrush and toothpaste so I can freshen up a bit, but when I catch a glimpse of myself in the reflection of the mirror, I suck in a breath. I'm not sure if I stare at myself in horror over my appearance or what I'm feeling.

My hair is a complete and total mess. It looks like I stood in a windstorm for about eight hours and never bothered to brush it out. But as scary as that is, it's my face and eyes that have me the most mesmerized.

My eyes don't look haunted. They actually have a sparkle to them, and I don't know if I've ever seen that before. Then there are my cheeks. They're flushed and almost cheery looking. In fact, I've never really felt joyful in my life, but I do right now, and I know it's not just the sex. It's him. It's Wells.

Then there's my neck. That causes me to pause. There are bruises there, on each side, finger-long bruises that have already started to purple slightly.

Once I've brushed my teeth, washed my face, and moisturized, I attempt to brush my hair and then throw it up in a messy bun with a claw clip to hold it in place. Moving into the bedroom, I don't even think about what I'm going to wear. I just do.

I reach into my dresser and take out a silk pajama set. It's a sapphire-blue silk shorts-and-camisole set. Pulling both of the pieces on, sans bra and underwear, I reach for a long sweater that I like to wear around the house. It's oversized, cream-colored, and fluffy.

Shuffling through the condo, I listen for Wells but don't hear anything. Frowning, I step into the living area and am surprised to find him standing at the window, staring with his chin tipped down toward the sidewalk below.

"Wells?" I ask.

He hums, bringing his mug to his lips and taking a drink. I assume it's coffee, and I smile at the fact that he helped himself. I know he shouldn't feel so comfortable in my place, but at the same time, this man made himself comfortable here. He walked right in, more than once, like he owned the place.

"I have a feeling I should be very scared of you," I say.

150

Wells doesn't turn to me immediately. His attention is still on the sidewalk below us. Then he lifts his head and slowly turns to face me. His eyes find mine, and his lips curve up into a grin that consumes his entire face.

"Yeah, cupcake. You really fucking should. Terrified even," he murmurs. "But you aren't."

Shaking my head once, I sink my teeth into my bottom lip and scrape them backward slightly. "I'm really not," I whisper.

He chuckles and takes a step toward me. He lifts the hand that isn't grasping the handle of the mug and wraps his fingers around my bruised throat and gently squeezes, just enough that it reminds me of the bruising there.

"You should be," he says before he dips his chin and touches his mouth to mine in a kiss.

It steals my breath.

When he breaks the quick kiss, he runs his nose alongside mine before he releases his grasp on me and lifts his head, his gaze finding mine before he speaks. "Lunch will be here soon. I hope you like Greek."

I frown. I find that an odd cuisine to like in the middle of downtown Dallas. Granted, I do like Greek and all different types of foods, but it's just not what you expect. Unless he is Greek? I shift my gaze to my feet slowly before I lift it up again to meet his.

"Are you Greek?" I ask.

He smiles, giving me a wink. "I'm not. My father's family is Scottish. My mother's is from Eastern Europe, where exactly, I'm not sure. But not Greece. Although Greece is a beautiful country and the food is amazing, they aren't from there."

Wow.

He's been to Greece.

I haven't been out of the East Texas area... ever. I have a

feeling that I am, without a doubt, out of my element with him. He is far above me in a million different ways. I feel like a newborn fawn trying to walk on wobbly legs beside a gazelle that is galloping gracefully through the grasslands.

That's what I am, too. A newborn animal compared to him. I'm not sure how old he is, but it's clear he's far beyond my years in experience. I decide I'm going to ask him some questions since he seems to be in a talkative mood.

"What do you do for a living, Wells?" I try not to sound like I'm prying, but at the same time, I think I should know a little more about this stranger who has just had sex with me… twice.

"Real estate."

That's all he says, and it's clear he doesn't want to elaborate on it. Which is fine. At least I know what he does now. That's more than I knew before. He gives me a smirk, then my buzzer for the front door sounds.

He turns away from me, and I watch as he walks to the door as if he owns my place. He answers the intercom, talks to the delivery man, and buzzes him up. I stare, unmoving, as all of this takes place, and wonder how on earth he is *this* comfortable in my place.

Maybe it's because he's just that confident. He is clearly aware of who he is as a man and in this place. He is in charge, he walks around as if he owns it, and he fits and moves well in here. I'm not sure why, but even though it strikes me as odd, I don't dislike it. In fact, I think that I actually like it.

A few moments later, with two bags in his hands, he turns toward me. "Hungry?"

My stomach makes a loud growling noise, answering for me. His lips curve up into a grin before he turns toward the kitchen. I watch him, moving closer, but not so close that I'm in his way.

Again, he moves through my kitchen as if he's been here a

million times. As if he lives here. And as I watch him, I think to myself that I wish he would never leave. Then I scold myself because that sounds just as crazy as the fact that I gave this stranger my virginity just a few hours ago, this stalker, this man who just appeared in my apartment.

I wonder offhandedly if I'm normal in any way. Between the anxiousness, my parents being murdered, living with my horrible aunt and uncle and being a twenty-three-year-old virgin. All probably oddities.

But then I wonder if anyone is considered truly normal? And what does that mean? Normal. The meaning: conforming to a standard. Aren't we supposed to, as humans, strive to perform above the standard?

"Parker, you want to eat?" Wells calls out.

Jerking my chin, I take a step toward him, then another. He's got food plated and on the table. There is also a bottle of water for each of us and two tablets beside mine. "Anti-inflammatory," he explains. "What are you thinking?"

Sinking down into my chair, I give him a small smile. "I was thinking about the definition of normal and wondering how, or rather why, people strive to be normal when it just means that they've met a standard. I don't want to just meet a standard. I want more."

WELLS

I CAN'T HELP but laugh at her words. She's not wrong. Normal is just meeting a standard, and there is nothing normal about her or any of us, really. Reaching for the bottle of water, I lift it to my lips and take a drink.

"No, cupcake. I suppose normal is not something to strive for. I'm glad you aren't, and neither am I."

For a few moments, we eat in silence, then she reaches for

me, touching the back of my hand with her finger. She traces the ink there. Her eyes watch the movement before she lifts her gaze to meet mine.

"Eat," I gently demand.

"Does it always feel this way?"

Instead of saying anything immediately, I watch her and lean back in my chair. I think about asking her what the fuck she means, but I already know.

"Do you mean, is it always this real, this comfortable?" I ask.

She dips her chin, reaching for the fork before she stabs a piece of lamb. I'm unable to take my eyes off her. She's breathtaking, and seeing the bruises on her throat, knowing that it was me who put them there and her body fucking loved it, makes me want to keep them there... always.

"Yes," she whispers.

"No," I state. I could lie to her, but what's the point? Instead, I tell her the truth. "Or maybe it is. I've never stayed overnight before with anyone, so I wouldn't really know."

"Never?"

"Never."

We don't say anything else for a few moments. We eat, and when we're finished, Parker cleans everything up. I watch her, loving the way she looks as she moves through the kitchen. She's brushed her hair, washed her face, and is wearing the sexiest shorts and tank set.

She's perfection.

"What happens next?" she asks, her hip leaning against the kitchen counter.

I open my mouth to reply, although I don't know what the fuck I would even say at this point, but I'm saved when my phone rings in my pocket. Standing, I reach inside and grab the device, frowning at the sight of the name on the screen.

Sliding my thumb across, I walk away from Parker, open the balcony door, and slip outside.

"Uncle Dean?" I ask.

"Need a favor," he murmurs.

A favor?

That sounds both ominous and like it would piss my dad off. When it comes to work, I try not to do that... ever. Even if I seem to accomplish it often.

"What's that?" I ask.

"Don't end the girl."

I know exactly who and what he's referring to. He doesn't want me to kill Shiloh. I let out a heavy sigh, then clear my throat before I ask him why, even though I'm not really sure that I want or need to know. I've already made a promise to my brother. I'm not someone who breaks promises or vows, ever.

"Why?" I ask, more for curiosity's sake than anything else.

He sounds desperate, almost panicked. "She shouldn't be doing what she's doing," he says.

"Uncle Dean?" I snap.

There is a moment of silence, then I hear him inhale a deep breath before he lets it out on a sigh. I wait, wondering what the fuck he's going to say and somehow knowing it's going to completely rock my whole fucking world when he does.

"Uncle Dean?" I ask on a rasp.

"Shiloh is my daughter."

CHAPTER
TWENTY

WELLS

I stare toward the window that I know is my apartment and try to force myself to breathe. I do not understand what he's just said. Because it sounds like he said Shiloh is our cousin. Yet Coleman had been fucking her, and everyone was trying to get him to marry her.

Jesus fucking Christ.

"Does Dad know?" I ask.

Another moment of silence before he speaks. "He didn't. I had an affair with her mother over twenty years ago. I was married. She was not. Ray was an associate, new to the scene and trying to make some fast money in real estate along with other endeavors. I introduced them."

Fuck.

"You're telling me that Coleman was fucking his cousin?" I hiss. "And you not only knew, but you encouraged a future marriage?"

If it weren't my family, if it were anybody else, I would be laughing my ass off at the whole situation. But since this is my fucking uncle and brother involved, I can't quite find the humor in it yet, but I guarantee I'll be calling my brother a *cousin fucker* soon enough.

I still cannot believe his words.

None of them.

"Dad will have you killed for this," I rasp. "Not only did you father a child that was not your wife's, but you also hid it, then you didn't say a fucking thing when Coleman started fucking her, or at least when Dad was trying to push the marriage between them."

Uncle Dean doesn't respond to me. In fact, he begins to sob like a bitch. I find that disgusting. Curling my lip, I clear my throat and wait for him to stop. It's fucking pathetic, and I can't believe I am related by blood to this man. If he were in front of me, I might kill him and put him and myself out of this misery.

"Are you finished?" I ask when I don't hear his blubbering any longer.

"She can't die," he whispers.

With a heavy sigh, I make him a promise. I have to get him off the phone and call my father. Regardless of what Coleman feels or how I feel, the director needs to know this shit.

"Just help me," Uncle Dean whimpers. "If I die, I die. But she can't. She's part of me. Help me."

"I will."

And I *will* help him. It won't be the way he thinks I should, but I don't give much of a fuck. A promise is a fucking promise. I'm going to help him, all right, I'm going to help him into a goddamn grave.

Ending the call, I do the exact opposite of what he wants, or maybe this is truly what he wanted and didn't want to admit it. I have no fucking clue. Finding my father's contact in my phone, I let out a grunt as it rings. He picks up almost immediately on the second ring.

"Wells," he rumbles.

I run my fingers through my hair, tugging on the ends before I begin. My first question is the only one I truly need answered to know if Uncle Dean was telling me the truth or not, although I'm not sure he has any reason to lie to me.

"Uncle Dean ever fuck Ray Randolph's wife before she married him?"

There is a moment of silence, then he clears his throat. "You're hearing this where?" he asks.

"He called me and confessed. Also said he was Shiloh's biological father. Which means Coleman was fucking his cousin, and you wanted him to marry her."

There is a pause, but I can hear the blood pumping through my ears because I know without a doubt that I've just not only confirmed this shit is true but also that my dad has no goddamn clue about Shiloh.

"She is his daughter." It isn't a question. It's a statement. He didn't know. "She is his daughter, and he was pushing for a marriage. He was the one who suggested it to Ray."

"Why the fuck?" I ask.

"That's what I would like to know. Emergency meeting. Just executives and managers at the club, one hour."

Fuck.

He ends the call, and I close my eyes, letting out a heavy sigh as I think about what this means for the night. I can't remember the last time someone in the family was under fire this way. And this is my father's brother. But I know that when it comes to the family, we are all related, and nobody is above anyone else when they've done something this fucked up.

And this is one of the most fucked-up things I've heard in

the ten years since my initiation, so I have no fucking clue what is going to come out of it. "Wells," a welcome, sweet voice calls out from behind me.

Lifting my head, I turn and look over my shoulder at her. She's standing there in the doorway, obviously apprehensive. Turning around completely to face her, I dip my chin in a silent order for her to come to me.

She understands that demand and her bare feet begin to move. Reaching out, I wrap my fingers around her hip and gently tug her toward me with a grunt. Tipping my chin, I look into her eyes, searching them for that sadness. That haunted look that I saw in my mother's office. It's there, but it isn't as prominent as it was then. I take full credit for that, me and the orgasms I gave her.

"I have to go in to work. I have an emergency meeting," I murmur.

She tilts her head to the side, her gaze searching my own. "An emergency real estate meeting?"

I hum, touching my mouth to hers before I speak, my lips moving against hers. "Yeah, cupcake. That's exactly what it is."

Pressing my mouth to hers, I give her a hard kiss, then release her. She takes a step backward, her eyes finding mine, then she steps to the side, holding her body a bit stiffly. It's clear that she thinks I'm leaving, and that's that. Which, under normal circumstances, would be true.

But like she said, she isn't normal.

And I fucking love that about her.

PARKER

I'M NOT sure I understand what's happening here. I start to ask him if or when he'll be back but decide against it, mainly because that sounds stalkerish, I think. So, instead, I take a step to the side, and he smirks as he continues to watch me.

"I'll be back later. Don't know when, but I'll be back."

Nodding once, I stay where I am. He walks toward me, lifts his hand, and cups my cheek. "I will be back sometime tonight. Don't worry, yeah? This isn't a one-night thing."

I want to believe him so badly, mainly because there is no reason not to, but at the same time, there is also no reason to. I keep thinking about it, but it's still the truth. This man is a stranger to me. I don't know what is going to happen with him, and it makes me feel anxious.

I feel the need to call Doctor Hamilton again. Then I realize I threw my phone on the floor earlier and never picked it back up again. Wells shifts his head back slightly, his eyes searching mine again before his hand falls from my cheek and he takes a step backward.

Without another word, he turns and walks into the condo. I watch him for a moment, then decide to follow behind him. Closing the door behind me, I watch him disappear down the hall to my room.

I take that time to find my phone and check the battery percentage. Five percent. Walking over to the charger, I place it down and sink my teeth into my bottom lip, then turn around when I hear a noise.

It's Wells walking into the living room, his shirt still unbuttoned and showing off both his muscles and tattoos as he carries his socks and shoes in one hand and his phone in the other. I watch as his thumb moves over the screen of his phone, and I think about asking him what he's doing, but know it isn't my place.

I'm unable to keep my gaze off him. Again, he moves through my condo like it's his, and he fits so well here that I don't want him to leave... ever. Except that's exactly what he's getting ready to do, and even though he said he would be back, I'm pretty sure he won't be.

I watch him put his shoes on, then he stands and buttons his shirt, tucking it in and hiding the view of his chiseled abs from me. When he lifts his head, his gaze finds mine and he smirks. There is a moment of silence as he searches again. It seems like he's always looking for something, but I don't know what.

He moves toward me, then stops again, his body so close that I can smell him. I can smell myself on him. God, how embarrassing. He dips his chin, touches his lips to mine, and murmurs a promise to return.

"Be good," he calls out as he closes the door behind him, then locks it.

As soon as I hear the lock click closed, it reminds me that he has a key to my place, and I never figured out how he got it. That should scare the absolute shit out of me, but like all things that include Wells, it doesn't.

My home feels empty. He wasn't even here for twenty-four hours, and he's placed his stamp on my condo. I want him back.

Instead of pining over him, I decide to do a little house-work to keep myself busy. I clean the kitchen, disinfect countertops and wipe down cabinets, then move to the bathroom and do the same, including scrubbing the master shower down.

When I start on my room, I stand at the foot of my bed, and I silently scream at the sight in front of me. My expensive flax linen sheets have blood on them. Blood that I didn't see and didn't realize happened. Blood from last night's loss of my virginity.

Ohmigod.

He had to have seen that. My face heats with embarrassment, and if anyone were here, they would no doubt comment on the color because I'm pretty positive that it's bright red. I cannot believe I didn't think about that and figure out a way to hide it before he saw it.

How freaking embarrassing.

Quickly, I move around the room, stripping the sheets and carrying them into the laundry room to try and get the dried blood off them. Then my stomach flips when I realize we slept in that and did it again on those.

Ohmigod.

I feel gross.

Like, it's disgusting, right? I also feel like I can't tell anyone about this or talk about it ever. It's not a question I can call Allison about. Almost anything else. But bloody sheets? Eeeww.

Swiftly, I throw the sheets into the washer, put some soap in, and press *Start*. Walking out of the room, I close the door behind me and hope that once the stain is gone, my embarrassment will be washed away as well.

As I grab my phone off the charger, I notice it's at thirty percent, which is enough for me to call Doctor Hamilton because right now, I'm feeling like I might be sick. She said I could call after hours for a price, of course, but right now, I would pay a million dollars not to feel this way.

The phone rings a few times before she picks up, and she sounds a bit confused, as if she wasn't expecting me to actually call her. Maybe she was just offering the service to be nice. I think about hanging up and curling into a ball in the corner of my sofa, but inhaling a deep breath, I let it out slowly and speak.

"Doctor Hamilton?" I ask. "It's me, Parker."

"Oh, Parker, talk to me."

Tears instantly fill my eyes and stream down my cheeks. That's when I spill everything. I tell her about the handsome stalker, though I don't say his name because it's not really imperative at the moment. I tell her about him showing up and how I just gave him anything and everything he wanted, but now that he's gone, I feel really... indescribable.

I don't know if I'm upset, sad, scared, or nervous, but I feel like I want to scratch my skin off. I feel like I want to hide. And Doctor Hamilton doesn't interrupt me at all. In fact, she lets me get it all out before she says a single word.

When she does speak, thankfully, she doesn't judge what I've done, but she does express concern for my safety. I don't know this man. I didn't give him access to my life, and now he's here. He's in it, not just inside of my home and body, but he has a key to make himself at home any time he wishes, and she doesn't think that's healthy.

Boundaries.

That's what I should have with him. And while I agree, I'm also not sure that Wells would accept a boundary he didn't set himself.

CHAPTER
TWENTY-ONE

WELLS

ONCE I'VE GONE HOME, SHOWERED, AND CHANGED, I HEAD toward the club to wait. I know without a doubt that my dad will handle this here. It's quiet today. There is nobody here, mainly because it's not a scheduled meeting time.

We only bring in groups of men and women when we're having a scheduled meeting. Otherwise, this place stays fairly empty.

Coleman is walking up to the door as soon as I park my car in my designated space. Only the director, executives and managers have designated parking. Everyone else is on their own. Throwing my car door open, I unfold from the seat and shove my phone into my pocket.

I jog toward my brother, and he stands to the side, his gaze following me as I approach. "Do you know what this is about?" he asks.

I shrug my shoulders. I want to tell him, but at the same

time, I think it would be better if he didn't know before it started. He'll probably try and kill Uncle Dean right then and there, but I want to know exactly what Dad, the director, approves for something this big. Call me an asshole, but I want to watch it play out because it's completely fucked up.

Walking into the club, I move through the halls until we reach the conference room. Dad is sitting at the head, and Uncle Dean is to his right. *Fuck*. Uncle Dean's gaze meets mine, and I can see the tears in his eyes. Then he narrows them on me and curls his lip.

He's pissed.

But I don't give a fuck about that. He fucked the fuck up.

This is on him, not me.

None of us speaks as we find our seats. Five minutes later, the room is filled with executives and managers, all my cousins and two more uncles. Leaning back in my seat, I wait for what is about to come. Although I'm not exactly sure what's going to happen, I am here for the fucking show.

Dad stands, his gaze searching the room and landing on nobody in particular. I glance over at Uncle Dean and watch him with my peripheral vision, trying not to laugh at him as he sweats buckets, knowing that he fucked up big time. An over-twenty-year fuckup is not going to fly with the director.

"I call this meeting to order. It seems there hasn't been a need for one of these in a while. I feel as though I treat my men fairly, do I not?" he asks.

There are murmurings of affirmation, and my dad jerks his chin, which quiets the room all over again. "I thought I did. Considering I haven't called one of these meetings in years, I assumed that all was well within our ranks."

Fuck, this is going to be bad. So bad Uncle Dean is sweating profusely and even starts to shift in his seat.

Pressing my lips together, I roll them a few times before I let out a heavy sigh and lean back.

"Then it boggles my mind..." my dad continues, "that someone in this room would think they could get away with something. It may have taken me twenty years to find out, but I will always find out, and in the end, the lie is not worth my wrath."

Uncle Dean jumps to his feet, and everyone's gaze swings to him. Silence. Uncle Dean wipes the sweat from his face, and without a single word, he drops to his knees. The thud of his knees hitting the concrete floor makes me cringe.

Coleman clears his throat, and Uncle Dean's two oldest sons stand as well. Dad doesn't speak immediately, his gaze searching his brother's, no doubt looking for the remorse in his eyes. However, I have a feeling that if there is any remorse at all, it's more along the lines that he's sorry he mentioned anything to me.

"Bring her in," Dad roars.

Hendrick, who I didn't realize was even here because he's standing by the door, jerks his chin, then opens the door and steps outside for a moment. As soon as my dad said to bring her in, I knew exactly who *her* was, or at least I thought I did.

But I didn't.

It's not Shiloh.

It's the wife.

My uncle's lover and Shiloh's mother.

She is gently pushed through the room and guided toward my uncle's side. He doesn't look up at her but instead continues to pleadingly focus on my dad. I wonder offhandedly if he was always this much of a pussy or if it's just because he knows what his fate is going to be.

"Dean, why don't you tell us who this is beside you?" my father calls out loud enough for the whole room to hear.

"She was my lover," he whimpers.

"Were you married at the time?" my dad asks.

"I was."

He hums. Then he gives Dean the real question. "Did you father a child with her?"

The woman lets out a loud sob, her body giving one single jerk as she lifts her hand to cover her mouth. I'm sure she doesn't want to draw more attention to herself, but it doesn't matter. She has half of the room's focus on her, along with Uncle Dean's.

"I did," he murmurs.

Coleman grunts, and I shift my attention to him, knowing that what comes next is going to send him reeling. And it does. Because as soon as my father says her name, as soon as the word *Shiloh* leaves his lips, Coleman is on his feet.

There is a hush across the room, and Uncle Dean stays on his knees, his head bowed as he waits for the imaginary sword to slice across his neck. It doesn't happen. Instead, Dad takes a step backward, almost as if he's washing his hands of the drama that he announced to the whole family.

I almost laugh, and if this didn't involve Coleman, along with the other topic, I would probably be laughing my ass off at the whole thing. Maybe one day in the far future, we can, but right now, Coleman fucked his first cousin... multiple times... for months.

"Are you telling me that Shiloh is my first cousin?" Coleman roars.

His voice bounces off the walls around us. He's angry. I don't blame him. I would be fucking pissed if I were him. In fact, I would be so angry that I would kill someone. Dad turns to him, arching a brow.

"You better ask your uncle that question."

Uncle Dean lets out a cry, and I wonder what the fuck kind of pussy this man is. How the fuck is he an executive for the family and acting this way? Dad takes the words right out of my mouth. He crouches down in front of him, lifts his hand, reaches out, and grips Uncle Dean's hair hard, wrenching his head back and forcing him to look up at him and Coleman, who now stands beside our father.

"Yes," Uncle Dean whispers.

Dad turns to look at Coleman. He's wearing an expression of complete and total disgust and anger on his face. The disgust fades, and eventually, there is only anger.

"What do you want to do with him, Coleman? He disrespected you. He was the one who was pushing the marriage to Shiloh. Pushing a marriage between first cousins. I don't know who he thinks we are… who you are."

"I'm not that," Coleman growls. "I am the family, and the family is me. What I do not do is marry family. Nobody does. We are given women as a prize. I don't know what you thought was going to happen, but you disrespected me, the family, and your director."

Uncle Dean's sons don't say a single word, but when I glance over at them, it's clear they do not think their father has done the right thing. In fact, they appear to be as disgusted as we are at the whole situation.

They have also no doubt done the math and realize that Shiloh was born between them, so it's clear he cheated on their mother, and when it comes to men of the family, they no doubt love and respect their mothers… always.

The women whom the men marry may be their prize, but they are treasures to their children. What they aren't are women to be cheated on in any way that results in a child, nor hiding said child for twenty years, and then doing whatever the fuck Dean thought he was going to do. I'm not sure what he had in mind for the end result, but I'm pretty sure death wasn't it. Although he brought it all on himself.

"What happens now?" the woman asks, speaking for the first time since being brought into this room. "I did what was asked of me. I married the man he brought to me. I did what I was supposed to do."

Biting the inside of my cheek, I try not to smile because it's clear that all of this was done by Dean, who thought he was going to get away with it for life. He would have, too, had he not said anything or pushed the marriage. Without another word, Dad reaches into his shoulder holster and takes out his gun.

He holds the gun close to Dean's forehead and pulls the trigger. None of the men even jump, not even Dean's children. This isn't a surprise. It's expected. Dean should have known that admitting to me what he did was as good as a death sentence. I'm not sure why he would think I would betray my father or my family. My oath prevents me from doing that, no matter who asks.

Dad lifts his chin to me, his eyes finding mine. "Kill the girl," he orders.

That's when the woman becomes hysterical. I don't even know her name. She starts to scream bloody fucking murder. Coleman takes a step toward her, his knife unsheathed from his hip and slices her neck. Blood sprays out all over the place, and then he jerks his chin to me, the bitch's blood all over his body.

"Shiloh is done. They cease to exist to me, all of them," Coleman growls.

Jerking my chin, I walk over to Hendrick and stop in front of him. "The girl, and then after the deal closes, the father."

"He won't cancel?" he asks on a whisper so low that nobody else can hear him.

"He could, but he won't. He knows what the fuck is going to happen if he does."

"Would he care? He'd be dead."

I laugh softly. "True. However, I don't think he loved his

family more than money. His business dealings tell the truth about him, whether he admits it or not. Plus, I've met him. That man is weak as fuck."

"Then let's do this," Hendrick murmurs.

We leave the club together, letting them clean that mess up, and head out to make one of our own. "Do you know where to find her?" Hendrick asks as we approach his car. I decide to leave mine at the club. He can be my chauffeur for the night.

"I do," I murmur as I pull my phone out of my pocket. "One of those nights that Shiloh came to Coleman's door begging him for sex, he took her phone and shared her location with my work phone. So, when we end her, we need to make sure we take her phone and dump it."

"Always," Hendrick murmurs.

I give him the area where the phone says Shiloh is located. I'm not surprised to see she's not home but instead dancing at a club. "Fuck," I hiss. There is no way I'll be able to get this done and get back to Parker in a reasonable time.

This just turned into a stakeout. Mainly because as easy as it would be to just walk into the club and seduce this bitch, our first cousin, and take her out of the club between me and Hendrick, that leaves far too many witnesses.

"So we just have to watch and wait for her to come out," he murmurs.

"We do. I want to catch her and finish this before she goes home to her father."

That's the hardest part about someone who still lives at home with their family or with roommates. They always have someone there to witness something like this. Then you have to kill them all, and it just makes a bigger mess to attempt to cover up.

So we'll wait.

As we watch the door of the club, I clear my throat and

ask Hendrick something I've been meaning to ask him. "You still fucking that Allison girl?" I ask.

He chuckles, shifting in the driver's seat of his car before he speaks. "Yeah, she's fun." I snort. *Fun* being the operative word. I know exactly what he means. "What about you?" he asks. "You get her friend you were being a total fucking creep about?"

I could tell him to fuck off or not say a single fucking word in response, but I'm not embarrassed about Parker and how I pursued her. I wanted to make sure she was a viable option. It's not as if I've ever really dated or spent time with the same woman more than once. I needed to know what I was getting into, plus I enjoyed it.

Although not as much as I enjoy being inside of her.

"Yeah. Parker. It's good."

It's all I say because, at that moment, Shiloh stumbles out of the club in a tiny dress and come-fuck-me heels. It's time to get to work. I can't believe this shit even happened. Holy fucking hell. How did my uncle think any of this was remotely even close to okay?

"You ready?" I ask Hendrick as she stumbles toward her car.

She's alone, drunk, and possibly high. We follow behind her, and after a few moments of silence, Hendrick lets out a sigh.

"Ready as I'll ever be."

It's not that killing someone is foreign or even that killing a woman is some taboo concept. It's this whole situation. It's really fucking bad. Between the building for sale, Coleman and this woman being our cousin whom he was fucking, my uncle being dead, and Shiloh's mother.

All of it is a clusterfuck that I was not expecting this evening.

CHAPTER
TWENTY-TWO

PARKER

After talking to Doctor Hamilton and finishing cleaning my whole condo, I take a bath to ease my still-aching center and read while I soak in the tub. I'm having a hard time concentrating as I think about Wells and Doctor Hamilton, plus all the things she gave me to consider.

I'm not sure I did the right thing by allowing Wells into my condo, my bed, and my life. He stalked me. He *hunted* me. She made it very clear that she was worried I'd allowed myself to be in such a dangerous position.

Her words are making me think... *hard*. I'm insane. I must be. Nobody who's normal does this and then tries to justify it by saying that nobody is normal. I don't know what's wrong with me. This is more than just my parents dying and my aunt and uncle being assholes.

When I took a good look at myself in the mirror, I couldn't stop staring at the bruising on my neck. Have I just entered some kind of abusive thing? I'm not sure it's a rela-tionship, but I didn't tell Doctor Hamilton about that part. I think she might have called the police or something if I had.

Now I'm lying in my tub, trying to think of what to say and do with this man. I'm scared. But I want to see him again. I love the way he feels. The way he looks at me. But Doctor Hamilton is right... I don't know anything about him.

I need to get to know him better before I have sex with him again. I need to know who he is, more than just his name and his career. I need to know what kind of man he is if this is going to go any further.

And that's where I want it to go, but I don't know if it's what he wants, too. There are a lot of unknowns with him, and this is my first attempt at any relationship. I'm trusting him to take the lead, but should I be?

When my bathwater runs cold, I go ahead and forget my book, climb out, dry off, and lather lotion all over myself before I head to bed. When I choose a pajama set, I keep Wells and his likes in mind.

Even though I know I shouldn't.

Choosing a dark-plum silk babydoll gown, I slip it on before I finger the panties that go along with it and decide to leave them in the drawer. I should not do this, and I almost laugh because I bought all these pajamas just to feel pretty for myself, and here I am, choosing them for a man.

It's like a dream come true, but I'm afraid that my dream might actually turn out to be a nightmare.

I just don't know how to wake myself up from it all.

Slipping between the sheets, I prop two pillows behind my back and grab the remote control from my bedside table. I can't concentrate on the book I was reading in the tub, so I turn on mindless television and hope it can drown out all the thoughts that swirl inside my head.

It doesn't work. Inhaling a deep breath, I let it out slowly and wonder where Wells is. He claimed he would be here, but I knew he wouldn't. Deep down, I knew that this was just a one-time thing, and once he left my condo, he wouldn't come back.

Tears prick the backs of my eyes, and I try to hold them back, but they fall. I'm an idiot. I'm a little girl and a fool. I shouldn't have even called Doctor Hamilton. Now she's going to think I'm as stupid as I already know I am.

Eventually, my eyelids become heavy, and then I get lost in dreamland. I'm not sure where I go, but I'm glad to be there because it means I'm not awake and thinking only of Wells. At least in sleep, I can get away from him for a brief moment. He's begun to consume my entire world, and it's only been a couple of days.

THE SUN SHINES on my face, and I push myself up to a seated position. The pillows are still partially propped behind me, and the television is still on, but I have no idea what's playing. I can't remember the last time I fell asleep watching television. My e-reader, yes. The television, no.

I blink a few times and hold my breath as I turn my gaze to the side. I expect to see him lying beside me, all tanned, tattooed, dark, and sexy. But the bed is empty. Not just empty because he's in the kitchen or on the balcony, but the never-been-slept-in kind of empty.

What I want to do is cry, but I don't because whatever tears I might've had, they're completely dried up now. Throwing my legs over the side of the bed, I place my feet down on the floor and stand up straight.

With a heaviness that I haven't felt in years, I make my way toward the bathroom and take another good look at my reflection in the mirror. The bruises on my neck aren't as purple. They've begun to fade. I'm not sure if I like or hate that.

This is why I'm fucked up.

I'm not sure if I love or hate the *bruises* a man left on me. A man who I don't even know.

Not truly anyway.

No matter how much I want to tell myself that he makes me feel a certain way, the truth is the truth, and I have to face reality. I don't know him, and so far, I don't think I could trust much about him. He's already breaking promises.

Taking a quick shower, I decide to drown myself in work today. Tomorrow begins a new week, and hopefully, I'll be busy enough that I won't think about him. Then, as each day passes, I can try to forget this whole thing.

It's clear that this was a fantasy for him. He got his kicks. He stalked and fucked a virgin. Maybe he knew that's what I was. I'm not sure how long he's been watching me, but maybe he's been doing it for a while.

Chewing on my bottom lip, I gather my computer and phone and sink down in my leather chair. Instead of opening my computer immediately, I think about texting Allison. I'm not sure I want to tell her. I'm so overwhelmingly embarrassed with myself.

Finding her name in my contact list, I call her just as the door to my condo opens. "Hello?" she calls out as Wells steps through my door.

He's wearing a pair of dark-washed jeans and a white T-shirt with sneakers on his feet and sunglasses on his face and is holding a little pink box in his hand. After he closes the door, he takes the sunglasses off his face, and his eyes find mine.

He looks exhausted.

"Parker? Are you okay?"

Allison's voice shakes me from my thoughts. "I am. I'm sorry. Can I call you back?"

She hums as if she knows exactly what's happening, then she lets out a heavy sigh before she speaks. "Yeah."

I can't take my eyes off him. He stays fairly far away from me, still standing across the room, and stares in silence. I don't know what to do, let alone what to say. The expression he wears is one I couldn't even attempt to guess at what he's thinking.

Wells takes one step forward, then another. He gives me a smirk, and I swear my entire being melts at the sight of him. Every single negative thought vanishes immediately. I open my mouth to ask him where he's been but snap my lips shut because it's not my business, but then again, isn't it just that?

"Work was rough last night," he murmurs. "I didn't even sleep. Just went home, showered, and came here," he says, lifting his hand that holds the pink box. "Made a stop at the cupcake shop on the way."

I feel like a total asshole now.

"Cupcake shop?" I ask.

He grins. "Cupcakes for my cupcake."

"Work in real estate takes all night?" I ask, trying not to swoon at the cupcake comment.

He lets out a low chuckle as he kicks off his sneakers, then makes his way toward me. He sinks down in the corner of the sofa, his head slowly swinging over to me, his eyes finding mine again.

"Come over here, cupcake. Had a shit night. Need you."

My heart stops.

WELLS

Parker hasn't said much to me, but I can tell she didn't expect me to show up at her place this morning. Setting the pink box of cupcakes on the coffee table, I watch her. Her sofa is comfortable, but it would be a lot more comfortable if she were naked and straddling my lap.

It wasn't a lie when I told her that I had a shit night. I did. After watching Shiloh leave the club, we followed her to another club, then we had to wait until that one closed before she left. At three in the morning, we followed her to a fucking trap house, where she bought some shit, then she got back into her car and drove to an empty park.

She knew we were following her, and she knew she was going to die. She took a hit of whatever the fuck she bought and OD'd. It was her last night, and she did what she wanted to make the most of it.

Then we had to clean it up.

Typically, we would call in a crew of corps to clean up shit like that, but I knew they were busy dealing with Uncle Dean and that mess. So Hendrick and I decided to take care of shit ourselves, but it'd been so fucking long since I'd cleaned a damn thing that it took for fucking ever.

Then, we had to have a meeting with Dad, giving him details and confirmation that she was gone. My next step would have been to come here, but I couldn't just walk away from Coleman, who looked like he'd seen a fucking ghost. He was white as shit.

None of this can I tell Parker. So, I leave it at *I had a shit night* and refuse to say much else. Parker sets her computer and phone down on the floor beside her chair and stands. She closes the distance between us, just a few steps and starts to make a move to sit beside me, but I reach out and grab hold of her hips, gripping her there and stopping her.

She's wearing another one of her silky shorts-and-tank-top sets. I don't know how many of these she owns, but I would be more than happy to supply a lifetime of them.

"Strip."

My word comes out just as I intend it. A demand. Releasing my grasp from her, I place my palms on my knees and wait. Her eyes widen, then she sinks her teeth into her bottom lip and scrapes it across as she does when she's anxious or nervous.

I don't say a word. I'm not here to comfort or coddle her. That isn't what she needs right now. I watch her fingers slide across the hem of her tank, and then she slowly lifts it up her body and bares her tits for me.

Fucking hell, it hasn't even been that many hours, but I'd almost forgotten how fucking amazing they are. My fingers itch to touch them, to feel their weight in my hands, to slide my thumbs across her nipples. To taste her.

She slips her thumbs into the waist of her shorts and slides them down her legs until they pool at her feet. As she stands in front of me, completely naked, I wonder if I'll ever be able to walk away from her.

There's something about her that draws me in. It's not just the fact that I followed her. It's not the fact that I was the first to have her. It's a little bit of everything that makes her a whole... mine.

"Free me," I demand, my voice gruffer than I expected.

Her eyes widen before they flick down to my hips, then slowly lift to meet mine again. "Wells?" she asks softly.

"Want your pretty mouth on me, cupcake."

"I've... never..." She exhales.

My lips twitch into a smirk. "Yeah, I got that. No better time to try."

Slowly, she does as she's told and reaches forward, unbuckling and unzipping my pants. Lifting my hips, I give her room to pull them down my legs. She takes them completely off, along with my socks. Reaching a hand between my shoulders, I tug my shirt off and toss it on the floor.

"On your knees."

Parker sinks down to her knees, but she has her head tipped down, and I chuckle as I reach out my finger and place it beneath her chin, gently forcing her head backward slightly so I can look into her eyes.

"Unless I tell you that I don't want to see your eyes, do not look away from me. I want your eyes, Parker."

Her breath hitches before she asks me why. Typically, I wouldn't explain shit to a woman I'm fucking, but since I don't really fuck them more than once, and this is my third time with Parker, this is a different situation.

"Wells," she breathes.

I love it when she says my name like that. I also love the fact that she's essentially breathless in this moment. Releasing my finger from beneath her chin, I use my thumb across her bottom lip and tug her mouth open slightly.

"Suck my cock, cupcake."

CHAPTER
TWENTY-THREE

PARKER

WHEN I FEEL RIBBONS OF HIS CUM SLIDE DOWN THE CENTER OF my chest, I know it should probably not make me feel powerful, but that is exactly what it does. I've never imagined this act could make the woman feel dominant, but that's how I feel.

Somewhere in the middle of the act, watching Wells while I moved up and down on his length, he tangled his fingers in my hair, and he hasn't let go. His eyes have darkened. They're no longer coffee-colored but now a deep dark chocolate as he breathes heavily through clenched teeth.

He lifts his free hand and places his palm in the center of my chest, where his cum drips down and wipes it. No... he rubs it into my skin as his nostrils flare and his gaze follows his movements. He doesn't speak, and I'm too enamored by everything about him and taking in this new experience to say a single word.

Wells's grip on my hair tightens, and he tugs upward. I straighten my knees, standing in front of him, between his legs, his cum drying on my skin and completely confused about what happens next.

Does this mean the sex is done? He got there, so that's it, right? I don't ask those questions, but they're running through my mind on a loop. Wells releases his grasp on my hair and moves it to my hips, and with both hands, he grips me and guides me closer to him.

"Straddle me, cupcake," he murmurs. "You're going to ride me until you come, and I'm going to watch."

Sucking in a breath, I hold it as I stare at him wide-eyed. I'm not sure why I raise my hands and place them on the center of his chest as I straddle his hips, but I do, and my eyes flutter closed when I feel his warm skin and hard muscles beneath my touch.

My lips part when one of his hands slips between my legs and I feel his finger glide through my folds. On an exhaled breath, my hands move to his shoulders, and my nails dig into his flesh there.

I can only hear our breaths surrounding me as his fingers continue to move between my legs, swirling around my clit before they move back to my center but never penetrate. I ache to have any part of him fill me. My pussy pulses over and over, begging for him to bring me some relief.

Digging my nails into his skin even harder, I open my eyes, my gaze connecting to his. I'm surprised to see that his eyes are back to their normal light coffee color, and he's wearing a smirk on his lips as if he knows exactly what he's doing to me.

"Wells, please," I whimper.

"Please?" he asks as if he doesn't know what I'm begging for when he knows exactly what I want. "Tell me, cupcake.

Tell me that you want to fuck me, that you want my cock filling up that sweet, tight cunt. Tell me."

My entire body breaks out in goose bumps, and my breath hitches at his dirty mouth. His fingers don't stop moving, and he lets out a chuckle. "You like that, Parker. When I talk like that and when I tell you what to do."

"No," I lie.

He hums, taking his fingers from between my legs before he glides them across my lips. "You do like it," he murmurs. "Your pussy doesn't lie. Taste yourself."

I could say no, but I'm too lost in him. Slipping my tongue out of my mouth, I slide it across my top lip, then my bottom lip, and do exactly what he asked—I taste myself. What I don't do is break eye contact with him, per his demands, and I'm able to watch his gaze darken at the sight of me tasting myself.

"Take my dick, Parker."

Lifting slightly, I look down as I align myself with his length and slowly sink down until he's completely inside of me. His hands shift, his fingers wrapping around my hips as he firmly holds me there.

Inhaling a breath, I hold it for a moment, then let it out slowly. I feel like I'm being stretched to the limits, but I don't feel like I'm going to be torn into pieces. I'm a bit surprised. His hands grip me so tightly that I know I'm going to have more bruising there tomorrow morning.

"Don't move," he demands.

I let out a heavy breath, biting the inside of my cheek as one of his hands leaves my waist and I feel his fingertips glide up my side and cup my breast. He gently squeezes me there for just a moment before his fingers grip me hard.

Crying out, I'm not sure if I like it or hate it. All I know is that it hurts. But when his fingers pinch my nipple and tug, it sends desire throughout my whole body, and I have the urge to move. I begin trembling as I try to keep my natural instincts at bay.

"I have to move," I moan.

"No," he grinds out as he continues to manipulate my nipple.

My thighs tremble as I try to hold back, as I try to follow his orders, but I don't think I can last much longer. My body begs to move. It demands that I do something. I can't just sit here while he touches me the way he does.

When his hand leaves my breast, I feel it between my legs, and I gasp. Sinking my teeth into my bottom lip, I whimper.

"No," he barks.

His fingers move. They play, they swirl and pinch, and I begin to sweat above him. I feel hot and almost sick to my stomach as I try to hold back. I have never experienced anything like this in my life.

It feels almost like a form of torture.

Maybe that's exactly what it is.

Torture.

"Fuck me, cupcake. Let me see you take what your body craves."

And I do.

I take and take and take. I'm close in what feels like seconds, my hips bucking over and over. Reaching down to the hand at my hip, I know I need more. I wrap my fingers around his wrist, lift his arm, and bring it to my neck. He lets out a groan, curling his fingers around the front of my throat.

My hips jerk, they buck, and then it happens. My belly turns warm and tingly, and my body feels as if it's soaring. He lifts his hips beneath me once, twice, maybe even ten times. I'm not sure because I am not even on this planet. I'm gone, completely and totally lost in another atmosphere.

"Fuck," he roars somewhere in the distance.

My vision begins to darken, then he releases his grasp on my neck, and my entire body falls forward. Burying my face in his neck, I attempt to catch my breath. His hand lifts to my hair, and I feel his fingers comb through the strands at the back.

"You're mine, Parker. You belong to me, all of you, and I'll kill anyone who tries to take you from me." His words are said on a whisper. I'm not sure if he even meant for me to hear them. Deep down, I know those words should terrify me, just like everything about him, but they don't, and he does.

Wells is a mindfuck, and I like it.

WELLS

CUDDLING.

I'm not sure what the fuck I'm doing here, holding her, my dick going soft inside of her wet heat, but here I fucking am. Parker lifts her head slightly, her lips sliding across my jaw before she shifts back and looks into my eyes.

"You're back," she whispers. I feel like an asshole for not at least texting her, but she wasn't really my focus at the time. "I don't know how to navigate this."

Her admission is vulnerable, and if I were going to be honest and forthcoming, I would admit the same thing. But I'm not honest, vulnerable, or very forthcoming. Sliding my fingertips up her spine, I tangle my fingers in her hair again. I love the way the strands feel—soft, silky, fucking amazing.

"I'm back. We take it one day at a time. Whatever we are only matters to us."

"Only to us," she says, the words coming out in a sweet little whisper.

Gripping her hair, I tug her head back, exposing her

throat for me. I lean forward, and my cock slips from her as I slide my tongue up her bruised throat. I lower her head again, my eyes find her, and I repeat my words.

"Whatever we are only matters to us, cupcake," I murmur. "Let's go get cleaned up, and I'll take you out to a late lunch."

"Really?" she asks on an exhale.

Giving her a grin, I dip my chin. "Yeah, cupcake. Really."

Before I can say another word, she has scrambled off me and is making her way toward the hall that leads to her bedroom. I watch her for a moment, then stand and follow behind her. I watch her heart-shaped ass as she makes her way into the bathroom, then starts the hot water.

I step in behind her and spin her around to face me, gripping the front of her throat with my hand as I slam my mouth against hers in a hard kiss. It's an owning kiss. Because I own her. Even if she doesn't believe it or truly realize it yet, I do.

"I could fuck you again, but I think I'll wait until later. Make you think about what I feel like inside of you all through lunch," I growl against her lips.

She lets out a trembling breath, then says my name on a whisper that goes straight to my cock. Fuck, but this is too goddamn much. I want her again. It's only been minutes, but I want to come inside of her all over again.

"Please," she breathes.

Shifting my head back slightly, I search her gaze with my own before I tell her exactly what's going to happen today. I want a laid-back Sunday, but I also want to fuck her again, and I want her to remember who exactly she's got in her bed.

"Not right now," I say. "I'm going to paint your pretty ass red tonight after I feed you. Fuck you until you're screaming my name. Every time you sit down at work tomorrow, in your little office, all by yourself, you're going to think of my hand on your ass."

Her eyes round, and her lips part as she stares at me. The water washes down on her skin, her sweet body wet and willing for me. She would do anything I asked. I've shown her exactly how good I can make her feel, and I don't plan on stopping anytime soon.

Without saying much else, we take a shower, towel off, then I wait for her to get dressed. I realize I've never gone anywhere with her. I've only watched her out in public and been with her inside of her condo.

Naked, I make my way back into the living room and grab my clothes. Dressing there, I glance over to my apartment across the street and decide it's probably about time I get rid of it. Probably. But I won't. Instead, I decide I'm going to keep it for a little while longer. Maybe forever.

I have a feeling that Parker is going to be a hard habit to kick.

Once I'm dressed and waiting for her, I take my phone out of my pocket and check my notifications. Coleman has texted me. I'm surprised. I figured he'd be piss drunk and passed the fuck out.

BROTHER 1: NEED TO TALK.

Calling Coleman, I hold the phone to my ear. "You with your girl?" he asks.

"Yeah," I grunt.

"Go where she can't hear you. I've been doing some research."

Looking behind me, I check the hallway, but she's nowhere to be seen. I decide to slip out onto the balcony to talk to my brother. I doubt he's slept since everything happened, so I know he may need this right now from me. As much as I want to tell him to fuck off, I decide not to, at least not yet.

"What's up?" I ask.

"That girl. I don't know why, but Nichols sounded famil-iar, and I couldn't sleep. I remembered Mom's note. *Henry*. I can't even fucking eat. I'm so pissed and disgusted and every-thing else. Anyway, I started doing some research. Wells," he hisses, rambling a bit.

"What?" I ask.

"The family killed her parents. It was us. Her father was an investor and her mother an heiress."

"I knew that about them, but are you saying we had something to do with their deaths?" I ask on a hiss.

"That's exactly what I'm saying," he grinds out. "Dad was a manager at the time. He did the hit."

Fuck.

Fucking fuck.

Mom was right.

The door to the balcony opens, and I turn my head, looking over my shoulder at Parker as she stands there watching me, a dreamy smile on her face. I don't know how to fucking react. So I don't say a fucking word.

"Gotta go," I murmur to Coleman. "I'll see you tomorrow."

"Fuck," he hisses before he ends the call.

Fuck is absolutely right.

CHAPTER
TWENTY-FOUR

PARKER

I'M NOT SURE WHAT ONE WEARS TO A LATE LUNCH/EARLY dinner with the man you're having sex with, who isn't your boyfriend and you've never been in public with. Judging by his dark jeans and clean white T-shirt, I figure I can be pretty casual, but I still want to look nice.

After slipping on my favorite black stretchy cotton spaghetti strap dress, I slide my hands down the sides of my thighs and smooth it out. The dress hits just above my knees and hugs every single part of my body, leaving nothing to the imagination. Naturally, Allison bought it.

Grabbing an oversized chambray shirt, I button it but leave a few undone at the top and then tie it at the waist. Instead of wearing heels, I grab a pair of white slip-on sneakers to dress it down and take another glance at myself in the mirror.

Turning away from my reflection, I make my way toward

Wells. He's standing with his back to me on the balcony, leaning over slightly. He's on the phone, and I wonder who he's talking to, but I know that at the same time, it's not my place to ask.

Watching him for a moment, I decide I'm going to make my presence known. I close the distance between me and the door. I reach out and wrap my fingers around the handle before I gently tug it down and open the door.

Moving forward, I watch him for a long moment before I hear him tell whoever he's talking to that he has to go.

Wells slowly turns to face me, his eyes finding mine, then slowly sliding down my entire body. It feels like every single second his eyes are on my body that his fingers are touching me. I suck in a breath, then let it out as he pushes off the balcony rail and moves toward me.

He lifts his hand to cup my cheek, and I can't hold back. My breath hitches as his light-coffee-colored gaze searches mine. "Are you hungry?" I ask, my lips touching his.

He doesn't speak right away but lifts his head slightly, his eyes connecting to mine, and then his lips slowly curve upward. "Starving. Always."

"For food?" I ask.

He growls, his lips curving into a wider smile. "Still starving, cupcake."

Reaching out, he takes my hand in his and walks past me, tugging me behind him as he moves through the condo. I grab my phone and my purse before we move out of the condo and into the hallway.

I wonder where he's parked, knowing I'm allowed to have one visitor spot, but I'm also wondering if he knows that or if he parked somewhere else. I don't know why I'm so focused on this. I can't think of anything else until he stops.

Lifting my head, I blink the daze away and glance around. "You parked on the street?" I ask.

He hums but doesn't say anything else. That is until he tugs me close to him. My body slams into his hard one. I lift my hands, place them on his chest, and tilt my head back so I can look up into his eyes.

One of his hands slides up the center of my back, his fingers tangling in my hair as he watches me for a moment. He bends down slightly, his mouth touching the center of my neck. I tried to cover the bruises as much as I could. But they're still purplish in color and dark.

"I love these," he rasps. "My marks on your body for the world to see."

"Wells," I exhale.

"This is fucking beautiful, Parker. Don't ever be ashamed of my bruises on your throat, on any part of your body. This is what you like," he grinds out.

It is, too. I wasn't sure I did. I sat and overthought the entire thing. I decided it was him manipulating me and nothing more. It was me being inexperienced and pathetic. Except, he came back, he did it again, and I would have crawled on my hands and knees and begged him to bruise me.

I love it.

I'm not sure what exactly is healthy or not, but I feel like this is probably not healthy in the slightest. I'm not sure I care. I don't give a shit, actually. I want his hands on me, everywhere, anywhere, and I want his mark.

I crave his brand of pain.

Over and over again.

He releases me, then takes a step backward and reaches out for the door handle without saying a single word. I watch as he tugs it open. Sinking down into the seat, I buckle myself in as he jogs around the front of the car. I don't even know what kind of car he drives, but it seems really nice.

When he starts the engine, he looks over at me, a smile

playing on his lips before he shifts his attention forward and guides the car onto the street. I watch as he drives, his tattooed hand moving from the gearshift to the steering wheel.

Instead of asking me where I want to eat, he moves through the city in silence until he pulls into a parking lot. I'm shocked when he pulls up to the front of a building instead of finding a spot, acting as if he owns the place.

My door is opened almost immediately. With more surprise, I turn my head and look up at the man who is standing in front of me. He's wearing a uniform, and there is a little pin on his chest that says *Valet*.

Blinking a few times, I now realize I am, without a doubt, not dressed for the occasion. I thought this might happen, but figured I would be safe with Wells wearing jeans and a tee.

Obviously, that's not the case.

I've never eaten anywhere that has valet, or if they did, I didn't realize it.

Shifting my legs over to the side, I place my feet flat on the ground, then I stand up from the seat, straightening before I take a step to the side just as Wells appears beside me. He wraps his hand around my waist before he tosses the valet the keys to his car, and we move toward the front door.

Wells doesn't even reach for the door before it opens. "Wells," I whisper.

He stops, turns his head, and flicks his gaze down to mine. He almost looks annoyed that I've stopped us, but thankfully, he doesn't say anything. His lips curve up into a smile as he watches me, waiting for me to tell him whatever is on my mind.

"Parker," he murmurs.

"I'm not dressed for this place."

He chuckles. "Cupcake," he begins, "you're only underdressed if you don't have the connections and money to get you in, which I do. Therefore, you're dressed exactly the way you need to be. Which means whatever you're wearing, sweats, cocktail dress, whatever, is exactly what you should be wearing."

WELLS

THE HOSTESS DOESN'T EVEN ASK me how many or tell us there's a wait time. She wouldn't. She knows who I am. Who the family is. And she takes us straight back to the family-reserved table for two.

Sometimes, we hold meetings here. Other times, we bring a date or have a birthday celebration. Placing my hand on the small of Parker's back, I continue behind the hostess until we reach the table. She dips her chin without saying a word and leaves two lunch menus and a drink menu in the middle of the table before she turns and walks away.

Before I can say a single word to Parker, waters are being set down in front of us, along with my favorite glass of whiskey. The waiter turns to Parker and asks her what she would like to drink. Her eyes widen at the sight of my glass, and she slowly lifts her gaze to meet the waiter's before she tells him that the water is fine for now.

When he leaves us, she sinks her teeth into her bottom lip. I watch her teeth scrape across it, and I know she has something to say, but I don't ask her. I wait it out. I'm not going to pull anything out of her, not when I know she can ask me whatever it is herself, and she will.

"Do you come here a lot?"

Her question is soft, almost too low for me to hear. Frowning, I clear my throat and lean forward slightly. "I do, with my family, my brothers. They know us well and treat us right. Is that okay with you?"

Her gaze flicks down to the table, then she slowly lifts it to meet mine. "You have brothers?" she asks.

Leaning back in my chair, I let out a small laugh. "Yeah, one older and one younger. My poor fucking mother. We still give her a run for her money."

Parker's eyes widen as she slides her finger across the top of her menu. She watches me. I'm not sure if she's trying to see anything other than what I allow her, but she won't be able to get inside. I was taught years ago how to show exactly what I wish to show to another person.

I'm only going to show her what I think she needs to see, which right now isn't much at all. Smiling, I reach across the table and take her hand from the menu, squeezing her fingers. "I don't date, Parker. *Ever.* I've never taken a woman out for a meal. So if you're thinking I am a regular here with women, you are thinking absolutely wrong."

Her body visibly relaxes, and she gives me a small smile before she dips her chin and looks down at the menu. A few moments later, she's ordered some kind of fucking salad, and I've ordered more than I can eat because I plan on giving her half. She doesn't eat enough, judging by her thin frame and the lack of food in her fridge.

"Do you like your job? Analyzing numbers and shit?" I ask, trying to get to know her better.

Granted, I don't have to know much else about her. I already know how she feels on my cock. But Coleman telling me who her parents were and that Dad probably killed them, I want to get as much information about her as I can. And before I start poking around into her childhood, this is as good as anywhere to begin.

"I do. I went to college on an academic scholarship. God knows my aunt and uncle wouldn't have paid for anything, and I didn't get anything from my trust fund until I was twenty-one," she murmurs. "Allison and a couple other girls let me rent half a room in their two-bedroom apartment. We had a lot of fun," she rambles.

It's cute. I can tell as she talks that she's thinking about her friends and her time in college. She acts as if it was so long ago, but I know it's only been about a year and a half.

"What about you?" she asks.

"I love my business," I say. "It's what I was raised in. It's the family business."

She opens her mouth to say something, but our first course arrives, and she snaps her lips shut. For the rest of lunch, we stick to movie and music topics, which I appreciate because those are things I can't find out about her without asking.

As I pay the bill, I can't help but smile at the empty plates on the table. She ate about a quarter of everything I ordered. It took some serious coaxing and a few stare-downs, but she did it.

I'm pleased with myself, but not just because she ate, more because she did what I told her to do, and that alone makes my cock fucking hard.

Taking her hand, I walk us out of the restaurant. I slip the valet a twenty and tell him I'll be back and tug her behind me as I walk down the street. There's a place I want to take her, but really, I just want to spend time with her.

I've never done anything like this before, and I like it, but I have a feeling it's because I'm doing it with her and not necessarily the act itself. "Where are we going?" she asks.

I hum, not saying anything immediately. It's a nice afternoon, not too hot or humid, which can be a rarity depending on the time of year.

"Just for a walk, cupcake."

Releasing her hand, I lift my arm and wrap it around her

neck, tugging her against my side. I feel her shaky arm timidly slide around my waist. Turning my head, I touch my lips to the top of her hair. She lets out a soft sigh, and that makes me smile.

"I like this," she confesses softly.

"Me too, Parker."

We aren't far from our destination, and as I approach, I turn our bodies to face the shop's window and stop.

"We're here," I murmur.

"Cupcakes," she breathes.

"For my cupcake. Even though you have some at home, you can save them for later. Eat these now."

And I know that's the cheesiest fucking pussy-ass shit to say, but somehow, it fits, and when she looks up at me, the smile she wears, it's worth the pussy-ass words. Every single one of them.

CHAPTER
TWENTY-FIVE

PARKER

THE SUN IS SETTING. I'VE HAD LUNCH, CUPCAKES, AND AN ICED coffee. I'm not sure if I should feel spoiled, but I do. I don't know if this is normal for people who aren't dating, but it feels like that's what we're doing—dating.

We've talked about work, movies, and music. Now, our fingers are laced together as we walk hand in hand back toward the restaurant to pick up his car. I feel like I'm in the middle of a movie.

My entire body is pulled to the side, and I let out a gasp as Wells tugs me into an alleyway. The sun is down. It's darker but not pitch black or anything. I don't know what's happening, and he moves toward me to the point where my back hits the wall behind me.

When he lifts his hands, cupping my cheeks, and his gaze searches mine, all thoughts and questions vanish. Slowly, he lowers his head, his lips touching mine, and I let out a moan as his tongue slips inside my mouth.

He releases my cheeks, nibbling my bottom lip before he breaks the kiss. Our breaths come out in pants as I look up at him, wondering what the hell is going on while at the same time wondering why I want him to touch me... there... now.

Wells takes a step backward, his gaze never leaving mine, and I open my mouth, ready to ask him where he's going, but then he lifts his arm, his hand cupping the back of my head before he tangles his fingers in my hair. I let out a gasp as he spins me around to face the wall.

My natural reaction is to lift my hands and place them on the cool, hard concrete wall in front of me. Pinching my eyes closed, I can feel my heart racing throughout my entire body and hear it in my ears, slamming hard and loud. There is nothing else in this moment but my heart racing.

I should be feeling absolutely sick to my stomach. I'm not someone who typically enjoys the unknown, but my body seems to thrive on it when Wells is in charge. I feel safe with him. I feel protected. And I know I shouldn't, but I do, and I'm trying not to overanalyze it.

Except that's all I'm doing, analyzing every moment and questioning myself, and him, and then myself and him all over again. Like right now, I want to trust him. I'm beyond excited about what is happening, and yet I'm terrified at the same time.

He tugs my head back. My neck arches unnaturally. It almost hurts, but the thrill of desire slides throughout my body, settling in my belly, and I feel it contract with what is to come. His other hand moves toward my thigh, and he wrenches the skirt of my dress up, then grabs the strings of my thong and breaks it off, letting the scraps of fabric fall to the ground at our feet.

"Wells," I call out.

I don't recognize my own voice. Not only does it sound odd from the way my neck is being held, but there is a tone of want there as well. I shouldn't want this—my ass being exposed to the world. I'm in an alley, not in a locked house or room. This is the wide open for all intents and purposes.

My thighs tremble, and my knees threaten to give out from beneath me, but he doesn't allow that to happen. He grips my hip, tugging me backward and tipping me just the way he wants me until I'm positioned like his little doll. That concept makes me moan.

He hasn't even touched me yet, and my pussy is aching for something—anything. He could blow on me down there, and I think I might come. When he has my body where he wants it, bent and arched, positioned like a clay model, I feel the head of his length against my center.

My pussy pulses. I want him right now. I don't care that I can feel the warm breeze from the wind against my body. In fact, I think it makes this whole thing a little more dangerous and sexier. It's forbidden. Slowly, he thrusts inside of me from behind.

I let out a gasp, holding my breath for a moment. He doesn't move, allowing me to adjust to his size, his intrusion, the way he has done before. Then his fingers gently dance across my hip to my belly and slip between my legs.

He swirls my clit. My fingers try to grip the stone walls, but my nails just scratch at the concrete. He chuckles behind me, knowing exactly what he is doing to me. Slowly, he pulls almost completely out of me before he glides back inside.

Wells moves with precision, slowly and steadily, in and out, over and over. Closing my eyes, I try to let my body relax, feeling the way he moves, the way his fingers lightly glide against my clit. This is different from the way he has had sex with me in private. This is sensual, almost as if he's putting on a show for the outside world.

"Are you going to come on my cock, cupcake?" His voice is low and rough. It sounds almost animalistic. Goose bumps break out over my skin.

I moan. Words wouldn't come out even if I tried at this point. He moves inside of me, his fingers continuing to make firm circles against my clit, over and over. I'm frozen in a position where I'm immobile. I am his to have. To use. To play with. And I wouldn't have it any other way.

"Yes, you are. Because you're mine. You get off on me controlling you, on me hurting you, on the way you feel when I'm fucking you," he says on a growl.

He's right. I do. I'm not sure I should admit that, but I do get excited about all those things. A thrill washes through me again, and I feel myself climbing higher and higher. I'm on the edge, ready to fall over, ready to finish chasing down my release and come, but I can't quite get there. I can't move. I can't search and make it happen.

Wells's words come out on a low growl against the shell of my ear. "Come, Parker. Squeeze me with your sweet pussy. I want to feel you pulse around me. Over and over."

There is a moment of silence while his fingers begin working between my legs harder, faster, and with purpose. That purpose is for me to come as quickly as possible. It's almost too sensitive, too fast, too much, but at the same time, I wouldn't dare ask him to stop.

"Open your eyes," he demands. "I want to watch you."

My eyes open, and that's when it happens. He's got sweat on his forehead. His eyes are that deep, dark-chocolate color that I already know means he's feeling something intensely. His hips move harder, faster, the sound of our skin slapping together filling the alleyway around us, the concrete absorbing the noises as much as it can.

His jaw is clenched, and I don't know if it's that, the way his eyes shine, the demand that I open mine to look at him. Maybe it's the combination of everything. But when he pinches my clit, that's all I need.

Every muscle in my entire body tightens. I can feel my pussy clamp down around him, trying to keep him still inside of me while I ride my release, but he doesn't allow that. He continues to move, his fingers even continuing to swirl around my clit.

"Too much," I whimper.

If he hears me, he doesn't even falter. He continues. Hard and fast. It almost hurts, but when I let out a heavy sigh, a breath, and I force my tight muscles to relax, warmth fills me. My whimpers of pain turn into moans of pleasure.

Seconds pass before he buries himself inside of me and stills and lets out a roar. He lowers his forehead to mine as his breaths come out in pants and his cock twitches inside of me.

"Fuck," he rasps, his hand still between my legs, his fingers having stopped moving as he found his release. "Fuck," he grinds out again. "Being inside of you feels out of this goddamn world, Parker."

I shouldn't be as pleased with myself as I am. But I am. Extremely.

WELLS

WATCHING her smooth down her skirt, I bend slightly and grab her panties from the ground, shoving them into my pocket. Her hair still looks perfect as fuck, her makeup not smudged in the slightest as she turns to face me.

Lifting my hand, I wrap my fingers around the side of her neck. She gives me a timid smile, but I know her. She's not as timid as she seems. She's wild beneath those anxiety-riddled, fearful green eyes. She's just waiting for the right person, the man she feels safe enough with, to let it out.

I am not that man.

I can't be that man, not for her.

My father killed hers. My family made her an orphan. My father is the reason she is so full of fear, anxiety, and loneliness. It's my fucking fault, and I should walk away from her right this fucking second.

Except I have no plans of doing so. In fact, I'm going to fuck her, own her, use her until there is nothing left to have. She is mine. That makes me beyond a fucking dick, and I know that, but it's what and who I am.

I am the family. The family is me. And she is mine.

"You ready to go home, cupcake?" I ask.

Sliding my thumb across her bottom lip, I smile when she lets out a heavy breath. She's flushed and fucking beautiful.

"Home?" she asks.

Dipping my chin in a single nod, I give her a smile before I lean forward and touch my lips to hers. "You have work in the morning," I say.

"I do," she murmurs.

"Home to your place. I need to fuck you again."

"Already?"

I smirk. My hand falls from her face, and I take a step backward. She slips her hand in mine, and I lace my fingers with hers and tug her gently behind me. There is nothing said between us. Nothing needs to be said, even though I can't stop thinking about Coleman's call.

Once we're back at the restaurant, I get the car from the valet and guide her toward the passenger side. Tugging the door open, I watch as she sinks down into the seat. I bend slightly, lean over her, and give her a grin.

"Got your panties in my pocket, cupcake. I think we'll have some fun on the way home."

Parker's eyes widen, and she sucks in a breath. I watch as her cheeks pink from my words. No doubt, she's thinking about my hand between her legs on the way back to her place. She squirms slightly, and I sink my teeth into the skin inside my cheek.

Straightening, I close the door and head over to the valet, slipping him another twenty and telling him I'll be back soon. He dips his chin, then I walk back over to the car and slip into the driver's seat.

I shift the car into *Drive* and head toward the condo. I don't want this ride to be over too quickly, so I make sure to take the long way home. I could reach between her legs, and she would probably open them immediately for me, as that seems to be her natural reaction to my hand near her cunt.

I don't want that this evening, though. I want a little bit of a show.

"Hike up your skirt, spread your legs," I demand without taking my gaze off the windshield.

I hear fabric rustling, and I shift my gaze over to her, but I don't move my head. She does as I've asked, though she doesn't bring it high enough so I can see her. Yet. But she will. Reaching my hand between her legs, I slide my fingers through her folds.

Parker's fingers wrap around my wrist and stop my movements. Turning my head, I glance over at her. She's watching me, her teeth sinking into her bottom lip.

"Parker?" I ask.

She sucks in a breath, holding it for a moment, then lets it out slowly. "I'm sore," she confesses.

Her cheeks are red, her eyes are wide, and she's breathing heavily. She's fucking beautiful right now.

"Just relax, cupcake. Don't think about the sensitivity,

about the aches, just feel. You already know the pleasure is coming with that pain."

I am a goddamn asshole. I should give her cunt a rest, but I can't. I'm fucking addicted to her. Every single part of her. But mainly that sweet pussy.

CHAPTER
TWENTY-SIX

WELLS

Cupping Parker's pussy, I grip her there as we drive out of our way, taking an unnecessarily long drive home. She's already wet with anticipation at just a single simple touch. Her panting breaths fill the cab of the car.

"Spread," I gently demand.

She does. Her legs open as far as they can, and if I were able to glance down for more than just a moment, I know I would be able to see her swollen pink center. Shifting my fingers, I slide two inside of her, my palm still applying pressure against her clit. She's still warm and sticky from my cum, and I can't help but moan at the sensation. I want to tie her to my bed and keep her this way always.

"Wells," she exhales.

I hum, not speaking as my fingers begin to make a come-hither motion inside of her. She lifts her hips, gasping as her clit grinds against my palm. I continue moving rhythmically inside of her as I drive. I can feel her pussy's wetness against my palm, and I know she's climbing closer to her release.

Smirking, I take my hand off the steering wheel for a moment to squeeze my own aching cock, then continue driving. I don't know how long I'm going to be able to make it on this road without pulling over so I can be inside of her.

As much as I want to fight it and wait until we get back to her place, at this point, I don't think I'm going to be able to make it there. She moans, her head moving from side to side, her lips parted, and her eyes closed.

She's climbing higher and higher. I know she's close, ready to tip over the edge, and as much as I want to take her there, I want to feel her come around my cock even more. Taking my hand from between her legs, I jerk the car over to the side of the road and touch the button for my hazards.

"Climb on," I growl as I unbuckle my pants, push them down my hips, and free myself.

Her heavy breaths fill the car, and I think she's going to tell me no. It's not like she's ever done this before, and I'm fucking her in public twice in one afternoon. But my girl is a good goddamn sport, and in the next breath, she's straddling my thighs.

Her knees sink into the leather of my seat on each side of my hips. Gripping her waist with one hand, I guide her down on my length until she's taken all of me inside of her. She hisses as she sinks down, her hands gripping my shoulders.

Slowly, she lifts her gaze to meet mine, her eyes wide as she watches me. Tangling my fingers in the back of her head, I use my other hand to grip her cheeks before I tug her forward, my mouth touching hers in a brutally hard kiss.

Holding her there, not deepening the kiss, I murmur against her lips, "Fuck me, cupcake."

A shiver breaks out over her skin, and slowly, she begins to move. I push her back slightly, my gaze connecting to hers as I watch her. My hand is tangled in her hair, my fingers gripping her face, and fuck me, but she's breathtaking.

Her body moves. She rises and falls on my dick as she tries to find her rhythm. I don't move, keeping my hands where they are, looking at her as she watches me. I am her world. There is only me, and I don't give a fuck what that makes me because she's my world, too, right now.

Parker whimpers, grinding her clit against my pelvis with each roll of her hips. She's climbing closer again. She's now where I left her off with my fingers between her legs. "Don't stop," I demand.

Thankfully, she doesn't. "I want you to feel me with every fucking move you make at work tomorrow, cupcake."

She shivers, sucking her lips in and pressing them together as her hips buck. I hear her gasp, then she cries out as she moves perfectly erratically. When she comes, I feel the gush of her wetness slide down my balls.

Pushing her backward slightly, I release her face with my hand but keep my fingers buried in her hair, holding her tightly as I lean forward and suck on the hollow of her throat. My hand grips her hip, and I use her body to jack my cock until I come deep inside of her.

It's this moment that I think about birth control. Something I had not a fucking thought in the world about because every woman I've fucked, I've used a condom. Every woman but this one. I knew she was without disease, considering I was her first everything. Though, I didn't think about babies. I'm not sure I care, though. The thought of her carrying my child makes me want to fuck her all over again.

I release her hair, and she falls forward, panting as she buries her face in my neck. I wonder if I should bring up birth control right now, but then I decide I'll do it later... maybe. After I've fucked her bare again in the morning before she goes to work... maybe.

I need one more time with no barriers between us just to feel her tight, wet heat once more. Then we'll talk about it. Letting out a sigh, I slide my hand up and down her back in a few soothing strokes.

"You ready to go home, Parker?" I ask.

She lifts her head, her eyes searching mine. Her lips slowly curve up into a smile, and she dips her chin in a single nod. I can see my fingerprints' red marks against her cheeks, and I wonder if she'll be wearing them in the morning. I hope she does.

Tapping my palm against her hip, I tell her to get up. "I don't have anything to clean myself up," she whispers.

"You didn't earlier either," I point out, knowing that her tattered panties are still in my pocket.

She sinks her teeth into her bottom lips, scraping them across her tender skin before she speaks. "I know, but your seats."

"They clean," I say with a shrug.

"Wells," she exhales. "I know this car is expensive."

I gently cup her cheek. Using my thumb, I tug her lip out from between her teeth and shake my head once. "They'll clean up, cupcake. I got money. There's nothing for you to worry about, Parker."

She climbs off me, pulling her skirt down as much as she can, then sinks down on the seat, but I can tell she's trying to keep her legs close together so that nothing leaks out. Chuckling, I pull my own pants up and fasten myself, then I shift the car into *Drive* and head for her place.

My thoughts shift to what is going to come next. Coleman. Parker's parents. My father. The family. There is a lot that needs to be discussed. A lot that needs to be said. But at the same time, a lot that needs to be kept a secret.

Maybe this will be my out when it's time for me to leave. I can tell her who killed her parents, and she'll never want to see me again. Fuck, if that's not the perfect end to a relationship like ours, I don't know what is.

Letting me take her virginity or not, she'll never want another thing to do with me.

That's what I'll do.

PARKER

STRETCHING, I reach for my phone and slide my thumb across the screen to turn my alarm off. I think about my new life. It almost seems like a dream. I can't believe I've spent the weekend having sex. So much sex. My body aches. Every single part of me, even my arms, back, and legs. Everything.

Wells's hand slides across my belly, and I think he's going to try again, but we just did it a few hours ago in the middle of the night, and it was amazing. Wild and sweaty. His hand glides up the middle of my chest, between my breasts, and then his fingers loosely wrap around the front of my throat.

"You going to get ready for work?" he murmurs in a raspy, sexy, gravelly, sleepy voice.

Turning my head, I look over at him. He's lying on his stomach, his face turned toward me, his eyes closed. I would guess he's asleep if his fingers weren't currently wrapped around my neck.

"Yeah," I exhale.

He hums, then opens one of his eyes. "I'm exhausted. I want to fuck you again, but I don't think I can. Trust me when I say I've never felt like that before."

Smiling, I wrap my fingers around his wrist and gently pull his hand off my throat. Turning my head, I touch my lips to the center of his palm.

"I need a few days of reprieve myself," I say on a small laugh.

He frowns. "Days?" he asks, then his lips twitch into a small smile. "You'll be lucky if I don't come get you for lunch and fuck you in the office, cupcake."

My breath hitches at his words, and my eyes widen just thinking about that. I envision closing the blinds to my small office and locking the door while he does whatever he wants to do with me because, let's be real, he knows what he's doing, and I'm just along for the ride.

The orgasm ride.

I'm not sure what to say, but he doesn't seem bothered by my surprise. In fact, I think he just said what he did for the shock value of it... but then again, it's Wells, and I'm not really sure he does much for shock value. At least, I don't think he does. He seems to do exactly what he says he's going to.

"But not today, Parker. I have some meetings I need to handle. Probably going to take my whole day."

"Are you coming here after work?" I ask, trying and failing not to sound like a lovesick puppy who is borderline obsessed with this man. A man who doesn't even have a title, and I sure as hell don't have one with him either, except *mine*.

And I don't know what that means. Not in the slightest.

"I'll try."

I hate that instantly. My nose wrinkles, and I clear my throat. He lets out a laugh and a wink before he rolls over onto his back and slowly pushes up, sitting straight before he leans against the headboard.

"I'll text you, yeah?"

I snort. "Will you?" I ask.

He turns to me, his smirk still playing on his lips. "Yeah, cupcake. I will. I'm busy, and sometimes my nights are as hectic as my days. I've never done this before, but I'm going to try."

"What does this make us?" I ask.

He seems to be in a talkative mood this morning, and I would love to ask for clarification. I haven't really been sure where I stand with him. One minute, it's comfortable and sexy, and I feel like being with him is perfection. The next minute, he is cold, closed off, and almost scary.

"We are what we are, Parker. You're mine," he simply states.

"And you're mine."

He doesn't answer me, and I know this is a familiar conversation, but I want to know what he is to me. I want to know everything. I want him to be my boyfriend, and I don't care how juvenile that sounds.

I want it.

"Sure," he murmurs, but his eyes don't meet mine.

I'm not sure what that means, but I decide to ignore it because when it comes to him, I find that I've been ignoring a lot of things, all of which are likely flaming red flags. Inhaling a deep breath, I give him a smile and shift to my knees before crawling over to him.

He watches me, not saying a word. Leaning over his body, I touch my lips to his. I don't say anything, mainly because I'm not sure what to say. Instead, I slide my tongue across his bottom lip, then move to climb off the bed and head to the shower.

I have to get ready for work.

As I make my way toward the bathroom, I can't help but give my hips a little more sway than I would normally because I can feel his eyes on me. He's watching my ass as I walk through the room, and I love it.

When I start the shower, I hear a noise. My heart slams against my chest, and I turn around to find him standing in the doorway, his shoulder leaning against the jamb, his eyes focused on me. I don't know how he got here so quickly. I haven't even put my hair up in a bun or put on my face cream.

Wordlessly, he moves toward me, lifting his hands to cup my cheeks. His mouth touches mine in a sensual kiss. I feel his tongue swirl inside my mouth, then he takes a step backward and grins.

"Shower time," he murmurs.

We take a shower, and much to my disappointment, he doesn't touch me again. Even though I'm too sore to even think about it, I can't deny that seeing him wet and naked makes my body feel all sorts of things.

In the end, I'm glad he didn't, that we didn't, because I'm almost late for work. Thankfully, nobody even notices me walking through the door, let alone that I am almost late to the office. That's what happens when you lock yourself in your office and just work numbers all day long and don't socialize much.

CHAPTER
TWENTY-SEVEN

WELLS

COLEMAN LEANS BACK IN HIS CHAIR AND STARES AT ME. I'M sitting across from him, coffee in hand, smelling the aroma and hoping it will wake me up. I wasn't kidding when I said that Parker completely exhausted me.

I don't know if I'm even going to be able to keep my eyes open the rest of the day. I'm thinking at some point, I'm going to need to take a goddamn nap to attempt to recover.

"So you claimed her as your own then?" he asks.

Shrugging a shoulder, I bring my cup to my lips and close my eyes as I inhale deeply before I take a sip. That coffee touches my soul, and I swear to God, if I had any cum left in my balls, I would make a fucking mess in my pants. It's that goddamn amazing.

"I guess," I say. "For now."

"And what are you going to do if she ever finds out? You

know, once Dad hears her last name, it's fucking over for you."

I hold my breath for a moment, then lean back in my chair. Lifting my leg, I place my ankle on my knee as I watch my brother. I'm trying to gauge him right now. I don't know if he's upset about Shiloh being killed.

I know that the fact they were cousins really pissed him off, as it would anyone, but I can't tell if he really gives a fuck that she's dead or not. Clearing my throat, I decide to end this conversation immediately.

"She finds out it'll be nothing other than pure luck for me. It will end what we have, and I won't have to worry about her ever coming back to look for me or wanting me again. So, yes, she's my woman for now. Until I'm ready to move on, and then I'll make sure she finds out the truth."

Coleman lets out a laugh. "You're fucking cruel."

"Yeah," I agree. "Necessary evil."

He dips his chin, then I decide to switch to the topic of Shiloh. It seems like a good transition. I open my mouth to ask him how he's doing when the door to his office flies open.

"I'm sorry, sir. I couldn't stop him," Coleman's secretary calls out, sounding as if she's seconds away from having a heart attack.

"It's okay, Danica. He can come in."

I watch as the secretary dips her chin, then turns and shuffles away. She's a nice lady, single and in her fifties. Never been married, as far as I know. She's also very attached to her three cats, which is a cliché, but she makes fun of herself. She's funny, and it's nice having her around the office, considering the rest of us, minus Hendrick, are serious and grouchy most of the fucking time.

"Ray," Coleman calls out. "To what do I owe this pleasure?"

Coleman is full of shit. He knows why Ray is here, and so do I, but neither of us lets on. Murder has no statute of limitations, and although the government and the police are all in our pockets, it's better that we don't flaunt any of the things we do during the night hours.

"Where is my daughter?" Ray demands.

Coleman lifts his hand to his chin, moving it from side to side as if he's thinking hard about the question. I almost laugh, but I know it won't go over well, so instead, I lift my cup to my lips again and take another drink as I watch the show before me.

"Shiloh?" Coleman asks.

Ray growls, taking a few steps forward, no doubt meant to intimidate Coleman, but it doesn't work. Nothing about Ray is intimidating. I've seen the man cry like a fucking bitch. Coleman doesn't stand, although I keep waiting for him to, but he acts as if he is completely and totally disinterested in this whole thing.

"Yes, where is she?" he demands.

Coleman looks at me, lifting his brows, then shifts his gaze over to Ray. "Am I supposed to know this?" he asks. "I haven't seen her in weeks."

"Weeks?" Ray asks. "You're a liar."

Wrong. Thing. To. Say.

At those words, at that challenge, Coleman stands straight at attention and slams his palms down on his black walnut wood desk. I watch, taking in the whole moment and wondering how in the fuck Ray thought this shit would ever fly.

Calling Coleman a fucking liar is the last thing I would ever do, but it did get his attention. Which is what Ray was going for.

"A what?" Coleman asks, giving him a second chance.

"A liar," Ray hisses.

If Coleman could kill him and it wouldn't fuck with the building escrow, I think he would right fucking now. But he can't. I watch as the realization of the deal, of Ray's part in it, flashes across his face. Then he sinks down in his chair, replacing the expression of anger with one of mild humor, which is totally fucking fake.

"She came to me, but it was days ago, and I sent her away," Coleman murmurs. "Thank fuck I did, too."

"Where is she?" Ray asks on a whisper.

Coleman shakes his head. "Don't know," he whispers.

Ray takes a step backward, his gaze flicking from me to Coleman, then back to me. "What do you know?" he asks, focusing on me.

Lifting my head slightly, I watch him for a moment. I don't say anything immediately. Rising to my feet, I lift my coffee to my lips and take a drink. I can hear Coleman in the back of my head, screaming at me to shut the fuck up.

I'm not a good listener.

Ever.

"All I know is that Dean Hamilton is Shiloh's biological father, and you are not. Which makes her first cousin to Coleman here. And me. Which means Coleman and Shiloh were fucking each other but are also first cousins. I don't know where she is, but maybe she ran away because of that?"

Ray's eyes widen, and he takes a step backward, then another, his back slamming against the closed office door. He knows... he knew. That much is clear, and he didn't tell Shiloh. What a piece of shit. He was pushing for the marriage to Coleman, too.

I thought that maybe he was innocent in all of this, but it's apparent he wasn't. If I could slit his throat right now, I would.

"You hurt her," he hisses.

Coleman stands and walks around his desk to stand between Ray and me. "Nobody hurt Shiloh."

His words aren't a complete lie. Shiloh's death was quick and likely virtually painless. But she did die. I won't admit it. Coleman won't either. She's gone, the mother is gone, and so is our own uncle. Nobody was safe from the repercussions of their actions over twenty years ago. But it wasn't just that. It was their continued lies and betrayal that did all three of them in.

"Shiloh was innocent," Ray whispers. "She didn't know."

And it doesn't matter. But she knew enough. Otherwise, she wouldn't have killed herself. Without another word, he turns and tugs open the office door, then walks out of the room in silence.

"He's going to be a problem," I murmur.

"More than likely," Coleman agrees. "As long as the deal goes through, I don't give a fuck what he says or does. I'll deal with him later."

My lips slowly curve up into a grin. I like the sound of that. Ray has been a pansy-ass issue for a while. It will be nice when he is dealt with, and we never have to worry about him again. Once we have the building and his contacts, he's no longer an asset.

PARKER

As I walk through the office, I wonder if anyone notices what is different about me. I'm wearing a high-collared silk blouse that is smooth up the front but has a bow at the neck. It hides the bruises there.

Bruises that are in different shades of healing even just after a few days. Some are from early this morning, some from last night, some from a few days ago. I'm going to have to tell him that he can't bruise me anymore. I don't have enough shirts to cover the marks, and I can't wear turtlenecks in Texas for more than a few weeks in the winter.

Slipping into my personal office, I close the door behind me and turn to glance out of the window. Nobody even noticed me, as usual. My heart starts to race, and I suddenly feel freezing cold. My body trembles and my knees threaten to give out.

I'm finding it hard to breathe as I force myself toward my chair, my palms pressing against the desk with all my body weight as I sink down in the seat. I'm not sure what to do. I am feeling sick, my stomach tingling and flip-flopping.

Maybe I should call Doctor Hamilton, but I'm supposed to see her after work. If I can't make it through an entire workday, then I'm not getting better. I'm getting worse. I don't want to say it's because of Wells, but I think it is.

I don't know how to handle him. He's too intense for me. I don't know what I'm doing, and it's making me sick. The back-and-forth, the *I don't know what we are*, then the complete domination and control. It's messing with me. When we're physically with one another, I'm good, but just like the last time I hadn't heard from him, we're apart, and I'm panicking.

This can't be healthy.

I already know that Doctor Hamilton is going to tell me to run away from him. She did the last time I called, but then he walked into my condo, and we spent the most amazing weekend together. And now it's Monday morning, and I'm questioning everything all over again.

Closing my eyes, I suck in a breath, then slowly let it out through my parted lips. I do it again, then again, until I feel better. *Calmer.* But my heart is still beating quickly, my stomach still a little turned upside down.

Sinking my teeth into my bottom lip, I get my computer

all set up, hoping my numbers will settle me the way they usually do. Once I get focused on work, I'll feel better. At least, that's the way it's always been.

I don't know how long I work, but there is a knock on my office door that interrupts my focus. I lift my head.

The only thing I can think is that it's going to be Wells walking through the door, but then I realize he wouldn't be knocking. That man would burst into the space like a hurricane, holding nothing back and demolishing anything and everything in his way. What he wouldn't do is knock.

"Come in," I call out, my voice trembling and sounding odd even to my own ears.

The door opens slightly, and I blink at the sight of Eira. He's one of the bosses here. Actually, he reminds me a lot of Wells. Not in looks but in the way he carries himself. He's tall, strong, dominant. But right now, he seems off.

Almost soft.

Maybe it's me who's off.

"We need your report. Meeting starts in ten."

I blink, then clear my throat as I press *Print* on the report, then I email it to Eira's secretary so she can add it to the presentation he'll be giving. "I finished it. I just totally spaced on the time," I murmur. "I'm so sorry."

Standing, I hurry over to the printer, take the papers that have printed quickly and turn to face him. He's standing in my doorway, his eyes watching me, a smile playing on his lips. He appears to be almost... *playful?*

My feet falter as I move toward him, and I almost trip on my heels and land flat on my face in front of him. Thankfully, I catch myself in time and clear my throat as I straighten and continue to move toward him.

He doesn't step out of the way, though. He watches me, tilting his head to the side, his eyes searching mine.

"You're beautiful," he states, and he appears almost

surprised by that confession, or maybe it's more because he said those words aloud.

I'm shocked, too, mainly because this man has said a total of a handful of words to me since I started working here. He's never knocked on my door, and he's never just stood and stared at me. I don't know what to do, and I can feel my heart begin to slam against my rib cage.

"Eira?" I ask.

"How have I never noticed how beautiful you are, Parker?" Then he shakes his head as if he's trying to forget what he's just said. His lips curve up into a grin, and he clears his throat before he takes a step to the side. "We have a meeting," he murmurs.

He doesn't say anything else as I brush past him and make my way toward the conference room. Eira may not speak, but I can feel his gaze on my ass as I walk. I'm wearing a pencil skirt today with three-inch heels. Definitely not a normal outfit for me, but I felt sexy as I got dressed this morning. I felt sexy because Wells made me feel sexy.

I might be regretting my choice.

CHAPTER
TWENTY-EIGHT

WELLS

BRINGING THE COOL LIQUID TO MY LIPS, I TAKE A HEARTY GULP and hiss as it burns my throat. I slam the glass down on the table, close my eyes, and let my head drop back. Dad is on his way here. Apparently, we have to have a family meeting with everyone. And it has to be this afternoon.

Talk of Uncle Dean has gotten around, and there are plenty of upset people. Then there's our aunt. She's been staying at Mom and Dad's since shit went down. Inconsolable, not just because he's gone, but because of the affair and the child.

Come to find out, she had no idea, and she was pregnant when Shiloh was conceived. It's a whole mess of family drama, and I personally want nothing to do with any of it, but I'm stuck in the middle because I am a manager.

Lifting my head, I take my phone out of my pocket and decide to send Parker a text.

ARE YOU SORE?

My lips twitch into a smirk as I wait for her to respond. She doesn't, at least not immediately, and my brows snap together in a frown at the thought that she is ignoring me or busy. Thumbing through my apps, I find the tracking one and touch her picture.

She's in the office building. Maybe she's just busy working. I know she'd been working on a big financial project for her company. Before I can dig further into where she is and why she isn't answering me, the door opens and Hendrick walks in.

"Morning cocktails? Yes, please," he calls out. "I have a feeling we're going to need them."

He's not fucking wrong. I have the same feeling. I hear my father's booming voice as he speaks with someone down the hall, which is our cue to get our asses up and walk into the conference room.

I can't take too long at whatever this is. I do have to meet with someone from the bank on this building deal. They have some paperwork they need me to fill out. Usually, an executive would handle that, but I'm a signer on the account, along with Coleman and Uncle Dean.

Since Uncle Dean won't be signing anything ever again, it's going to be up to me because my father refuses to fill out any paperwork anymore at all whatsoever. He delegates now, which is hilarious, but also I aspire to become him because I fucking hate paperwork.

Hendrick slams his drink in one gulp. As I stand, Coleman grabs his phone and shoves it into his pocket. Together, the three of us make our way toward the conference room. It's full. Thankfully, Coleman and I don't have to stand since we're managers. We have assigned seats.

One chair sits empty, and I wonder who is going to be the next executive.

My father is sitting as we enter the space. None of us sits out of respect as we wait for his instructions. Slowly, he stands to his feet. Right now, as his gaze searches the room, he is the director. He is not my father.

"Be seated. The meeting is beginning now."

The room goes silent, and then he begins. He's got a whole speech prepared, and I almost laugh because he's being so fucking serious. Granted, it's a serious issue. Uncle Dean betrayed the family and then tried to get Coleman to marry his first cousin.

"So there is an empty seat in the executive section of our family. I want to ensure that this decision was not made in haste. It was not something that was even made emotionally. Dean Hamilton clearly betrayed his family. Our family. And paid the price that any of us would have to pay if we did the same.

"This is a reminder to all of us. None of us is above the rules of the family, not even my own brother. A life for a life," my father says, finishing his speech.

The entire room repeats his words. "A life for a life."

"Next order of business before I let all of you go for the day. I would like to nominate Coleman for the empty executive position. He will be wed in a few short months, and I believe it is time to move him up within the family. Does anybody disagree with this?"

There is silence, and while I'm not surprised that Coleman has been nominated for the position of executive, I'm surprised that my father is not only suggesting it but also asking for a vote today. I figured he would leave the position empty for a few months, at least until after Coleman's wedding.

"Welcome to the executive position, Coleman."

The room erupts in applause, and then my father dismisses the meeting, knowing that on a Monday afternoon, we all have things we need to do. Standing, I reach into my pocket and wrap my fingers around my phone, taking it out to see if she's texted me.

She hasn't.

Frowning, I decide I'm going to have to pay her a visit. There's no way in fuck she isn't sitting at her desk with her phone in her hand. Has she already talked herself out of this between us? It wouldn't surprise me. She's like a timid, terrified animal. She's ready to sprint at any given moment.

Seems I'm going to have to remind her that she's mine. Maybe I didn't fuck her enough this weekend. I figured every single move she made would remind her of me and at least she'd be aware enough to check her fucking phone.

"Are you going to the bank?" my father asks.

Lifting my head, I jerk my chin. "I am," I murmur. I'm distracted. I know I am, but this woman, she is already driving me fucking crazy. I need to check on her, even if it's without her knowing.

"You've met someone," he announces.

My body jerks, and I lift my gaze to meet his. "Huh?" I ask.

His lips twitch into a smirk. "You think I don't know what my boys are doing?"

Pressing my lips together in a thin line, I watch him for a moment, my brows knitted together. He watches me with a cocky smirk on his face. The room has filtered out. It's mainly Coleman, Hendrick, and a few executives left milling around.

"She's beautiful."

"Dad?" I ask.

He shrugs a shoulder. "You took her out to eat. It was

reported back to me. Nothing to be embarrassed about. Have your fun before you marry your prize."

I'm not sure why his words surprise me, but they do. "What if she's my prize?" I ask.

He arches a brow, the smirk disappearing from his lips. I don't shock my father very often, but I can tell he wasn't expecting that. He leans forward, placing his hands on the expensive conference room table, his eyes finding mine and holding my gaze with his own.

"What are you telling me?" he asks.

Sinking my teeth into the corner of my lip, it's my turn to smirk. "She was a virgin. I like her. I think she could be my prize."

Coleman clears his throat, then lets out a cough. "What?" my father snaps, turning his attention to him.

"You killed her parents. Wells is fucking with you," Coleman announces.

Slowly, so slowly that I think he's moving in slow motion, my father blinks, then swings his attention back to meet mine. "What?" he asks, his voice almost cracking.

"The Nichols. Don't know why or what happened. All I know is that she remembers a man standing over her bed the night her parents were killed, and Coleman did some research to find out it was the family. We're assuming you indeed were that man."

My dad runs his fingers through his hair. His usually cool, calm demeanor has been shaken, and I'm a bit surprised. I've not known my father to show any kind of reaction like this before. This is as close to panic as I've ever witnessed.

"Dad?" I ask, unsure if he's going to be okay. "You know she's one of Mom's patients, right?"

His face pales, and then I start to worry that maybe I'm fucking my sister or something, judging by his reaction. Thankfully, he puts me out of my panicked misery and takes a step toward me. He leans forward slightly, his gaze on mine and unmoving.

"Stay away, Wells."

"Why?" I ask.

I'm on the verge of freaking the fuck out, but of course, I show him nothing. He's giving me more in his expression than I've ever seen before from him, especially with other family around.

This shit is goddamn worrisome.

Coleman takes a step forward to stand beside me. I'm not sure if it's in solidarity and support or if he's going to hold me back when I try to beat our old man's ass over whatever the fuck he's dreading telling me.

"Because she is not for you."

"You're going to need to give me more than that. I've taken her. She's mine for now."

Silence washes over us. It hangs in the air, thick and impenetrable. Then Dad sucks in a deep breath, holding it for a moment before he releases it slowly. He clears his throat as he slowly sinks down in his chair.

"It was almost twenty years ago. I wasn't the director. My father was. Hell, I was just a manager. I was married, of course, to your mother. I had this investor. He was dicking us around. He'd promised the family something or other. It wasn't my pay grade to know."

I'm not sure how I feel about this story. It sounds fairly normal. I'm not sure why the fuck he's acting the way he is.

"Wife wasn't supposed to be killed. She and the kid were supposed to be gone for the weekend. I had my orders. They weren't even to kill him. They were to scare him and get the deal to go through, whatever it was."

"Like with Ray," I murmur.

He jerks his chin in a nod. "Like Ray. And we all know how that situation turned out. This was similar. He woke up, pulled a gun on me, and I had no choice. I ended them both. I knew there was a girl in the house. I went to do her, too, knowing we can't leave any witnesses."

"But she was six," Coleman says.

"She was six. I hated myself for that, leaving her with no parents. It was the one and only time I hated my job. Hated the family. So you can't be with her. I can't see her."

It's my turn to stare at him. I can't hold back my expression. I can't just stare at him and give him nothing. Lifting my hand, I rub my palm down my face and let out a sigh. I'm not sure what the fuck to say about any of this except I have one question.

"You watch her, don't you? You knew it was her at the restaurant."

It's not a question. It's a statement. I know he's watching her. He's been watching her. I wonder if he knows about her neglectful aunt and uncle. I wonder if he knows that they tried to take her money.

I wonder a lot of things, but I don't voice them. Instead, I wait for my father.

"I did know it was her, and I have. Which is why I know that she isn't for you. I didn't think it was that serious. Just walk away."

Pressing my lips together, I lean back in my chair. "I don't want to. Give me some other reason. I don't care about the dead parents thing. She might, but I don't give a fuck."

"Wells," my dad warns, "this is an order. Leave her alone."

Standing, I plan to do something I never do. I plan to defy my father. I could appease him and tell him I'll stay away from her, but I decide against it. I'm going to defy him and tell him it's what I plan on doing.

"I'm not going to stop seeing her," I say.

My dad stands, and I hear Coleman groan beside me. I don't give a fuck. I'm not going to stop fucking her just because he tells me to. It's not my fault he fucked up and feels guilty. I've fucked up plenty in my life, especially when it comes to the dealings of the family.

"So you're choosing to marry her?" he asks.

I snort. "No, I'm not marrying her. I'm fucking her."

My dad's lips curve up into a grin. "You're marrying her," he says.

"Why?" I ask.

Coleman chuckles. "Because if she's your wife, she won't be forced to testify against you in court."

Fuck.

"Do you think it would ever go that far?" I ask.

My dad takes half a step toward me. "There is no statute for murder. It's a possibility, and I got no fucking plans to go to prison for murder. Not now, not ever," he says. "You'll marry her. I'm glad she was a virgin because she is your prize."

CHAPTER
TWENTY-NINE

PARKER

My boss, Eira, watches me during the meeting. As much as I try to avoid his gaze, it's almost impossible. I've never had a man directly openly stare at me this way before, and I'm beyond confused. Is it because I've finally had sex, and a lot of it? Do other men sense that?

When the meeting is finished, I hurry out of the conference room, trying not to run but also not taking my time. I slip out and focus on heading to my office.

I need a moment to just breathe.

Luckily, nobody seems to notice me as I make a beeline straight for my office. Ducking into my space, I lock the door behind me and close the shades before I sink down in my chair, closing my eyes with a heavy sigh.

Alone, at last.

My phone buzzes on my desk with a new notification. My eyes slide open as I reach for the device. I have a new text message from Wells, but it's over an hour old. I cringe, feeling bad for not answering him.

He also changed his name in my phone, and just the sight makes me smile.

SEX GOD: ARE YOU SORE?

I start to type back a simple response of yes but then decide against it because he's probably pissed that I haven't responded in so long.

I'm sorry I didn't respond. I was in a meeting. Yes, I am.

Staring at the phone, I wonder if he's going to respond immediately. Those little bubbled dots don't appear. And as I sit and stare at the screen, I realize they aren't coming. He's probably going to punish me for not responding right away.

It's not like he said he would or anything, but this man is clearly used to getting what he wants the way he wants it, and I didn't respond in time. My heart beats fast and then faster with each passing second, then there is a hard, loud knock on the door, and I jump.

"Parker," a woman's voice calls out.

Standing, I make my way over to the door and unlock it before tugging it open. It's Rachel, who works at the front desk.

"There's a Titus Atticus here to see you."

I must stare at her in confusion because that's exactly what I'm feeling in the moment. I have no clue who Titus Atticus is. I've never heard that name before in my entire life. Opening my mouth, I start to say that when she just gives me a shrug.

"That's what he said his name was." She turns around and walks away.

I'm not sure what I'm supposed to be doing now. I stay where I am, then decide I should go out and talk to this Titus person. Taking a step out of my office, I glance from left to right to see if Eira is still lurking around, but he isn't anywhere to be seen.

With a grateful sigh, I head toward the reception area of the building. When I see him, my breath is stolen from my body. My heart skips a beat, and then every ounce of anxiousness just vanishes.

"Titus Atticus?" I ask, my lips curving up into a smirk. I'm relieved to see him, but that relief quickly vanishes.

He takes a step toward me, then another, until he's directly in front of me. "The one and only," he murmurs. "You're in deep shit, cupcake."

"I texted you back as soon as I could," I quickly blurt out.

Wells chuckles but doesn't look like he truly finds any of this funny. I'm not sure what happened, but there is a darkness in his eyes that wasn't there when I left this morning. He appears to be angry, but I'm not sure it's at me. Although, by the way he's watching me, I have a feeling he's going to take it out on me.

"Your office," he grinds out.

Turning my back to him, I begin to walk toward my office, taking him with me, when I hear Eira call out my name. My feet falter, and I stop at the sight of him standing at my doorway. "I was looking for you," he says, either not seeing Wells standing next to me or not realizing what and who he is to me.

"You were?" I ask, hoping he doesn't say anything that will cause Wells to become angrier than I think he already is.

"I was going to ask you if you wanted to join me for lunch," he murmurs.

Wells growls. I know this is going to be very bad. I open my mouth to say something in an attempt to stop whatever is about to happen, but Wells beats me to it. He releases my hand, takes a step forward, and slides to the side to be a barrier between me and Eira.

Placing my hand on the center of his back, I start to tell him that this is my boss, but again, I don't get the chance because he starts speaking before I can give him a single word of warning.

"Why?" Wells demands.

"Why?" Eira repeats.

This man is unused to anyone questioning him about anything, and I realize Wells is the same way. They are without a doubt going to butt heads, and soon.

"It's not your business."

Oh no.

Wells leans forward slightly, and I have no doubt that the bit of anger I saw in his eyes has grown exponentially. I hold my breath, unsure of what to do or say. I bite my bottom lip, finding a bit of dry skin and pulling it off my lip as I anxiously wait for whatever is going to happen next.

"Parker is very much my business," Eira announces. "Very much so."

"Since she's mine, I very much doubt that," Wells growls.

"Yours?"

I feel like I'm listening to a verbal, volleying match between them. I can't see Wells's face, but I don't think I want to right now anyway. I have a feeling I would probably be scared.

Holding my breath, I wait for Wells to clarify the statement. I want to know exactly what he is going to say. I know what he tells me when we're alone, but this is different. This is in public.

"My woman. My fiancée."

His words catch me by surprise, and my breath hitches. I blink, my throat going dry instantly.

Fiancée?

What on earth?

WELLS

Fiancée.

Fuck.

It just slipped out, but I'm fucking committed now. Sucking in a deep breath, I hold it for a moment as I wait for this pencil-dicked motherfucker to say some fly shit. He doesn't. His brows rise, and he takes a step backward, his chest no longer as puffed up as it was just moments ago.

"I… I didn't know," he mumbles.

He doesn't say another word. I watch as he spins around and walks away, his shoulders a bit slumped, and for whatever reason, that makes me smile. Turning, I face Parker. Her face is white as a sheet, her eyes wide and her lips parted in surprise.

"Take me to your office," I murmur.

She nods her head, snapping her lips closed, and brushes past me, making her way toward the closed door. I ignore the looks from every single person as we walk by. It's clear they heard the whole conversation and are intrigued by what's just happened.

Parker opens a door and stands aside to allow me inside. Walking past her, I stop in the middle of her small space and glance around. It's clean, just like her home. Fresh and tidy. Everything is not only in its place, but it also has a place to be in.

She closes the door behind me, and I hear the lock click into place, the sound causing my lips to twitch into a smirk. I wait for her to walk toward me, but she doesn't. Instead, I can hear her panting breaths behind me.

Turning slowly, I face her. She's got her palms pressed against the door. Her eyes are wide, and her lips parted as she breathes in short, quick pants. She's having a fucking panic attack. I watch as wetness fills her eyes and slowly rolls down her cheeks. If she notices, she doesn't wipe it away.

Wetness streams down her cheeks, her jaw, and onto the little bow at her throat. "Talk to me," I demand.

She pinches her eyes closed, shaking her head from side to side. She opens her mouth to speak, but nothing comes out except some little squeaks. She's deep in her panic, and I'm not sure how to bring her out of it.

There is only one person who can help, and she's going to be pissed off that I even know Parker is her client. Shoving my hand into my pocket, I take out my phone and find my mom's name. She answers on the second ring.

"Wells, I'm at work. What is wrong?"

She knows I never disturb her workday. Not ever. It was a rule enacted when Coleman was about twelve and would call to ask if he could have a snack after school, about once an hour, every hour for a week. She lost her mind and banished us from calling her at work.

"Parker is having a panic attack. I don't know what to do."

"Parker?" she asks.

"Mom," I snap.

"Wells," she warns, "you haven't done anything you shouldn't, have you?"

Clearing my throat, I try to calm myself down. I need to have patience with her, as much as I want to scream at her. This isn't the time or the place. I inhale a deep breath. Thankfully, my mom takes this for what it is and begins to talk me through bringing Parker back.

It doesn't take long. My mom is not only an expert at what she does, but Parker is also amazing. Once my mother is finished with me, she demands that I hand Parker my phone. I do, reluctantly, mainly because I won't be able to hear what's going on between them.

"Yes," she whispers.

I watch as she slowly sinks down onto her ass, her back resting against the door as she brings her knees up to her chest. I stand above her, watching and wondering what the fuck is going on. She inhales deeply through her nose, then lets it out slowly out of her mouth. Once, twice, three times, before she speaks again.

"Yes, I'll still be there at five thirty. Okay."

Parker holds out the phone for me to take, and I place it against my ear. "Mom?" I ask, unsure if she's still on the phone.

"You will come with her at five thirty to my office. I want to know what's happening."

She ends the call, and I shove my phone into my pocket, knowing that when five thirty comes, I'll be properly chastised by her without a doubt. There is no way I'm getting out of this unscathed. I'm lost in thought when I hear Parker's soft voice call out my name.

Blinking, I dip my chin slightly to look down at her. "Parker?"

"Why did you call me that?"

"My fiancée?" I ask.

She nods her head, rolling her lips a few times. She sucks in a breath, then lets it out slowly. She still hasn't wiped her cheeks, but her tears have wiped all her makeup off, and I can see a little bit of the bruising on her cheeks from my fingers.

My cock twitches at the sight, and I know this isn't the right place or time for it, but I can't deny that I would love to fuck her right now. Crouching down in front of her, I give her a grin. I reach out to cup her tearstained cheek before I slide my thumb across her bottom lip.

"Yeah, cupcake. Marry me."

It's not a question. It's a demand. It is going to happen. My father made it clear that I did not have a choice. I've come to terms with it. She's a good match. A virgin. She comes from money. She also has no immediate family to cause issues. It's really a decent choice. I just wasn't sure I was ready to commit.

I thought I had five more years.

CHAPTER
THIRTY

PARKER

"Yeah, cupcake. Marry me."

I stare at him. I can't believe he just said that. More than once. And it wasn't a question. It was a demand. We have literally known one another for a week.

One week, plus or minus a few days.

I know I don't love him. I don't even know him. But I also know that my body is already obsessed with everything about him.

"What happens if I say no? We don't even know one another."

Wells's lips curve up into a cocky smirk. He lets out a chuckle, then slides his palms beneath my arms and hauls me to my feet.

When I'm steady—though I don't know how steady I really am because my knees are wobbly, and the only reason

I'm able to actually stand on my own is because my back is propped against the door—he takes my hands in his.

"There isn't an option for you to say no."

I blink. I knew that's how he felt, but the fact that he's actually saying it out loud? That makes my whole body jerk. "Wells?" I ask.

He hums but doesn't say anything else. Instead, he lifts his hand and cups my cheek. It's a soft touch and surprises me. I open my mouth to whisper his name again, but he doesn't allow me. Wells dips his chin and touches his lips to mine. His tongue slips inside of me, and he tastes me with one swirl.

"Marry me, Parker." His voice comes out gruff, rough.

When he slides his nose alongside mine, my breath hitches at the tender move. He bends and slightly wraps his arm around the backs of my thighs and picks me up, carrying me over to my desk.

Slowly, he lets me down on my feet. My ass is pressed against the edge of the desk, his hips holding them in place there, and I feel his length against my lower belly. It's hard. That doesn't surprise me because I'm pretty sure he's hard all the time.

I think he's going to tell me again to marry him. He doesn't. He reaches down, gripping the sides of my skirt, and tugs it up to my waist, exposing my panties. I let out a gasp as his hand dives into said panties.

Wells chuckles, snorting once before he clears his throat. He leans forward slightly, two fingers sliding through my folds once, twice, swirling my clit and then slipping inside of me. I grip his shoulders, my nails digging into his skin through his shirt.

"Wells," I hiss. "There are people right outside."

He chuckles. "I told you I would fuck you here. I'm going to."

My hips jerk as he presses his palm against my clit. His fingers inside of me make a come-hither motion. My eyes roll into the back of my head as my hips buck, my body climbing higher and higher.

My body tingles, and I know I'm getting there.

So close.

So close to my release when there is a knock on my office door.

Freezing, I think he's going to stop, too, but he doesn't. He continues to move his fingers inside of me. My nails dig into his shoulder even harder, and I open my mouth to say something, but nothing comes out.

That's because I come. It rushes through me like a freight train with no brakes. My muscles freeze, then my body starts to tremble. I hold my breath for one beat, maybe two before I exhale and lean forward, my forehead resting against his shoulder.

Whoever is on the other side of the door knocks again, and I lift my head, my eyes widening. I stare at the closed door, waiting for it to open, then my gaze flicks to the knob, and I let out a relieved breath that it's locked.

Wells gently slips his hand from between my legs and takes a step backward. I straighten my skirt and try to calm my panting breaths. I don't have a mirror, and I hope I don't look too sweaty... and I don't know what... *sexed*?

Is that a thing?

Making my way over to the door, I really hope it isn't Eira on the other side to say anything else that will cause Wells to get pissed off and make any other life-altering declarations.

Engaged.

I still want to clarify that because he has said I'm marrying him more than once now, and I have no idea what he's even talking about.

Opening the door, I half expect Eira to be standing on the other side, but instead, it's Allison with Eira standing behind her. My eyes widen as I flick them from one to the other, then land on Allison, whose eyes are as round as saucers. Eira clears his throat, then spins around and marches away.

Slowly, I turn my head and look behind me to see Wells sucking on his two fingers. My eyes widen because I know exactly where those fingers have been. Exactly. And just seconds ago. Sucking in a breath, I turn back to Allison. She no longer looks shocked. Instead, she's got a cat-ate-the-canary smirk on her face and brushes past me into the office.

"I didn't expect to see sex on a stick here from the bar. Nice to see you again…" Her words trail off, and Wells clears his throat.

"Wells," he says, introducing himself.

She laughs softly, and I don't know why, but I expect her to flirt with him. Maybe because men have always gravitated toward her and not so much me. She's sultry and sexy. I'm obviously naive and don't know how to be either of those things.

So when she stays where she is and just says it's nice to meet him, I am surprised, although happily surprised. I shouldn't be. Allison has always been a good friend to me. The best I've ever had, actually.

"Nice to meet you. I'm Allison. Parker is my best friend," she states.

He hums, turning his head to face her. I watch as he gives her a smile and then shifts his attention to me. "Are you going to tell your friend the news?" he asks.

My eyes widen, and I shake my head, no doubt appearing as if I'm going to lose my mind. He laughs, almost as if he thinks I'm cute or something, then he gives me a wink and shifts his attention back to Allison.

"News?" she asks.

"Parker and I are getting married."

His words are loud, boastful, and even proud. But I can't help but feel like I need to curl into a ball and breathe, or at least attempt to breathe. I'm not quite sure I'll be able to in a few moments.

I start to pant, my eyes pinch closed, my lungs squeeze, and my feet falter backward a few steps. I'm not sure who wraps their hands around my rib cage, but I'm hauled over to my chair, and I slowly sit down in it. When I open my eyes, I see Wells crouched in front of me and a worried Allison standing behind me.

"Married?" she asks as her gaze finds mine.

Opening my mouth, I start to tell her no when Wells speaks for me. "Engaged. Married. Yeah."

There is silence. A silence that is almost deafening. I wish I could scream, but nothing comes out. I wish I could speak, but nothing comes out. I suck in a breath in an attempt to calm myself. Releasing it slowly and focusing on Allison.

"Not married. Not engaged," I whisper.

Wells lets out a laugh, lifting his hands to cup my cheeks. "Yeah, cupcake. We are."

WELLS

I'M NOT sure what Parker thinks is going on, but she and I *are* getting married. I've declared it, but before that, my father demanded it, and my father always gets what he wants, especially when it comes to his boys and the family.

He's also scared—something I've never seen in my entire fucking life. So, I'll do what he's demanded because I can't stand to see him like that.

I've never even imagined my father *could* be scared of anything, but I suppose he is of being pinned for the murder of Parker's parents. Taking her hand, I lace my fingers with hers as the elevator climbs up to my mother's office.

She is breathing heavier and faster with each floor we climb. I almost stop the car to check on her but decide she needs to keep going. I've already seen what happens when she is too stressed out too quickly. I want her in my mother's care when she has another panic attack. I don't know how to handle that shit. At all.

If it were up to me, I would have killed that motherfucker dead. And I would have done it publicly to make a fucking point—Parker is mine. Not anyone else's. She's not even available for their viewing pleasure.

She doesn't fucking exist to them.

When the elevator dings and the doors open, I step out, keeping Parker's hand in mine. She shuffles forward, although I think that if it were up to her, she would have stayed in that car and gone back down, then run the fuck away.

But she won't be doing that because she's got to get her shit sorted so we can get married. There is no choice in it. As I reach for my mother's office door, Parker tugs on my hand. Turning my head, I look back over my shoulder at her.

"You ready?" I ask.

She shakes her head without saying a single word, her eyes wide and her lips pressed together in a short line. Tugging the door open, I take a step inside without giving her the option of verbally answering or walking away.

She's going inside.

As soon as we step into the waiting room, I turn to her to say something, but my words fall flat because I hear my mother's door open and her voice calling out for Parker. My eyes search hers for a moment, trying to gauge how she's doing, but I can't tell. Either she's completely fucking shut down, or she's about as good as I am at hiding her emotions. Which I don't think she is.

"Parker, please come inside," she calls out, sounding so sweet and happy.

"Wells, you can stay out here," she deadpans.

Stepping to the side, I turn around to face her. "Mom," I murmur.

My mom's eyes narrow on me, and her lip curls. She doesn't say anything, although I can tell she's waiting for Parker to walk into her office. I watch as the door closes, then she takes a step toward me, and I can tell she's going to scold me.

"What is happening?" she hisses.

"We're getting married," I state. "Dad's orders."

Her eyes widen as she sucks in a breath. "Dad's orders?" she asks.

There is a moment of silence as she stares at me. She leans forward, extending her finger and poking it into my chest. I stay where I am. My face stays expressionless as I stare at her. I can see the wheels turning, and I'm sure she has a million questions, all of which she will make sure to ask.

One by one.

Torturingly so.

I inhale a deep breath. "Sit right there," she snaps as she extends her finger and points to one of the chairs in the lobby. Jerking my chin in her direction, I brush past her and sink down onto the sofa.

Holding my phone in my hand, I start to play a game and wait for my turn to get called into the principal's office. My mother walks away from me, slipping back into her office, and I hear the door click closed as I continue to play the app.

I don't know what the fuck she thinks she's going to say to me. She knows Dad is in charge of this one. She won't state that I can't marry her, but I can tell she isn't happy about any of this. Honestly, I'm not that excited myself, but this is my fucking life.

CHAPTER
THIRTY-ONE

PARKER

DOCTOR HAMILTON STARES AT ME FROM ACROSS HER DESK. She usually doesn't sit behind it, but apparently, this session is a bit different. She watches me without saying anything after I've spilled the whole situation to her... in detail... *extreme detail*.

"So, anyway, I haven't even known him two weeks, and he's already announced to my boss that we're engaged. And he told my best friend, too. I don't think he's going to take no for an answer and to be quite frank, I'm pretty scared about this whole thing."

My words come out all rambled, and I don't know if she even understands what I'm saying or if I'm expressing myself the right way. I feel confused and upset. She doesn't comment whatsoever, and now I wish I hadn't told her.

I should have lied about the whole thing. I could have said my panic attack was about anything. I could have chosen a random thing, like the fact that my boss asked me out for lunch and was flirting with me out of the blue. That was really weird.

Doctor Hamilton stays silent as she slowly rises from her chair. I keep my gaze focused on hers, and she does the same. Then she closes her eyes and inhales deeply before she exhales slowly, her eyes opening. They connect with mine again, and my heart skips a beat.

The woman who I thought was a friendly face, who I considered my calm from the storm that is my mind and body, has morphed into something, someone I don't under-stand. The expression she wears now is no longer the kind and sympathetic woman I walked in to meet.

Fierce.

That's how I would describe her expression right now.

Fierce.

Pressing my lips together, I lean back as far as I can against the back of the couch cushion, but I don't get far. I'm not sure why. It's not as if she's anywhere near me as she stands on the other side of her desk, but I can feel her mood shift the entire room.

"Doctor Hamilton?" I ask when she doesn't speak.

There is a moment of silence. It weighs heavily in the air, and I break out in a single shiver that rolls through my entire body.

"Listen to me, Parker," she begins, her voice coming out barely above a whisper. I nod, too afraid to reply. "If I could help you out of this, I would, but you're stuck now, so you may as well just submit. Things will be easier if you do."

"I don't understand," I exhale.

She gives me a sad smile, the only expression that hasn't been concerning this entire session... which in turn kind of scares me. She begins to move around her desk until she stands in front, resting her backside against the edge of the wood as she crosses her arms over her middle and tips her nose down slightly, her gaze holding mine.

"Yes, you do," she whispers. "Deep down, you know that this situation is dangerous, and there is only one way out of it and only one way to live."

"Doctor Hamilton?" I whisper, my lips trembling as my breaths become shorter and shorter.

"You will not panic right now, Parker. You have entered a world where you cannot be scared or weak. I will help you as much as I can if you still want me to after this."

I'm so confused. I don't know what any of this means, and I have a feeling that if I asked, she wouldn't clarify anyway. I suck in a breath and hold it, then let it out slowly as I continue to stare at her. I'm not sure if she's going to explain anything else, but I wait in hopes she will.

"Wells is my son," she announces.

The room spins. My hand shakes as I lift it, wrap my fingers around the front of my throat and close my eyes.

Ohmigod.

Ohmigod.

This is too much.

It's beyond too much.

As soon as I open my eyes and my mouth to say just that, the door opens and Wells walks into the room. He carries himself as if he owns the place. He is broad, tall, strong, confident, all the things that draw me to him, and right now, I hate them all.

"Got everything figured out?" he asks, his deep voice rumbling throughout the small office.

"Well, not really. We still need to talk," Doctor Hamilton announces.

Wells chuckles, almost as if he's just appeasing his mother. His mother. I still cannot... and then reality hits me.

It slams through me. It causes my entire body to jerk so violently that I jump to my feet.

I can feel their eyes on me, and I know I won't make it past Wells to run out of this room. I can feel the walls closing in on me. They seem to actually move, and I rush over to the window and slam my hands down on the glass.

I'm disgusted. Embarrassed, and then I feel something slither up my spine. I turn my head when a horrifying realization slams into me. Not only does Doctor Hamilton know exactly every single disgusting detail of my sex life with Wells, but he also knows she is my doctor.

I didn't tell him where I was going. He brought me here. I didn't tell him to call her. He already knew. He didn't just watch me. It wasn't a happenstance moment of him seeing me at a club and following me.

It was so much more than that.

He targeted me.

He stalked me.

Like, for real.

I open my mouth to scream, cry, do whatever I need to do to get out of this room, but then I remember that it's well after five. This is one of those buildings that basically shut down after hours, much like my own.

"You stalked me. You targeted me. Why?" I whisper.

Wells's lips curve up into a nonchalant grin. "It's not as salacious as that. I saw you from afar. I thought you were gorgeous. I found you."

I'm not sure if I believe his simple explanation. There must be more to this. My stomach squeezes, and my heart races, and I can't just ignore my body's response to this man. To this situation. To the whole thing.

"Anything else, Mom?"

Doctor Hamilton's gaze flicks from Wells to me, then

back to Wells. "Family dinner tomorrow night," she snaps as her response.

Wells chuckles. "Sounds good," he murmurs before he shifts his attention from her to me. "Let's go home, cupcake. You had quite a day."

As much as I want to tell him to go away, I don't think I can. I need more answers, clarification, information, everything and anything. The only way I'm going to get that is if I go with him.

So, against my better judgment, that's what I do.

WELLS

MY MOTHER IS PISSED. She probably knows that I looked up Parker's files in her office. She's not stupid, and she knows it's something I would do without feeling the least bit guilty for it. And I don't. Not when it comes to Parker. Nothing about what I do with her, to her, or anything that concerns her makes me feel any kind of guilty.

Dinner tomorrow? When my mother said *family*, she meant me, my dad, her, and my brothers. She did not include Parker in that, and as much as I want to bring her with me, I know it would be a shit show.

But after tomorrow's dinner, Parker will always be at my side. This is a new beginning to a life that I didn't expect, but I'm going to go in wholly. She is mine. There is no her and me anymore. We are no longer individuals.

She is now part of me.

Instead of driving straight back to her condo, I decide it's time she sees my penthouse. It's only a few blocks from her place, and I know she'll love it. She has a high-class, simplistic style, and everything in my condo is sleek, expensive, and sexy.

"Where are we going?" she asks on a whisper.

I can tell she's both scared and nervous. I almost tell her not to worry about it, but I decide to tell her. She's had a stressful day. I can't imagine discovering all the things she did today, plus the pure physical exhaustion the panic attack brought on, then therapy with my mother. Her portion lasted well over an hour.

As much as I want to be a hard-ass, I know this isn't the moment. Tomorrow, I'll be back to my normal self. Tonight, I need to take a little more care with her. "We're going to my place tonight," I offer.

"I don't have any of my things," she exhales. "I have to work tomorrow."

I hum. "Why don't you take tomorrow off? I feel like you had a day. Maybe you and Allison can relax?"

Parker stays silent for a moment. She sucks in a deep breath and holds it for a long moment before she lets it out slowly. I flick my gaze to the side and watch as she sinks her teeth into her bottom lip. She scrapes them across her tender flesh, and I know she's upset.

"How many personal days do you have?" I ask.

"I've never taken one," she mutters.

I figured she hadn't. Reaching across the center console, I wrap my fingers around her hand and give her a squeeze. "Take the day, cupcake. Nobody is going to say shit."

"At this point, I don't even know if I'll have a job to go back to. Considering you challenged my boss and made a spectacle. You embarrassed him."

"Was I supposed to let him ask you out in front of me?" I growl.

There is silence as I pull into my parking garage. I am ready to take her ass home for even suggesting this shit, but at the same time, I know she's just stressed. I'm giving her this evening as a pass, but I will not give her the same pass tomorrow.

"No," she whispers. "I don't know."

Shifting my car into *Park*, I turn to face her, my hand releasing hers and instead cupping her cheek. Her gaze searches mine, and I smirk. "I don't give a fuck if you get fired from your job. I have more money than I can spend, and soon it will be half yours."

"Wells," she breathes.

I hum and lean forward, my lips touching hers. "I know you have money. It's yours. I'll never touch it. I don't need it, and even if I did, I would work my ass off to make sure we never needed it."

Sliding my hand from her cheek, I tangle my fingers in the back of her hair and grip her as I press my mouth hard against hers. Every single word is the absolute fucking truth. She is mine, and that means she is mine to take care of. I know exactly how much money she has, what she's worth, and I don't want a goddamn penny. To me, her inheritance does not exist.

CHAPTER
THIRTY-TWO

PARKER

I'M SHAKY. MY BODY IS ON EDGE, AND I KNOW IT'S BECAUSE I'm in this strange place with this man who I don't know. This man who stalked me for God knows how long. I don't know what he knows and doesn't know about me. Especially considering his mother is my therapist.

I am so embarrassed.

She knows everything up until now about our sex life, even the choking stuff.

God.

I want to crawl into a hole and cry.

Wells doesn't seem bothered in the slightest. He's happy just moving around his gorgeous condo, but I can't enjoy it because I am so stressed out about everything that's happened today. All day long, it's been one thing after another.

"You're watching me, but I can tell that if you don't speak, you're going to explode," he murmurs as he turns around to face me.

He's in the kitchen, watching me from across his breakfast bar. He arches a brow, his gaze holding mine. He is silent while he waits for me to say something. I don't know what I'm going to say. I feel a million different things bubbling inside of me, but I don't know where to go first.

"You stalked me. You know everything about me, and I still know nothing about you. I mean, I know you followed me. You got a key to my condo, and I thought it was sexy, so obviously, something is wrong with me. So fucking wrong."

Tears fill my eyes, and they start to roll down my cheeks. I didn't think I had any tears left, but I must have replenished them because they're falling in streams onto the silk bow at my neck. Wells's eyes search mine, but he doesn't speak. Instead, he lifts his glass of amber liquid to his lips and takes a drink.

"Cupcake," he murmurs. "I'm giving you this night for all this shit," he says as he lifts his hand and waves it around slightly.

My spine straightens at his words. All this *shit*. This isn't nothing. He is acting as if I'm being a silly, emotional girl. I'm not. What I am is freaking the fuck out. That's a whole different story. I'm freaking out for a good reason. A damn good reason.

"You could have killed me, and I was stupid enough to think it was sexy. I was a virgin," I whisper.

He places his glass down on the counter, although I expect him to slam it down, but he doesn't. He sets it down gently, then moves through the kitchen as he makes his way toward me.

My entire body freezes as he stands in front of me, then wordlessly reaches out, cupping my cheeks with his hands. His eyes focus on mine, unmoving, unwavering. Then he leans forward slightly, his forehead pressing against mine as he closes his eyes and inhales deeply through his nose.

I close my eyes, too, wrap my fingers around his wrists, and inhale slowly, then exhale before he speaks.

"I choose you, Parker. None of the shit matters. Not how I found you, not what I know about you, not what you don't know about me. None of it matters because I choose you to be mine."

My breath hitches.

Those words. They're powerful.

WELLS

I DIDN'T PLAN on fucking her tonight. I was going to have some whiskey, get some dinner, and maybe call it a night early. But with my lips on hers, my hand tangled in her hair, her sweet body bowed toward me, and her tits pressed against my chest, my cock begs to be inside of her, my balls aching for release.

Nibbling on her bottom lip, I gently break the kiss, leaving my hand where it's most comfortable—in her hair. I look down into her eyes, watching her for longer than is probably comfortable, but I can't get past the fear there.

Sure, the desire she feels is always right in front, but the fear is close behind that, and right now, I know it's directed at me.

"Parker," I rasp, "you gotta forget all the shit and think about how you feel when you look at me, when you kiss me, when you fuck me."

Her tongue slowly slips out of her mouth, sliding across her bottom lip and wetting it. She looks fucking amazing. Her lips are puffy and wet, and I imagine them sliding down my cock as she takes me inside her sweet mouth and down her throat.

Biting back the groan at the thought, I try not to laugh. But I'm not laughing at her, just at my fucking self and how hard up I am for her. I fucking want her every second of every day. It's all I fucking think about anymore.

I'm sure it will fade, but right now, all I want is her. Just her naked body splayed out for me to ply and pleasure. *Fuck.* My cock presses against the zipper of my pants so goddamn hard that I'm sure there will be an imprint later.

"I feel beautiful," she whispers. "I feel seen. I feel special."

My lips curve up into a smile, a genuine fucking smile, and I know it is because my goddamn insides warm at her words. Tugging on her hair, my fingers tighten as I expose what little of her throat isn't covered by her shirt.

I touch my lips to the center of her neck and nip her there, then use my other hand to grip her skirt before I jerk it up to her hips. "Wells," she exhales. Driving my fingers beneath her panties, I cup her center.

"You're already wet," I growl against her skin as I kiss up her neck, her jaw, and over to her ear. "I'm going to fuck your tight cunt until you scream my name."

Her entire body trembles from my words. Slipping my fingers inside of her, I curl them and begin to move them in a come-hither motion. She whimpers as I jerk her head back even more. She cries out, her hips bucking as I press my palm against her clit.

Hesitantly, she begins to ride my hand. I can tell she's uncomfortable, but as she begins to move, her hips rolling over and over, she trembles with a heavy exhaled breath, and I know she's close.

Quickly, I remove my hand, causing her to growl with frustration. She lifts her head, her eyes finding mine. I release my grasp on her hair so she can move. "Wells, I was close," she exhales.

"Yeah," I chuckle. "I know."

Reaching down, I wrap my hands around her thighs and pick her up to carry her to my bedroom, where I slowly release her until her high heels hit the floor. Cupping her cheeks, I touch my lips to hers gently, just a brush, before I take a step backward.

I wrap my hand around my cock from over my jeans and squeeze, trying to relieve the ache there. Releasing my hand, I reach behind my shoulders and tug the shirt over my head. I look at Parker. I can't help but smirk at the sight of her standing in front of me with her skirt around her hips, her disheveled hair, and flushed cheeks.

"Take your clothes off, cupcake."

She blinks. Her parted lips snap closed, and she nods her head once. All business, I watch as she strips out of her clothes. I finish undressing, wrap my hand around my now bare cock, and begin to stroke myself at the sight of her nakedness.

Her tits beg for my mouth, her neck screams for more bruises, and I know her cunt weeps to be filled.

Moving toward her, my cock in hand, I don't look away from her. I can't. She is there, a gift just for me. Even if she doesn't know it, she is my prize, my reward for joining the family.

"Wells," she calls out softly.

"Parker?" I murmur as I reach out and cup her tit.

My fingers flex around her breast, my thumb sliding across her nipple as I smile at the sight of her sweet bud hardening. Leaning down, I ignore the ache in my balls, the way my entire body is screaming to be inside of her, and I suck her nipple into my mouth.

I watch her through my lashes as I swirl my tongue

around her nipple, then suck her in deep before I sink my teeth into the soft flesh of her breast. She whimpers, her back bowing toward me, her soft flesh smashing against my face, almost suffocating me. Which would not be a bad way to die.

Releasing my dick, I slip my hand between her legs and begin to work her again. Her hips roll, searching for more friction from my fingers. I almost chuckle, but my focus is now on her tits and marking them.

I want to mark her entire fucking body. I want to see my bruises on her skin, every fucking inch of her, and know that she came with each of them repeatedly, that she begged me for more.

I sink my teeth into the flesh of her other breast as my fingers continue moving through her folds, swirling her clit, then dipping inside of her in an unbreakable rhythm that I know she's quite enjoying. Her hips jerk, roll, and tilt with each stroke.

Releasing her tit with a pop, I slip my hands from between her legs and lift my fingers to her lips. She's panting, no doubt close to her release. Smiling, I slide my fingers across her puffy, gorgeous mouth before I slip them inside.

She does exactly what I want her to do with zero instruction. She sucks on my fingers, her tongue tasting herself on my skin. Slowly, I glide them out of her mouth and wrap my other hand around her waist as I pick her up and set her down on the edge of the bed.

Guiding my length to her center, I pause before I bury myself inside of her. I dip my chin and look down at her. She's gripping the sheets at her hips, her feet propped up on the railing of the bed, her ass on the edge of the mattress, her tits red and marked with teeth imprints. She's also flushed, panting, and on the edge of an orgasm.

She looks downright fucking perfect.

"Please," she whimpers. "Please."

One of her hands releases the comforter, and I feel her fingernails dig into the flesh of my shoulder. Dipping my chin slightly more, I look down at her cunt. She's soft and pink, warm and ready. Her pussy is pulsing with aching desire, and I know she needs to come. I've already brought her to the edge twice. I don't think she could handle a third time without some sort of relief.

"Touch yourself while I fuck you," I growl.

With one hand on my shoulder, her other immediately slips between her legs, and she strokes her clit. All it takes is for me to bury myself deep inside of her, and she cries out, her head falling backward between her shoulder blades.

Without another word, because nothing else needs to be said, I fuck her.

It's hard and relentless, her body taking what I give hers and almost silently begging for more, to which I happily oblige. We stay that way, me pounding into her sweet body as her fingers work her clit until I feel her pussy squeeze around me.

She comes with a sound that is more than a cry—it's a guttural scream emanating from deep inside her belly, and that alone would have been enough to make me come if her head hadn't straightened and her eyes didn't open to look into mine at the exact same time.

I still, bury my cock deep inside of her and fill her with my cum. I wonder and hope that my seed is planted deep inside of her womb and she's knocked up with my kid, making her completely and totally mine—forever.

Tilting my head to the side, I slam my mouth down against hers, and I kiss her. Hard and owning.

Mine.

CHAPTER
THIRTY-THREE

PARKER

Something has changed, and not in a bad way. In fact, this man is different in all the best ways. He looks at me a bit kinder. Maybe he's even a little softer. I'm not sure what it is, but I'm falling deeper for him with every passing moment we spend together.

He rolls over, wrapping his arm around my waist, and hauls me against his chest. "You are supposed to be sleeping," he rumbles gruffly.

Smiling, I reach behind me and slide my fingers through his hair. My entire body is sore, sated, and deliciously bruised. Turning my head, I touch my lips to his jaw before I speak.

"How am I going to work with all these marks on my body? You can only wear so many scarves in Texas before people start asking questions."

He grunts, his hand gripping my breast tightly, squeezing. It aches from his fingers, his teeth, and with need. All the above. Sucking in a breath, I arch my back, pressing my ass against his front. He shifts his head slightly, his teeth nipping my earlobe.

"You push that ass against my dick much more, cupcake, I'm going to fuck it."

My whole body freezes, which makes him laugh softly. He's still very much waking from sleep, and his voice is rough and sexy.

"I'm going to fuck it one day anyway. You may as well get used to the idea."

Turning around in his arms, I tip my head back slightly to look into his eyes. "Will it hurt?" I ask, my voice barely above a whisper.

His arm wraps around me, pulling my front against his chest as he touches his lips to mine at the same time. The kiss is a quick brush of the lips, then he lifts his head, his eyes finding mine before he speaks.

"I'll oil and stretch you. It won't be exactly like your cunt. It will probably hurt, but you like that, don't you, cupcake?"

God, why does this man using filthy words make me want to climb on top of him and beg him to have sex again? He lifts his hand, extending two fingers and slipping them beneath my chin before he tilts my head back slightly.

His gaze searches mine, then he smirks. "You do. You get off on the pain I give you."

"Just you," I confess.

His expression turns dark, and he tangles his fingers in my hair, tugging my head back with a snap. "There is only me, Parker, nobody else. Not ever."

"Yes," I whisper. "Only you."

I've come to the conclusion after speaking with Doctor Hamilton that my decision in this is not valid. There is no decision. I'm not sure how I feel about my choices being taken away from me, but at the same time, I don't think I overly mind, especially when I'm with him.

I want to ask a million questions, but maybe they'll all be answered in time? I have to hope that, because I've never done anything this crazy before. When I look into his eyes, I know this is better than anything else I could have imagined.

"Lie low today," he murmurs. "Call Allison, order some food. Just take the day. Don't worry about your boss. I'll handle it."

Sucking in a breath, I watch him for a moment, then frown and shake my head once. "What are you going to do? Are you going to get me fired?" I ask.

"Do you love your job?"

I don't even have to think about his question. I do love my job, but I didn't like my boss lingering today. I didn't like him noticing me. It all made me extremely uncomfortable. Then there was their encounter, which I didn't like much either.

"I love the work," I say.

He grunts but doesn't say anything else. Instead, he releases me, then rolls off to the side, throwing his legs over the edge of the bed. Sitting up, I tug the sheets over my breasts and wonder what the hell he's thinking and also what he's going to do. I can't even guess.

Wells stands, then turns to face me. Tipping my head back, I look up into his eyes. He grins as he looks down at me. "Shower with me, cupcake."

And it is all dropped. Whatever it was. I think about asking him some more questions but decide against it. Sliding off the bed, I leave the sheet there and follow naked behind him. I've never felt as comfortable in my skin as I do with him.

He starts the water in the shower, and I use the moment to take in his all-marble bathroom. It's beautiful. White marble with gray veins and matching matte gold fixtures everywhere. The vanity isn't just a counter with double sinks. There is also a makeup counter with a bench. Then there is a gorgeous freestanding tub that makes my knees weak at the sight.

"You comin'?" Wells asks.

I'm standing in the middle of the room, gawking at everything and wondering if I should remodel my bathroom when he speaks. My body jerks slightly, and I turn toward him, following him into the shower.

The warm water hits my back from the showerhead behind me, and I'm surprised there are two. Pleasantly surprised. "I think I could live in your bathroom," I mutter.

Wells chuckles. "You act like your bathroom is shit, which it is not."

I snort. Looking around this space, I have to argue with him because it does look like shit compared to this place. We don't say another word. Our shower quick and to the point. He is on a mission. I just don't know what it is.

"You can pick whatever you want from my drawers and closet to wear. Maybe Allison can bring you over a few days' worth of clothes," he says as he begins to dress. I'm standing in the bedroom, wrapped in one of his white, extremely fluffy towels. Something that is so sumptuous I decide I need a dozen in my place, too.

"A few days?" I ask.

"A few days."

I open my mouth, unsure of what to say or what to ask. I suck in a breath, then decide to let it out slowly and let it go. What's a few days? I shouldn't make it a big deal, but I'm curious. Far too curious as to why I would need to stay for a few days.

I decide to ask.

"Why a few days?"

He's pulling up his pants when he pauses and looks up at me. His lips curve up into a grin, and he jerks his chin and clears his throat.

"Want you here, cupcake," is all he says. "I got dinner tonight with my parents, though. No doubt, my mom is going to have words about this quick engagement. But it'll be all good, cupcake. Then I'll come home, and we'll eat dessert out on the balcony."

Home.

I almost swoon at the word and what that implies. Home. Our home. Together. God. And then the thought of dessert on the balcony, when I know that dessert likely entails both of us getting naked… I might just expire at this very moment.

"Okay," I exhale.

"Keep your phone close. Call Allison, have a girls' day."

His words are probably an order, but the idea sounds so good that I decide to just go with it. He leaves a few moments later after giving me a long, deep kiss that leaves me weak in the knees all over again.

WELLS

I'M NOT SURE WHY, but leaving her alone today, even in the safety of my monitored condo, makes me feel uneasy. It's stupid, probably only because I've never had a woman in my place, ever. Not even my mother has spent more than a few moments there, and that was when it was first given to me, then again after I had it remodeled.

Sinking down into the driver's seat of my car, I touch the button to start the engine and then slide my finger across the screen to find the phone icon. Touching that, I call my brother, who I know will handle some shit with me.

Coleman is great and all of that, but Hendrick will fuck

some shit up with me, then ask questions later. Coleman is too cool-headed for that. He asks questions first, and I don't need that this morning.

"You are not calling me before eight in the fucking morning," Hendrick growls.

"I'll be at your place in fifteen. I need some help."

"We fucking shit up?" he asks.

I laugh because I knew he would be down for this. "We are," I confirm.

"I'll be ready in five."

Hendrick ends the call before I can say another word. I laugh as I shift the car into *Reverse* and head toward his place. The good thing about the family getting us our own places, they thankfully do not buy them in the same buildings.

We're all spread out in the downtown area of Dallas, which makes it good for us if there is ever an issue. Someone is always close by to anything going down. It doesn't take me long to get to Hendrick's, and when I do, he's not only standing on the corner but putting a woman in an Uber.

He gives the car a wave and then turns toward me with a smile playing on his lips. It's clear that he's ready to do whatever it is I have planned, and I love him even more for it. He tugs the door open and sinks down into the seat with a heavy sigh.

"What are we doing?" he asks.

I don't answer him but clear my throat instead and jerk my chin toward the leaving car. "You have a date last night?"

I noticed the blonde hair but didn't see her face. I can guess, though. "It was Allison. I'm not hiding anything."

"You dating her or just fucking?" I ask as I pull out into traffic.

"I'm not sure," he replies. "It's definitely more than fucking, but less than dating. Why?"

I'm not sure why I want to know. I'm not sure why it feels

important to me. But we're the family, and the family usually does not date. Hell, the last time someone dated, it was Coleman, who was fucking his own cousin.

Not a good idea to date anyone in this world.

"I don't know. Doesn't seem like a good idea to get tangled with anyone."

He hums, clearing his throat as I move through the busy morning commuter traffic. "Is it because you're getting married now? You fucked around and found out."

"Basically," I chuckle.

I could tell him that I'm happy as fuck to have Parker as my own, but I'm not sure I am quite there yet. Yes, I love watching her. Yes, I love fucking her. Yes, I'm discovering that I like her. But I am not in love with her. I'm not sure she is who I'd choose for my life, and yet, I don't have the choice.

Perhaps that is what has me suddenly feeling unsure about the situation. The choice was taken from me. It is no longer mine, and I feel stuck. Completely and totally stuck. The family was a choice that I made, then they chose everything for me until marriage. In marriage, I am to choose who I wish. That is my prize.

The reward has been stripped from me, and even though I would have likely chosen her, that choice was taken, and I'm bitter about it. I'm sure the feelings will pass, but that doesn't mean I feel as if I had any other opportunity to take what I was promised.

Pulling up to the building, I shift the car into *Park* and turn to look at Hendrick. "I fucked around and found out. But this asshole who we're going to pay a visit, he thought he could not only flirt with Parker but challenge me in public. He thinks because he's the boss, he has a big dick."

"And you're going to show him exactly whose dick is the biggest in the room?"

My lips curve up into a grin. "Biggest dick in the whole fucking world, brother."

Hendrick chuckles, then he opens the car door. "Second biggest dick," he snaps, then slams the door shut, and I'm the one left laughing. This is why I brought my little brother with me. He's fucking hilarious.

THIRTY-FOUR

PARKER

PICKING UP MY PHONE, I SEND A TEXT TO ALLISON ASKING HER if she'll come over to Wells's condo today... and bring me clothes. Sinking my teeth into my bottom lip, I sit on the couch, my feet up in the cushion, my chin resting on my knees as I wait for her response.

> ALLISON: You slut. I love it. Pin me the location, and I'll be there as soon as I take a shower after spending the night with my own hot guy.

> Who's the slut?

> ALLISON: Always me. I'm always guilty. Be there soon!

Laughing, I slide my thumb up the screen and find my

Kindle icon. I touch it and let out a sigh as my book opens. I'm not sure what the rest of the day will bring. I don't know what Wells is doing at my work, but as for right now, I'm going to get lost in my book.

I read for longer than I probably should. I'm sure I ought to go look for food, maybe even something to drink, but I can't. I'm at the good part where she is running from the love she has for the hero.

He is denying his love, but when she becomes so distant that he feels the loss like a living, breathing thing, he chases after her. He insists that she is his. He confesses his love.

Swoon.

These are my favorite love stories. The grumpy-sunshine trope, the denying feelings, and then suddenly something forces the hero to declare them not only to the heroine but also to the world.

There is a knock on the door that causes me to jump. My phone flies out of my hand, landing somewhere on the carpet. I laugh to myself, unsure as to why I am the way I am. I'm a mess.

Standing, I tug down Wells's shirt, thankful he's so much taller than me, but he's obviously thinner than I am, and the shirt barely covers my ass. But it doesn't matter because it's Allison on the other side, and she's seen it all, plus she'll have some clothes for me to change into.

"You're finally…" My words die at the sight of the man standing in front of me.

A man.

Not Allison.

He doesn't look surprised to see me, but I am sure as hell shocked to see him. Taking a step backward, I try to close the door, but I fail. He chuckles and moves into the condo, slamming the door behind him.

I shake my head. I am pissed off that I dropped my phone. I open my mouth to say something, but he speaks first.

"The Hamilton family has ruined my life, specifically Wells. Now, I am going to ruin his."

I press my lips together, not sure what to say. I don't know anything about Wells's family. I only know his mother and him. But I have no idea how he could ruin someone's life with real estate. That's what he does. How could he ruin anything? I start to ask that, but I don't get the opportunity.

The man leaps toward me and wraps his fingers around my shoulders. I open my mouth to scream, but he releases one of my shoulders, reaches his hand back, and brings it down across my face.

He holds my body upward, not allowing me to fall, but my knees tremble and threaten to give out beneath me. Tears prick my eyes at the pain radiating across my face from the backhanded slap.

I've never been hit before.

My aunt and uncle were assholes who wanted to try and steal my money. They acted like I was a burden, but they didn't physically abuse me. Wells chokes me, pulls my hair, bites me and leaves bruises, but it's not out of anger, only for pleasure. This is different, and I can feel my face heat immediately from the assault and want to cradle it, but I don't.

"You say a fucking word, and I'll kill you. Come on," he barks as he jerks my shoulder forward.

I look around for a way to leave some kind of sign that I've been taken, but there's nothing. I'm literally in panties and a T-shirt, no bra, no pants. My phone sits on the floor, and I cringe at the sight, wishing I had kept a better grip on it when this asshole was knocking on the door.

Without another word, he drags me out of the condo and heads straight toward the elevator. I can only hope that someone will see us and call for help. But as the elevator car door opens, we step inside, and it rides straight down to the bottom without a single stop in between. My hope begins to wane.

As soon as he forces me out of the elevator and toward the door, I try to plant my feet because I know that if I am taken out of the building, the odds of me coming back will be zilch. But my efforts are for naught. This man drags me right out the front door, and nobody says a damn word to him.

Although there is nobody around to actually say anything, but still. He forces me out of the place without a single person seeing us. A car is waiting at the curb, and this man opens the back door and shoves me inside, then locks it behind me.

I think about trying to break out of the door. I look at the panel and chance reaching for the door handle and tugging on it just as he opens the driver's side and sinks down. He must see my attempt because he lets out a loud boom of a laugh that bounces all around the cab of the car.

"I'm not as much of a fucking idiot as they think I am. Child locks are on, bitch."

"Why me?" I ask on a whisper.

Not that I would want Doctor Hamilton to be kidnapped, but seriously, why me? I don't even know anything about Wells's business. Nothing. All I know is that Doctor Hamilton says I'm stuck with him and in the family forever now.

"Because as hot as the mom is, I don't want to fuck her."

WELLS

HENDRICK and I walk into the office building where Parker works. The girl at the front desk asks if she can help me, then she recognizes me under my alias of Titus Atticus. Hendrick

272

chuckles as she practically sprints around the reception desk to greet me.

"How can I help you?" she purrs as she arches her back slightly to push out her small chest.

Flicking my gaze down to her slight amount of cleavage, I almost laugh but decide I need her... at least I could use her for today. Lifting my hand, I run the back of my fingers down her cheek and grip the back of her neck before I lean forward.

"Be a good girl and tell me where Eira is today," I murmur.

"He has a meeting right now, but his calendar is clear after that," she exhales.

"Good girl," I rasp as I slide my hand from the back of her neck to the side of her throat and down to the center of her chest before I stop, keeping my palm there.

Her heart is racing, and if this were a few weeks ago, I would give her a quick fuck in the back room somewhere before I killed Eira, maybe after. The adrenaline of a kill always makes for a good orgasm.

My hand drops from her chest, and I take a step backward. "Which office is his?" I ask, keeping my voice soft.

She lets out a long sigh, then sinks her teeth into the corner of her bottom lip. "Step out of the elevator, turn left, and it's all the way down at the end of the hall," she murmurs breathlessly, her eyes focused on mine.

She's trying hard to be sexy, and it works, except my dick is completely sated and wants absolutely nothing to do with her. Giving her a smirk, then a wink, I say thanks and head straight for the elevator banks.

I hear Hendrick chuckling behind me, no doubt laughing at the whole thing. Once we step into the car, I look over at him and find him grinning at me like the fucking asshole he is. Jerking my chin, I give a smile.

"Yeah?" I ask.

He shrugs a shoulder, kicking the carpet with his foot, then his gaze searches mine. It's bright, his eyes almost sparkling. I narrow my gaze on him. "Are you high?" I hiss.

"Yeah," he says with a snort. "You just noticed?"

"I did," I grunt. "What the fuck?"

"Just some coke. It'll be fine."

Shaking my head, I wonder if he was doing that shit with Allison. I'm sure he was. I slide my palm down my face with a heavy exhale.

"It's all good," he murmurs. "I'll be fine."

I know he'll be fine. We've both done jobs for the family, on and off the books, high as kites. But that's not what concerns me. It's the fact that Allison is with Parker right now in that state. It shouldn't bother me, but it does.

Parker is the most important person in my life, other than my family.

That itself bothers me.

She should not be on the same level as the family. And yet, she is. I'm worried about her. Seriously fucking worried about her. The elevator door dings before the doors open, and I see it's Parker's work floor.

I'm going to have to think about her later. Right now, I need to deal with this motherfucker who thought he could look at her, let alone openly flirt with her. Hendrick and I square our shoulders and step out of the elevator simultaneously.

One step, then another. Staring straight ahead, we make our way down the hall. I can feel people's eyes on us, but none bother to approach. It's for the best. This isn't going to be pretty. Although, with this many witnesses, I may not end this fucker's life... *yet*.

Reaching for the door handle of his office, I turn the knob and step inside. It's empty, just like she said it would be.

Since I'm an asshole, I make my way to his cushy leather chair that sits behind his desk and sink down.

I'm surprised to find that the chair is comfortable, and the leather is buttery soft. Hendrick smirks at me from across the room, lifting his leg and pressing his foot against the wall as he stares at me.

Placing my palms against the wood of the desk, I slide them across the smoothly polished top. It doesn't have any fingerprints on it. Well, until now. I smirk as I smear them around. I shouldn't have as much joy as I do by fucking up his perfect desktop.

Lifting my legs, I place my heels on the desk and lean back in the chair. If I had a cigar, this would be the perfect position. With a chuckle, Hendrick takes his phone out of his pocket and begins scrolling on it. I can tell he's antsy and ready to get this shit done, probably so he can find Allison to fuck away his high.

The doorknob begins to turn, and I grin as I watch it open. Eira takes a step inside. He's looking down at his feet, and I hear the door lock click closed, then lock. I watch him, waiting for him to lift his gaze, and when he does, the appearance of shock almost makes me burst out in laughter.

"What the—"

His words are cut off by Hendrick pushing off the wall and taking a step toward him. Then he growls and reaches into his pocket. "I would probably not do that if I were you," he rasps. "This won't take long, and whoever you call won't be able to get here in time."

"Parker isn't here today," Eira grinds out.

"I know," I state. "I also know exactly where she is."

"What do you want?" he asks with a snap. He's feeling brave. It makes me chuckle.

I hum, clearing my throat before I speak. "I don't want

anything," I say. "Except for you to leave my woman alone. I also want her fired."

His eyes widen. "Fired?" he asks.

Lowering my feet from the desk, I slowly stand and place my palms on the desk again, leaning forward. My eyes find his. They focus on his own, and only when I know he's completely and totally focused on me do I speak.

"I want her fired. I want you to forget she ever existed. And if I ever, and I mean *ever*, find out that you even looked at her, let alone spoke to her again, I will kill you—slowly."

He blinks a couple of times, then he jerks his chin and places his fists on his hips. I move toward him until I stand just a few inches from his body, tipping my chin slightly as I look down my nose at him.

"Is this going to be a problem?" I ask.

Eira stares at me, his lips curved up into a smart-assed-looking smile as he tilts his head to the side. He appears as if he has some kind of secret, but I couldn't give less of a fuck what that is. He could have the cure to world hunger, and I wouldn't give a fuck in this moment.

"I'm not firing her."

His words sound so brave, but I can hear his voice waver just slightly underneath his breath. I lean forward. I could kiss him if I were into that, but I don't. Instead, I stare into his eyes, wondering if he's stupid or if he really does have massive balls.

Instead of waiting for his answer, I reach my hand back, make a fist, and thrust it forward into his gut. He stumbles backward a few steps, letting out a grunt. I reach over, grab hold of his hair and snap his neck back so he can look into my face.

"I know you think you're Billy Badass, but you aren't. Do not fuck with me."

Without another word, I release my grasp on him before

Hendrick and I walk out of the room, down the hall, take the stairs to the main floor and waltz out the back. I avoid the receptionist and slip away into my car, which is still waiting for me at the front curb.

"That motherfucker better not even try my ass," I growl.

Hendrick chuckles. "Can I be there when you really teach him a lesson?" he asks.

"Of course."

The conversation is dropped, and we head over to see Coleman and start our workday. My phone buzzes in my pocket with an incoming text. Glancing down, I grunt at the message. It's from Coleman, and it means we have some serious fucking work to do today.

CHAPTER
THIRTY-FIVE

PARKER

THE CAR DRIVES THROUGH THE STREETS OF DALLAS, BUT I have no idea where we're going. I tried to sit up once, and the man who took me swerved and threatened to hit me again, so I lay across the seat, and now I'm way too scared to even try to sit up again.

Sucking in a breath, I pinch my eyes closed as I try to keep from not only getting carsick but also because I'm not sure that I want to see what's going to happen. I try to stay present, not let myself get lost inside of my own head.

I'm not sure if I'll be able to do it, but I inhale a deep breath nonetheless and hold it for a moment, then exhale. Over and over, I do this in an attempt to keep my brain occupied. I'm not sure if it works at all. I want it to because the last thing I need right now is to have a panic attack. I need to stay alert and figure out a way out of this.

I refuse to be a pawn in whatever game this asshole is playing, at least not by choice.

I inhale and exhale again and again until the car comes to a stop, and my eyes pop open. I stay still, waiting for my instructions. The man opens the door, then I hear it close. I hold my breath, waiting for my door to open, and it does.

I feel his hand wrap around my ankle as he drags me out of the back seat. With a gasp, I land on the hard concrete floor. I glance around and realize that I'm in a garage. Frowning, I open my mouth to ask him where we are but snap it shut when he grabs hold of my hair and hauls me to my feet.

Trying not to whimper, I clench my jaw tightly as he drags me behind him. I try to find my footing, but it doesn't happen because he doesn't stop moving. He drags me through a house, and I can't even take in the space enough to find the exits. Then he tosses me into a room.

I hope he closes the door behind me and locks me inside, but I'm not that lucky. Instead, he moves into the room with me, closing the door as he stands in front of it. I open my mouth to ask him where I am, but I don't get the chance because he begins to speak.

"Listen, you little bitch. You'll sit right here and not make a fucking sound. You do, and the slap to your face will be the least of your worries."

"Where am I?" I finally ask, but my words come out sounding as terrified as I feel.

My entire body is trembling as I stare at him and wonder how in the hell I'm going to get out of this. I don't think I am. I honestly think I'm going to die here. In this room. Alone. And it wouldn't necessarily be a bad thing. In fact, it would make sense.

My parents were murdered, leaving me alone, and it

would be logical that I would be taken the same way. It just seems like it's the way it would happen. I should embrace it, but there is something inside of me that is still here and ready to fight.

That something inside of me is, without a doubt, Wells.

He is the little voice in the back of my head telling me to fight.

No way would he just lie down and take anything, and neither would the woman who he chose to marry. I still can't believe I'm going to marry this man who I've only known a few weeks, this man who stalked me, still for reasons unknown.

This man who probably knows a lot more than he should about me.

This man I've completely and totally fallen for.

"It doesn't matter where the fuck you are," the man sneers.

I almost forgot about him. I was lost inside of my own head. Which can be a dangerous place to be, not just because I'm trying to stay on the defense and forget about that but also because I could get lost and have a hard time finding my way back.

"Who are you?"

"Ray Randolph," he states proudly as if I'm supposed to know what that means. I don't. I stare at him, blinking, unsure of what I should say. I have no idea who this man is, and he clearly thinks I should.

His lips curve up into a grin, and I realize he is going to tell me something that he knows will bother or upset me. Pressing my lips together, I roll them a few times and try to keep my face expressionless, but I'm sure I completely fail, especially judging by the excited expression he's wearing.

"My daughter was Shiloh Randolph, and she was dating

Coleman. She's gone now, though I don't have a body to bury. But your boyfriend killed her, which means you're going to suffer for that. You're going to pay for it. A life for a life."

A life for a life.

Wells has that tattooed on his chest.

That means something, not just to him but to this man, too. That means something huge. I'm too scared to ask, though. Instead, I continue to stare at him. He's telling me that Wells killed his daughter.

Killed his daughter.

"You get comfortable. I'll be back later."

Without another word, he turns, opens the door, and slips out, slamming it behind him. I hear the lock click into place. The only positive thing I can think about in this whole situation is that I'm alone.

It's also dangerous because being alone means that I'll likely freak myself out, but in this case, I think it's the best alternative. I don't know what Ray Randolph has planned for me, but I do know that it is nothing good at all.

Lying down on my side, I bring my knees up to my chest and face the door. The room is completely empty. I'm alone. And I'm possibly in love with a murderer who definitely stalked me.

I'm lost.

I'm broken.

I'm not able to be fixed.

Ray should just end me for his justice.

A life for a life.

WELLS

Pulling up to the office, I'm not surprised to see Coleman's car in his spot. Hendrick doesn't even ask me to take him back to his place for his ride. He doesn't need it. He's going to dinner tonight, just like me.

Dinner with Mom, and I'm in the hot seat. I want to find a way out of it, but I know it's inevitable. I wasn't able to tell her about the engagement in a tactful way. How she found out was not how I had planned at all.

But it doesn't matter anymore. It's out in the open, and Dad is the one pushing it, so she won't really say shit to me about my choice. She will, however, have some shit to say about me breaking into her office, something that I'm sure she's figured out by now.

"That guy," Hendrick begins.

"Was Parker's ex-boss. He isn't shit, and if he even thinks about her again, I'll find out, and I'll kill him."

Hendrick chuckles. "I didn't realize it was so serious with you. Allison told me she was a virgin and all. I figure she's not now. But you're really going to marry her?"

Hendrick and I don't typically have somber conversations. I can tell he's been thinking about this for a while. Shrugging a shoulder, I lean back in my seat. Lifting my eyes to the ceiling of the car, I let out a heavy sigh.

"It wasn't serious until it became that way. Dad says that I have to marry her."

"Yeah?" he asks. "Have to?"

Jerking my chin, I clear my throat. "Family shit," I murmur.

He hums. His gaze straight ahead. "When do I get to be part of the trusted inner circle of the family?" he asks.

I think about his words. At his age, I was just becoming a manager. I have a feeling once Coleman gets married and moves up, he will, too, but I don't tell him that. Instead, I reach out and pat his hand before I speak.

"Not everything that glitters is gold, brother."

I open the car door, step out, and close it behind me. I can hear Hendrick moving as well. He doesn't say anything else. The conversation is now dropped, and we head into the office. The Ray Randolph deal is supposed to close today, a text I received when I was leaving Eira's office.

Walking into the building, we make our way over to the elevator banks. We step inside, and I stare at the numbers as they climb up to our floor. When we reach our floor and the elevator doors open, we step out, and I'm surprised to see Danica waiting for us with two cups of coffee, one in each hand.

"Coleman said you might need these for today," she says brightly.

Arching a brow, I take one cup from her as Hendrick takes the other. This is out of character for her. Although she's nice, Danica doesn't usually do shit for me. She's Coleman's assistant, not mine. This makes me suspicious as fuck.

Shaking off the thoughts, I thank her, as does Hendrick, and she jerks her chin, turning as she begins to make her way toward the conference room, where I assume Coleman and maybe Dad are waiting for us.

My assumptions are correct. Danica doesn't enter the conference room. She diverts and heads toward her desk. When we walk into the room, Dad and Coleman are bent over some papers, talking.

Jerking my chin, I take my seat and sink down onto the cushion as I lift the coffee to my lips. "Good morning," Coleman mutters. "I'm surprised to see both of you up and moving so early."

I don't take offense at his words. I don't like to wake up early if I don't have to, and I know Hendrick doesn't at all. Chuckling, I bring the cup to my lips again and take another sip.

"Wells had an offer that I couldn't refuse this morning," Hendrick quips, taking a drink from his own mug.

"Do I want to know?" Dad asks.

"Probably not. Now, why are we closing this right now?" I ask.

Dad clears his throat as he leans back in his chair, his eyes finding mine. "Ray suddenly became very motivated."

I'm sure his daughter and wife being killed had nothing to do with it. Although he would never be able to prove that we killed either of them. No bodies will ever be found. It doesn't matter. None of it does. We need this building and the contract with the government. We need all of this done and without this man causing waves.

I feel like he's going to be a fucking problem. I don't think he's going to just slip away quietly. I'm not sure why exactly. I just don't see him doing that. I think a lot more noise will be coming from him. Not just showing up and making it, but also fucking with the contacts and the contract with the passport agency.

"Let's get this shit done, then. I don't trust him, though," I point out.

"None of us does," Dad mutters.

The paperwork is easy to sign, and a few moments later, Danica is brought in as a notary to certify the signatures. When it's all finished, the four of us go to lunch together, and then we separate for the rest of the day and promise to see one another at dinner.

Coleman and I have a couple of deals we're working on for the family on our own, so we head out together to handle our shit. Thankfully, Dad takes Hendrick home, probably to sleep his night off before he has to face Mom.

It's a good and productive day. Maybe it's just the Ray thing, but I'm not sure. I feel... off.

Something is off.

I think about texting Parker a few times throughout the day but end up getting distracted, and by the time I think about it again, I'm already at dinner with my family. My mom is ready for a discussion. She wouldn't take to me texting very well, especially since I'm the focus of the dinner.

CHAPTER
THIRTY-SIX

PARKER

A NOISE AT THE DOOR STARTLES ME. I DON'T MOVE. KEEPING my knees up to my chest, I wonder what is going to come now. I've been here for hours, and I know there is something coming for me… or rather, someone.

He's going to hurt me. I know he is. There is no way around it at this point. He's locked me up in here for hours. And hours. He's not just going to let me walk out. He's going to take his anger out on me.

It is his plan anyway.

I'm not going to survive this, and I hope that when Wells discovers what's happened to me, he doesn't get put in prison over it. Sinking my teeth into my bottom lip, I wait for him to say something. He's standing in front of me. I can see his feet, but I'm not going to move yet.

I don't want to look into his face. I don't want to see any part of him if I don't have to. He crouches down in front of me, reaches out to grab hold of my hair again, and snaps my neck awkwardly so I'm forced to look into his face.

"You're all bruised, and it's not from me. He beats you?"

Refusing to answer, I continue to stare at him, trying to keep my face completely expressionless. I'm sure it doesn't work, and I know without a doubt that my eyes show exactly how terrified I am in this exact moment.

Ray's lips curve up into a grin. "He doesn't beat you. He hurts you when he fucks you, and you like it."

I don't say a word. He's right. That's exactly what it is, but I'm not going to admit it to him. Not fucking ever. His fingers tighten in my hair as his eyes search mine. I'm not sure what he's looking for, but whatever it is, he's sure happy about it.

He hauls me up to my feet with his tight grip on my hair. I cringe but don't cry out the way I want to. Instead, I keep my mouth closed and sink my teeth into the skin inside my cheek. He doesn't say anything else but instead drags me out of the room, down a hallway, and then stops.

"Look up," he growls next to my ear.

Slowly, I lift my eyes to face the room. My breath hitches at the sight in front of me. Not one or two, but three men are sitting between a sofa and a love seat. I'm still braless, wearing only panties and Wells's T-shirt. Their eyes roam over my body, not one of them looking above my breasts.

My stomach sinks, my heart races, and I know this is it. I will not survive this, and even if I do, Wells won't want me anymore, so I may as well be dead. Nobody would want me. Not after whatever torture they have planned is enacted on my body, my heart, and most of all... my soul.

Ray shifts behind me. I can feel his lips against the shell of my ear before he rasps.

"See them?"

Staying quiet, I wait for him to finish, knowing he's all hot to scare the absolute hell out of me, and it's working.

"They are going to tear you from asshole to pussy. They're going to fuck every single hole you have, and then they'll leave you a bloody, cum-stained mess. And what do you think I'm going to do?"

There is a long pause, one where I don't say a damn word, mainly because I have nothing to say. "I'm going to record it and send it to Wells so he can watch his pretty little woman be violently violated right before his eyes. And then, only then, will it be a life for a life."

"Do you think I should warn him that it's coming? Should I call him, or should this be a surprise?" he asks.

I still don't answer. I can't. My throat doesn't work. My brain is gone. Every muscle in my body is completely frozen. All I can do is imagine everything he's described, and I'm horrified. I bite the inside of my cheek even harder. I can't stop the metallic taste of blood from touching my tongue.

"Not yet," Ray rasps. "I want you to imagine it all tonight. They'll stay here until I give them the order."

Without another word, he takes a step backward, then turns, his fingers still tangled in my hair as he drags me down the hallway and back toward the room. He tosses me inside, and I land hard on my side. I don't bother attempting to brace myself. It doesn't matter.

Nothing matters.

"Don't get too comfortable. Twelve hours and that body will be fucked so hard it will be ripped to pieces."

The door slams and locks, and then there is silence. I try not to cry. I try hard to be brave, but the moment I hear the door lock into place, everything inside of me breaks. Tears roll down my cheeks as my entire body trembles. This is it.

My last hours of peace before I am tortured and ripped to shreds.

My last hours of being whole before I am no more.

My last hours of being Wells's.

My last hours.

WELLS

"You DIDN'T TELL your mother why," my dad murmurs after the family meeting.

We're sitting outside, me, my brothers, and my dad, enjoying a whiskey and a cigar. Though I passed on the cigar, choosing only the whiskey. Hendrick doesn't chime in. He knows that if he does, he'll be dismissed because he doesn't know exactly why I'm marrying Parker yet, and he wants to.

Sucking in a breath, I look across the firepit at him. It's a gas one, but it still puts off enough heat that I'm ready to kill it. As much as I like the ambience, Texas is too fucking hot for this shit. Leaning forward, I place my forearms on my knees and turn my head to look at my father.

"I didn't tell her because she didn't need to know. It's family business, and family business is where it stays. All she needs to know is that I've chosen Parker because that's what I've done."

My dad jerks his chin. "I did something right with you boys. Even if it wasn't everything."

"Nobody does everything right," Coleman murmurs.

We all snort, although more because we all know what Coleman is referring to. Shiloh. She'll never be spoken of again, but that doesn't mean we have forgotten that he not only fucked his first cousin but that there was a push for them to be married.

"What happens now?" I ask.

Dad shrugs his shoulder, takes a puff from his cigar, then brings his glass to his lips and takes a pull. He lets out a heavy sigh, looking up at the stars, and grunts before he turns to face me. His gaze searches mine before he speaks.

"Now we work," he rasps. "We work our asses off, and we reap the rewards. A life for a life," he calls out.

"A life for a life," my brothers and I repeat, holding out our glasses.

We all take a drink before I hear Hendrick's phone ring. He picks it up, then in a tone that I've never heard from him before, he asks. "What? You're where? For how long? I'll be right there. *We'll* be right there."

Turning my head, I look over at him. "All good, brother?" I ask.

His gaze finds mine, and it feels like it does it so slowly that my entire body stands on the edge of a cliff, teetering. When he speaks, that teetering stops, and I fall completely over, rolling down the rocky canyon until I land, boneless and sweaty, at the bottom.

"Parker is missing," he announces.

I frown. "What do you mean?" I demand.

"Allison. She was supposed to go over today. She hasn't been able to get hold of her all day long."

"And she's just now saying that?" I roar.

He shakes his head. "I just turned my phone on after dinner. She's been calling me but didn't want to bombard me with messages."

"Are you fucking kidding me?" I ask. "She's missing?"

"Missing."

Without another word, both Coleman and my dad stand. "We must find her, then," my dad states.

I know this is just because he doesn't want her to find out about him and go to the police. But I'm still a bit taken aback that he would care to help. He usually lets us handle the dirty work these days and just sits back.

"We must," I agree. "Now."

Without another word, the four of us rush out of the house. Mom is upstairs in her bath with her book, and I watch as Dad sends her a text. I climb into Coleman's SUV, knowing I'm not in a state to drive. Apparently, everyone else had the same idea.

Minutes later, we are at my building. As we rush up to the penthouse, for the first time in my life, I wish I didn't live on the top floor.

When I arrive at the hall, I see the back of Allison's blonde hair, and when she spins around, the look of absolute worry, stress, and pain that is etched across her face tells me this is really fucking serious.

My entire body deflates.

My heart sinks, and my spine straightens.

Something has happened to my woman.

Someone dies tonight.

THIRTY-SEVEN

PARKER

MINUTES, HOURS, SECONDS, I'M NOT SURE HOW QUICKLY OR slowly time passes, but I stare at the door, waiting for Ray to open it and take me back out into the living room. Take me back out to those men and to my fate.

My stomach lurches, thinking about the pain that will no doubt fill both my mind and body. If I had anything to throw up, I would probably do that right about now. But I haven't eaten since yesterday sometime, at least I think it was yesterday. I'm not quite sure at this point how long I've been here.

I close my eyes but don't fall asleep, but I do rest. It's not like I can do anything else. I must doze off because I'm startled by the sound of the door opening. The initial excitement of who it could be disappears after realization sets in of where I am and what's going on. I had a moment of forgetfulness, and it was beautiful.

"He hasn't responded to me," Ray announces. "I guess he

doesn't give a shit." He shrugs a shoulder as if it's all the same to him. "Maybe he'll care once he sees the video. Maybe he won't, but I'll feel better no matter what."

I take a moment to really take him in. Fear aside, the man isn't what I would consider manly. He's thin, a little shorter than Wells, and seems almost frail. If I saw him walking down the street, I wouldn't even look twice.

He looks like he works behind a desk, like he's worked there his whole life. I don't think he goes to the gym, and if I had to guess, his diet doesn't include much protein. I shouldn't judge him, except in this moment, I feel like judging him is appropriate since he's about to torture and likely murder me.

Ray takes a step into the room, then another. I've tried to think of several different scenarios of how I could try to get out of this, but none of them play out with me coming out the winner in my mind, so I decide against them. I should just take whatever fate I'm handed and shut up about it.

It's not like I've done anything exceptional in my life to warrant being saved. When Ray is directly in front of me, I brace myself to feel his fingers in my hair, but they don't come. Instead, he grunts, and then I hear him let out a laugh.

Lifting my gaze to him, my eyes widen when I see that he has his phone to his ear. "So you got my message?" he asks. "Yes. I'm looking at her. She's breathing for now. Untouched as well," he states.

I want to scream that isn't exactly true. He's a fucking liar. My scalp has never hurt so badly in my life, and my cheek is still pulsing from the back of his hand. His eyes sparkle as they watch me.

Either he can tell the defiance is building inside of me, or he's excited about whatever it is that Wells is saying on the other end of the line. I'm not quite sure. I'm going with he's excited about what is going to happen next because, deep down, this asshole is sadistic as shit.

"You better hurry and find her. I have plans already set into motion."

I doubt that Wells can respond because Ray ends the call seconds after he finishes speaking. His sparkly eyes search mine for just a moment before he lets out a chuckle of laughter, then he crouches down in front of me.

"Let's get you cleaned up. They want a pretty package to destroy."

My heart squeezes at the same time my stomach drops. I force myself to stand, my knees trembling, threatening to buckle as I stare straight ahead. It takes everything I have to follow this man into another room and then into a bathroom.

I think he's going to leave me alone to shower, but he doesn't. He leans against the vanity counter and watches my every move. He demands that I shave my legs, my armpits, my pussy, and the crack of my ass before I get out.

I've never been so embarrassed in my life. I've never been watched and scrutinized like this before. As much as I want to tell him to go to hell, I don't. It's as if I'm in a trance, but more like I'm terrified of what's coming, the impending doom too much for my mind to accept or even contemplate.

Once I'm clean, toweled off, and standing in front of Ray completely naked with the towel wrapped around my wet hair, I wait for my next instructions. Modesty is now something of the past.

This man watched me take a shower and demanded that I shave every part of myself while he observed. I don't know if my brain has taken a step back and can't handle this, so it's shut down, or if I'm somehow actually coping with this.

I'm not sure how to feel right now, and as much as I want to think that I'll be able to get out of this without completely breaking, I'm not holding my breath. If I survive this at all, I don't think I'll ever be the same as I was before. I don't think I'll be anyone Wells will want. I need to face the music, the fact that we're over. That my life is over.

"Let's go," Ray announces, reaching for the towel and yanking it off my head before he lets it drop to the bathroom floor.

It lands on the tile with a swoosh. My feet pad behind him. Thankfully, he doesn't push or pull me. He just moves through the house, knowing that I understand my place and my fate. The living room comes into view, and he takes a step to the side.

The three men who were there earlier are in different seats, but it's still just them. Their eyes widen at the sight of my nakedness. I watch as one of them licks their lips, and I can't look anymore.

Dropping my gaze to my bare feet, I cringe at the sight of toenail polish. It was red when I painted them, probably three weeks ago, maybe longer. But now it's all chipped up and a complete mess. At least it matches the rest of me now.

"How much for her mouth?" Ray calls out.

My spine straightens. He's going to have a bidding war right here for my body parts, in front of me, as if I'm not standing right here. A human auction.

What the hell?

Lifting my head, I look at his profile, watching him smile as his gaze scans the men sitting in front of us. One of the men grunts something that I can't quite make out, and then he continues.

He auctions off every single part of my body. Then, he auctions off the destruction of those parts. And as much as I want to be stony-faced and act as if it doesn't affect me, silent tears begin to fall down my cheeks at the comprehension of what is coming next.

. . .

WELLS

RAY RANDOLPH HAS HER.

"Do you know how to find him?" I ask.

He left me a message on my phone, and when I returned the call, he gave me a bunch of nothing, except that he was planning on hurting her, but he hadn't yet. I can only imagine how he plans on doing that.

But as we sit in front of his house, it's clear she isn't here. Nobody is. This place is abandoned. Turning my head, I look over at my father. If anyone will know where he keeps a safe house, it will be my dad.

"Do you know where he could be?" I ask.

Silence fills the cab of the SUV as I wait for an answer. I'm not letting this go. That fucker has my woman. Even if I wasn't sure that I wanted her, even if I wasn't ready for the commitment and wasn't a hundred-percent okay with her being my reward. Ray doesn't know that, and it's not up to him to decide when he can and can't take her away from me.

Fuck that.

"This is because we killed Shiloh," Coleman mutters.

"Yeah, I know," I grunt. "But it wouldn't have mattered. Once the truth came all the way out, she was as good as dead anyway."

"How?" Coleman asks.

I can feel his gaze on the side of my face, but I'm still focused straight ahead on this fucking house, knowing that there is something else going on, something that I can't quite put my finger on, but it's there.

"She just was. Coming to your place the way she did, trying to make the two of you happen. Being manipulative. There was no way she was coming out of this deal alive. Not with the antics she was pulling. You asked me yourself, and I was ready then, with or without permission."

Dad clears his throat but thankfully doesn't say anything about my obvious disregard for the rules of the family. Instead, he pretends as if he didn't hear it at all and answers my question from a few moments ago.

"There is one place where he could be. Maybe."

"Then let's go," I grind out.

"Wait," Hendrick calls out from beside me in the back seat. "I know where he is."

Slowly, Dad turns around from his place in the passenger seat to look back at him. His gaze locks in on Hendrick's, and I can tell he is not only concerned, but it also appears that Dad is more than slightly pissed off.

"You need to explain this. Now," Dad roars.

Hendrick shrugs a shoulder, acting completely and totally un-fucking-bothered, but when Dad is pissed off, I know there is something concerning happening. Coleman doesn't speak, but I can see him grip the steering wheel tightly. It seems that everybody knows what's going on here except me.

"I just wanted something different. I haven't done it in weeks."

"You bought a woman who was not willing?" Dad asks.

"What?" I demand.

The air in the room goes completely static. We aren't good men, the family isn't some sweet group that helps little old ladies and saves puppies, but we have rules, and rape is high on the list of don'ts in the rules. I cannot believe what I'm hearing. And from my own brother.

"Sounds worse than it is, or maybe it's worse than it sounds, I don't know. I was high as fuck every time I've ever been there."

Hendrick gives Coleman the address, and I watch as he types it into his GPS. I don't know exactly what the fuck we're going to be walking into. I am still too floored by Hendrick's confession to even think.

There is just no way that he paid for anything. I can't comprehend it. He has women falling at his feet at clubs, and here he paid this asshole money for women who were unwilling. Frowning, I look at my brother and start to ask him what the fuck is going on when my dad's voice fills the cab of the SUV.

"I'm not going to ask you why you did it. I just want to know why you did it with Ray."

There is a moment of silence, but I can tell that Hendrick isn't thinking about why he did it. He's just thinking about doing it in general. Hendrick leans back in his seat and lets out a sigh.

"I was bored. I'd done everything. I'd fucked everyone willing. I needed a thrill, and I was high. It was fun for a while."

"Until?" I ask.

"Until I wasn't high, and I looked into her eyes once. That sucked the fun out of it. Then I met Allison."

Fuck.

Fucking fuck.

"Get there now before someone hurts Parker," I grind out.

CHAPTER
THIRTY-EIGHT

PARKER

THE MEN MAKE THEIR BIDS, BUT NOT BEFORE THEY STAND UP and circle me like sharks. They poke me, palm me, cup me. Anywhere you can think of, that's where they touch me. Thankfully, they don't stick anything, finger or otherwise, inside of me, but I don't think anything will ever erase their fingers' touch from my body.

Then one of them reaches up, his fingers digging into my cheeks and forcing my lips apart as he leans in to check my teeth. I am an animal for their inspection, nothing more, nothing less. I am not human in this moment. They are not thinking of me as their mother, sister, or daughter.

They are thinking of me only as a thing.

An animal.

Ray wheels and deals. It's clear that this is not his first time doing this, not even his tenth. This man is a profes-sional, and my heart sinks at the thought of the sheer number of women who have been used in the way he's just about to sell me into.

I watch as hands shake as money is exchanged. Everything is going forward. My life is going to end. Ray wraps his hand around the back of my neck and guides me into the middle of the living room before he pushes me down, forcing my knees to buckle.

I wince in pain as I slam against the hard floor. Ray slides the coffee table over to me and places his hand at the center of my back, pushing me over so that my chest hits the table and my bruised cheek is smashed against the hard wood. It's warm and scratched. I hate that when I close my eyes, I almost feel a sense of comfort.

"Chin on the table," Ray growls.

Lifting my head, I place my chin on the table and close my eyes. It's going to start soon, and as much as I want to scream and run, there's nothing I can do. I'm completely and totally stuck here without an ounce of protection.

I am done.

I know I am.

"What the fuck?"

A deep voice roars from somewhere behind me. I ignore it, assuming it's another one of Ray's little friends. I've given up. There is no hope for me, not anymore. I just hope that if Wells ever finds me or learns what happened to me, he gets rid of Ray in any way possible. I don't care how it's done or what happens. I just want Ray to suffer.

When I feel movement around me, only then do I open my eyes. The men who were on the couch, who circled me, they're on the move and looking really panicked. I don't try to sit up, even though that's my natural reaction. I stay where I am and hope that whatever happens, that I survive it.

Then I hear a shot.

It's loud and vibrates off the walls. I hear a few grunts

302

right before there is a shadow over me to the side. Turning my head, I look over and gasp at the sight of Wells standing above me. His eyes are dark, so dark that they're black, as he looks down at me.

He looks angry. Pissed off, exactly. Letting out a breath, I lift my chest from the coffee table and turn to face him. I start to stand, but he lifts his hand, his palm facing me.

"Stay," he murmurs.

I do as I'm told, looking up at him from my place on the floor. Nodding with a single jerk, I stay where I am. What feels like seconds later, I watch as Wells drags Ray right in front of me.

"Did he touch you?" Wells asks.

I slip my tongue out, slide it across my bottom lip, and nod once. "He hit me, but nothing else too bad."

"He hit you?" Wells growls.

Jerking my chin, I lift it slightly and look straight toward him. "He hit me," I confirm.

Wells hums, and before I realize what's happening, he slides a knife across Ray's throat and blood spurts everywhere. Wells moves toward me, and the rustling around the room stops. It's just him and me. There are just the two of us. Nothing else exists in this world but him and me.

He reaches down, slides his hands beneath my arms, and lifts me slightly. I don't know what I expect, but it isn't to be picked up and have my ass set down on the coffee table. "Wells?" I ask softly.

"I don't know what you went through, and I'm not going to ask you today. Right now, I'm going to fuck you. Whatever the fuck happened, you can work on that later. But right now, there is just you and me."

"And the dead guy behind you," I whisper.

He chuckles, his lips curving up slightly. "Fuck him. He doesn't fucking exist. It's just you and me, cupcake."

Lifting my hands, I ignore the blood that covers his face and neck as I feel the warmth of his skin beneath my touch. "Just you and me," I repeat.

He reaches out, wrapping his fingers around the front of my throat as he leans down slightly and touches his mouth to mine.

"You're mine," he growls.

He wraps the fingers of his other hand around my wrist, moving it so it slides across his skin, where the blood is dripping off his face. "He needs to know that," Wells states.

"I think he's dead," I whisper.

Wells lifts his head, chuckling as his gaze finds mine. "I know he's dead, cupcake. I'm going to fuck you in his blood."

WELLS

PARKER LOOKS UP AT ME, her eyes wide, and the fear that I remember from our first encounter at my mother's office has returned. I stare at her for a moment. I know I look horrifying, with blood dripping from my face and body.

"I want your ass on that table, cupcake," I demand, though I keep my voice soft, almost as if I'm purring to an injured animal.

Slowly, she places her hands on the coffee table and pushes herself up to stand. Standing still, I watch as she walks around the small table and sinks down until she's sitting on the edge. She watches me, seemingly not scared by the sight of the blood soaking my body.

Opening my mouth, I start to tell her to spread her legs, but I don't need to because she does it automatically, as if she already knows exactly what I want and the way I want it. She's mine in every way, and she knows it.

Sucking in a breath, I unbutton my pants, watching her as

I do and gauging her response. I place my palm in the center of her bare chest and slide it down to her belly, stopping there as my gaze flicks from hers to the blood that is now on her skin.

My lips twitch into a small smile at the sight.

Dropping down to my knees, I lean forward and slam my mouth against hers in a hard kiss. She gasps, opening her mouth, and as much as I want to make this a sensual thing, it's not. Instead of sliding my tongue inside of her mouth and tasting her, I break the kiss, grab hold of her hips, and pull her across the small table.

Her head hangs over the edge, and her back slams down against the wood as I bury myself inside of her with one swift thrust. I don't move. Instead, I reach out, wrap my fingers around the back of her neck and force her to sit up slightly.

Leaning over her body, I look into her eyes. That fear is gone, replaced with desire. "This is done after tonight. I fuck you in his blood, and then we wash it away," I growl.

"Yes," she exhales.

"And nobody will ever touch you again, cupcake." Rolling my hips, I fuck her, transferring blood from my body to hers.

Gripping her hair, I turn her head slightly.

"I want you to look at his body," I growl against her ear. "He is dead. He will never hurt you again. Not fucking ever. I want you to watch his lifeless body as I fuck you, as you come all over my cock. I want you to burn that image into your fucking head that he is dead."

My hips move, my pelvis grinding against her clit with each stroke, and I hear her breath hitch against my ear each time. I know she's climbing higher and higher. Parker lifts her legs, wrapping them around my hips as I continue to move inside of her.

Her nails dig into my shoulders through my shirt, and I'm

sure I'll have bruising there, but I don't give a fuck. I want her bruises, her marks on my body. Everywhere. Touching my lips just below her earlobe, I exhale against her skin before my tongue snakes out and I taste her there.

"Wells," she breathes.

"Come for me, Parker. Come all over my cock. Remember who you belong to."

I feel her thighs tremble, and then all the muscles in her body freeze. "You," she whimpers right before I feel her cunt clamp down around my dick.

Instead of stopping and allowing her to take in her full orgasm, I continue to move. I pound into her harder, faster, and when I find my release, I bury myself deep inside of her and fill her with my cum.

Lifting from her neck, I shift her head so I can see her eyes. Tears have spilled down her cheeks, the wetness sliding down her neck and chest. With a smirk, I search her eyes for that terrified fear that was there when I arrived, but it's gone.

Touching my mouth to hers, I brush my lips across hers before I lift my head. "We leave here together, and we leave this whole thing here, yeah?" I ask. "It doesn't fucking exist. I've taken care of it all."

Her gaze flicks to the body behind me, Ray's lifeless body, then she shifts her attention back to me. "It's done," she exhales, but I'm not sure if she believes it.

Slipping out of her, I stand and right my pants before I begin to take my shirt off. Parker sits up on the coffee table, her gaze once more shifting behind me to Ray's body. She doesn't say anything, her attention slowly shifting from the body back to me.

"It's done," she says again, this time a bit firmer.

I slide my shirt from my body, slip it up her arms, and button it at her chest so it covers her nakedness from everyone else's view. She starts to stand, but I don't let her.

She's covered in Ray's blood, her body trembling from her fear and her orgasm.

Gliding my arms beneath her back and her knees, I pick her up and carry her out of the shitty house and straight to the SUV. Hendrick is standing outside at the car door and opens it immediately for me.

He already has the third row ready for her to lie down. She should probably be in the second row, but I want her safely in the car while we deal with the rest of this shit. "I'll be back soon, cupcake. You're safe here."

She jerks her chin, lying down on the seat and staring straight ahead toward the front windshield. I am under no impression that she is going to be perfectly back to her normal self tomorrow, no matter how many times I try to tell her that she needs to be. She is human. She was kidnapped, she was abused, and she was almost raped by three to four men. I just hope I was able to stop irreversible damage to her.

"Where are Dad and Coleman?" I ask.

"Inside, dealing with the three buyers."

"Buyers?" I ask.

He hums. "Buyers. They didn't want to kill them before they got as much information as possible out of them."

Jerking my head in a nod, I push off the car and start to walk back into the house, shirtless and still very much covered in now-drying blood. I only make it a few steps before I turn and look back at my brother.

"You'll probably be punished for your part in this, but had you not known about it, my woman would have been ruined from the inside out, so thank you, little brother."

Admitting that. All of it. It isn't easy for me. We aren't married yet, we don't know one another well, but the fact that she was almost taken from me, and it was my fault? That it had to do with the family? That is what has me shaken more than anything.

Ray wasn't afraid of the family, at least not enough. We have failed somewhere along the way, and it's time to rectify that. He should have been so scared of getting caught that I could have told him I killed Shiloh in cold blood and laughed as I did it, and he would have said thank you to me instead of kidnapping my woman.

That shit was unacceptable from start to finish. This whole thing was unacceptable, starting twenty-something years ago with Uncle Dean.

Never fucking again

CHAPTER
THIRTY-NINE

WELLS

I REENTER THE HOUSE AND WALK INTO AN EMPTY BEDROOM, where I find Coleman and my father standing in front of the three men who were circling Parker when I found her in the living room. The men are sitting on the floor, their backs against the wall, their heads tipped backward, their eyes on my father and brother.

"The whole underground world is run by a man, but that man wasn't Ray," Coleman states.

"And these fuckers won't tell you who?" I ask.

My father clears his throat. "They don't know. They only know when there is a live one and get an address texted to them if they are willing to pay the entrance fee."

"Which is?" I ask. Although I could probably ask Hendrick these questions, I don't care. I want to know everything they found out.

"Twenty-thousand-dollar buy-in, then bidding for whatever they want from the girl."

"Who makes the bulk of the money?" I grind out, unable to open my mouth all the way to speak.

I'm seconds from losing my fucking shit and killing all three of these men immediately instead of waiting for whatever my father has planned. I try to suck in a breath, hold it, and let it out slowly in an attempt to take calming breaths, but I don't feel very calm right now.

"You know it's the man in charge," my father mutters. "But that doesn't mean Ray didn't walk away with a good chunk of the change. Which makes sense. I didn't think the passport angle he was working was making as much as he was spending."

"Should we be changing our direction?" Coleman asks.

My spine straightens at his question, but my father chuckles before he speaks. "Our direction is just fine. This is a darkness that I don't wish to invite into my life or the family's. But we definitely need to find out as much as we can. And all of the players, so we can avoid this in the future."

"These pencil dicks don't know shit," I say, jerking my chin toward the three fuckers sitting on the floor like little bitches.

One of them scrambles to his feet, his chest puffed up as he takes a step forward. He's daring and stupid, this one. My lips twitch into a smirk at just how fired up this asshole is that I called him a pencil dick.

"Or do you, Pencil Dick?" I ask.

"Fuck you," he sneers. "I know exactly who is in charge. You better watch your fucking backs, too. Messing with his money will get you dead."

I almost laugh in his face. If I didn't want information from him, I might just do that. Instead, I arch a brow as I bite the inside of my cheek and wait for him to tell me exactly who the fuck is the head boss of this shit.

"You're going to get your family killed," one of the men on the floor hisses.

My father lifts his gun and shoots him in the head. "Guess what?" he asks, looking at the one who is standing and talking to us. "Your family is already as good as dead whether you tell us or don't. Doesn't really fucking matter. Getting involved in this shit signed their death sentence."

The man gulps. He's trembling now, and I'm sure if I looked at his pants, he's pissed himself. What a pussy. Staying back, I try to let my father and Coleman handle this, considering they're both higher ranking than I am, but I'm starting to get impatient.

"Who is in charge?" my father growls.

His patience is waning as well, and somehow, that causes me to chuckle. I'm not sure why. It shouldn't. But it does. Maybe because my dad doesn't really lose his patience very often anymore.

"The richest person in Texas," he says, his lips curved up into a grin. "A trust fund heiress. You will never get to her, you will never ruin her, and you will never best her."

Maybe he's right. That being said, I know exactly who he's talking about. Rosalinda Dalton. She is the heir to a massive candy company. Fuck. She is untouchable, but not in the exact way that this fucker is thinking.

Sure, she's rich, she's famous, and she's in the spotlight, but she's also a huge human trafficking activist and involved in politics. She is on committees and brownnosing with all the biggest and most powerful people in the country.

We'd never be able to publicly expose her. Not with who and what we are. It would be a gigantic shit show, and we'd probably all end up in prison over some fake bullshit... or maybe real bullshit. Either way, we would end up in prison, and she would have the last laugh.

"Kill them," my father grinds out as he takes his phone out of his pocket and walks out of the room.

I'm sure he's going to call a family meeting about this. I know I would if I were him, at least with the upper executives and managers. As soon as my father walks out of the room, Coleman lifts his gun and takes one shot at the guy who was talking and ends him quickly.

The lone man against the wall cries out when his friend drops to the ground in a pile of twitching flesh. Lifting my gun, I end him before he makes any more noise.

"Cleanup crew?" I ask.

Coleman chuckles before his eyes find mine and he speaks. "Already called and pin sent."

Together, we walk out of the house, a fucking home of horrors no doubt filled with the ghosts of dozens of women who were tortured to death. We should just burn the whole place to the ground, making a completely clean slate and a place for the spirits to find peace as much as they can.

As I walk up to the SUV, I see my father shove his phone into his pocket, his head turning to look back at us.

"Take me home," he states. "Tomorrow morning at ten, we have a meeting, the entire family." He stops at the front passenger door and turns to Hendrick. "You're staying at home for a while."

That is that.

Hendrick is, without a doubt, not coming out of this completely unscathed. He fucked around a little too hard, and he's about to find out what happens. Granted, I've never done what he has, but I've been in enough trouble in my days to know he'll come out of it a better member of the family, even if he's without a doubt going to be a little broken.

PARKER

I FEEL MY BODY MOVING, and I jump, almost falling out of Wells's arms and onto the ground. He grips me a bit tighter as he moves into my building. I let out a sigh as he opens the front door, then walks straight toward the elevator bank and touches the button for my floor.

Wrapping my arms around his neck, I rest my head against his shoulder as I let out a heavy sigh. The silence around us should probably feel uncomfortable, but it doesn't. I will take this silence with him over the quiet of that hellhole any single day.

The doors open, and he heads toward my condo. We slip inside, but he doesn't let me down, not even when he locks the door behind him and carries me straight toward the bathroom. I expect him to start the shower, but he doesn't.

Instead, he turns the handle of the bathtub faucet before he gently sets me down on the cool tile floor. I don't drop my arms from around his neck, though. Tipping my head back, I look up into his eyes, searching them. For what? I'm not sure, but whatever it is, I don't find it.

"Wells?" I call out on a whisper.

He hums but doesn't say anything as he waits for me to speak. "Am I too damaged for you?"

There is a moment of silence as he stares at me before he jerks his chin. He clears his throat, then shakes his head once.

"Why would you think that?" he asks. He cups my cheeks gently, one of his thumbs sliding across my bottom lip, the other one lightly brushing across the bruised area of my face.

Slipping my tongue out, I wet my bottom lip where his thumb just traced my flesh. "I was kidnapped, I was held, and they were going to hurt me. Really hurt me. I might not ever mentally get over this, Wells. I already have issues, and now this?"

His lips twitch into a small smile before he dips his chin and touches his mouth to mine. "Luckily, I know a wonderful therapist."

He takes a step backward. My arms are forced to fall from his shoulders, and I watch as he turns toward the tub. He switches it off, then turns toward the shower and starts the water there.

"Rinse off," he murmurs. "Then soak."

Looking toward the mirror at the vanity, I suck in a breath at the sight of my body. I unbutton the shirt he put on me earlier and sink my teeth into my bottom lip as I take in the entire picture of my reflection. I'm covered in dried blood... everywhere.

Shifting my gaze to him, I watch as he sheds his shoes and pants, and I see he is covered in dried blood as well. We make quite the pair, and I can't seem to feel bad about the fact that this blood was once inside of a living body and now it no longer is.

I step into the shower behind him, and Wells turns to face me, one of his hands wrapping around the back of my neck, the other he places flat against the center of my chest. My breath hitches as I wait for him to speak.

I'm not sure what he's going to say, so I hold my breath as I wait. His gaze searches mine, then he gives me a small smile before he speaks.

"I almost lost you before I ever truly had you, cupcake. I didn't know what I was feeling, but I didn't like any of it. I never want to be in that situation again. You're mine. Everything is going to be okay."

His mouth touches mine, his lips brush against my own, then he lifts his head as the water washes over us. The blood rinses down the drain, washing away the entire day and evening.

"I've never loved anyone other than my family, Parker."

"I've never loved anyone other than Allison," I confess.

His lips twitch into a smirk. "Be my wife," he murmurs as he rests his forehead against mine.

"Yes," I exhale.

I'm not sure if this is the right thing to do. Someone he knows kidnapped me, and I still need to know what happened there. He killed a man, and we had sex in his blood. That should terrify me, except it didn't. Instead, I felt loved. I'm not sure that this relationship is anywhere near normal, but I'm also not sure I care.

No, wait.

I know I don't care.

When I thought that I was going to die, all I cared about was the fact that I would not be able to live a life with Wells. I wasn't going to learn more about him. I wasn't going to kiss him or touch him again. I was sure that what we had was going to be over.

Regardless of the reasons behind my kidnapping, behind that man's murder, I no longer care. I'm going to hold on to this life with both hands, on to this man with both hands, and I'm never letting go... no matter what I discover about him.

He is mine, and I am, without a doubt, irrevocably his.

Always.

EPILOGUE

PARKER

ONE MONTH LATER

GLANCING DOWN AT THE LETTER IN MY HAND, MY EYES CATCH the ring on my left finger. My engagement ring. Smiling, I move it around so the light catches it just right and causes it to sparkle.

It's beautiful. I cannot believe that just a few months ago, I was single and full of anxiety to the point that I couldn't even make it up to Doctor Hamilton's office. Now I'm engaged to her son, and I call her Brenda.

She's also helped me through the second most terrifying moment in my life. My kidnapping. But I feel better. I feel like I'm a whole person. I have a man who loves me. And he does. He tells me at least once a day, if not more. I would have never guessed him to be a man who openly expressed his love, but he does—often.

Looking down at the envelope again, I scan the outside and try to figure out where it came from. There is no return address, not even a stamp. Someone scrawled my name across the front and dropped it into the mail slot in the lobby of the building.

Sliding my tongue across my bottom lip, I sink my teeth down and scrape them across, looking for a piece of dry skin to peel off. Extending my finger, I flip the envelope over and glide my finger beneath the flap.

As I open it, I try to gulp down the lump in my throat, but it doesn't work out too well. I'm not sure why I'm nervous, but I really am. It's the fear of the unknown that has me so on edge. This could be anything. Maybe I should wait until Allison comes over.

Placing it down on the counter, I decide to do that. She's going to be here any minute. Standing from the barstool, I take a step backward and let out a heavy sigh. I hold my breath for a moment as I stare at the envelope for another beat before I turn around and walk away from it.

I don't go far. Just to the living room so I can pace. And wait. And pace some more as I wait for Allison to arrive. She's supposed to come over and help me look through wedding websites and magazines.

I'm not sure why we're even doing it. Wells already told me that we were going to do an all-inclusive wedding deal with a planner, and all I had to do was choose colors, try on dresses, and show up.

I know I'm supposed to be excited about the wedding. I'm supposed to want to plan everything. But I really don't. I'm glad to have it taken off my plate, especially since I've never even been to a wedding.

There is a knock on the door, and my spine straightens. I turn my head to look at the closed door before I realize who it is. I hear her call out to me, something she's been doing since I was kidnapped. I won't even walk to a door and look through the peephole again until I know who is on the other side.

I'm sure it makes me unhealed, broken, or whatever. But I don't care. I'll probably never blindly open a door again for as long as I live.

Looking through the peephole, I double-check to see if it's really Allison and make sure that she's alone. She's on the other side of the door, a smile on her face, knowing that I'm looking at her through the peephole.

I open the door, step to the side, and let her walk past me. Closing the door, I lock it, then turn to her. "Okay, I came prepared with sticky notes and everything," she says chirpily as she makes her way over to the breakfast table and sets everything down.

Making my way to the counter, I grab the envelope and take it over to the table. "Before we get started," I say, "I got this in the mail. I don't know what it is, but it feels wrong."

Allison looks down at the envelope but doesn't touch it. Instead, she stares at it like it's going to jump up and bite her. I feel the same way. I already opened it. But I haven't looked inside. I don't think I can. This is dumb.

It's a piece of paper. It's not going to actually hurt me.

"But what if it does?" Allison asks. "What if it does?"

I didn't think I said that aloud, but apparently, I did. It doesn't change the way I feel, though. What if the contents hurt me in some way?

It could.

Opening the envelope, I hold my breath for a moment, then let it out slowly as I pull the folded piece of paper out. Opening it, I find a newspaper article. Sliding my tongue along my bottom lip, I stare at the words.

"It's the news article from when my parents were killed," I murmur.

Allison reaches for it and scans the worn words. She lifts her gaze, her eyes finding mine. "What does this mean?" she asks. "Why would someone send this to you?"

Shaking my head, I look at the other paper, the one that was wrapped around the article. It's a typed-out note. It's just a few lines that cause me to pause.

I don't know what to do or say.

Taking my phone out of my back pocket, I open up the camera and take a picture before I attach it to a text and send it to Wells.

Allison takes it out of my hand once I'm finished and reads it out loud to me.

Ask your fiancé's father who killed your parents.

He knows.

"What does this mean?" Allison asks again.

"I don't know," I whisper.

The phone alerts me to a new notification, and I slide my thumb across the screen to see what Wells has to say.

WELLS: IGNORE THAT SHIT. I'LL BE HOME SOON.

"He said to ignore it," I mutter as I lift my gaze to Allison.

Her eyes are wide, and she sinks her teeth into the corner of her lip. I watch her for a moment, then suck in a breath before I let it out. She shrugs a shoulder before she speaks.

"You know what? Some people just don't want others to be happy. Some people are just assholes, and your old boss, he was one of those, I think. He was causing problems, right?"

"He was," I whisper.

"Well, then. I bet this was him. What a dick."

What a dick is right. I know that nobody down there had any idea about what had happened to me, but he made a big deal about having security watch me empty my desk and then made them escort me out of the building. It was so humiliating.

Deciding that I don't want to make a big deal about it, I respond to Wells's text.

> Don't worry about it. I think I know who sent it. I'm pretty sure it was Eira.

> WELLS: I'LL HANDLE IT, CUPCAKE.
> LOVE YOU.

> I love you, too, Wells. So much.

Setting my phone down, I smile across the table at Allison and ask her to help me with this wedding stuff. It takes my mind off that note, off that article, but I can't stop thinking about Eira and wondering why he would care enough to even send it to me.

Why is he trying to hurt me like that?

What is the point of it?

I don't even know him that well. It's not like we dated or spent any time together. He only noticed my existence that one day. I just don't understand any of it, and I don't know if I ever will. When we're finished figuring out color schemes and have a list of about fifty dresses for me to try on, Allison leans back in her chair, her eyes searching mine.

"You're okay, right?"

Sinking my teeth into my bottom lip, I lean back, too. "I am," I say just as the door unlocks.

Turning my head, I watch as Wells walks through the door. I didn't expect him so soon. His eyes find mine, and he holds my gaze for a moment. I know he's trying to gauge my mood. He doesn't say anything, then he moves closer to me, crouching slightly when he's in front of me.

He lifts his hand, wrapping his fingers loosely around the front of my throat. "You good, cupcake?" My gaze searches his, and my lips curve up into a small smile. "Yeah, she's okay," he rasps.

Wells leans forward and touches his lips to mine. I hear him crumple the article and the piece of paper in his fist, then he chuckles against my mouth. "Love you, Parker. Nothing, nobody, not a single person, comes between us."

"Never," I exhale.

"In two months, we get married, and this shit is just that… shit."

WELLS

LIFTING the phone to my ear, I step out on the balcony while Parker and Allison say their goodbyes. He picks up on the second ring, and I feel it's my obligation to tell him what's happened.

Shoving my hand into my pocket, I feel the papers there. I wadded them up, but as soon as her back was turned, I picked them both up and shoved them into my pocket. I don't know why. I'm sure there's nothing identifying on them, but throwing them away didn't seem right, not when I don't know who sent them.

"What had you in a rush out of the office this afternoon?" he asks.

"Parker received a letter. It was dropped in the box at the condo. No return address and no stamp. It was an article from the day her parents were killed and a note that said: *Ask your fiancé's father who killed your parents. He knows.*"

There is nothing except breathing and silence on the other end of the line. I almost ask him if he's okay, but then he decides to speak. "Your wedding cannot come soon enough," he murmurs. "Is everything okay?"

"I handled it, Dad. But do you know who it could be?"

I have no clue. Eira isn't a bad guess, but I highly doubt he is worried about it any longer. He didn't know her enough to give a shit. He didn't even kiss her, let alone fuck her, so I doubt it's him.

It's more than likely an enemy. Possibly one of my father's, likely one of mine. Instead of trying to figure out who it is, I hand it over to my father. This is his shit. Not mine. He's the director of the family for a reason.

"I'll see to it," he murmurs. "The wedding planning going well?" he asks, slightly veering off the subject at hand.

"All on course," I murmur.

"See you in the morning. Managers' meeting. Plus, tomorrow night, we all meet Coleman's bride and her family for dinner. Your mother is in a tizzy."

"I'll send Parker over early. She can help."

"Thanks," he rasps. "All will be well, Wells."

I don't know if he tells me that because he is trying to convince me or himself. I'm not sure. There is a noise behind me, and the door opens. Turning my head, I watch as my beautiful bride-to-be makes her way toward me in the cool Dallas night.

"I have to go now," I murmur.

"Keep her mind off whatever that letter is, Wells."

I almost laugh.

Keeping Parker busy is my absolute favorite pastime. I love every second of it, and I hope she does as well. Although, judging by the way her eyes watch me as she moves across the balcony, I think she does.

"Parker," I murmur. "Stop there."

She's a few feet from me, her eyes wide as she watches me, waiting for her next instructions. Sucking in a breath, she holds it. My lips curve up into a grin.

"Take everything off," I demand.

A light sparks in her gaze. She enjoys our moments together. The way I demand things from her. The way I make her beg for pleasure, for pain, for everything and nothing all at the same time.

Parker strips down to nothing, leaving her bare to me so the cool Texas breeze kisses her skin. I watch as goose bumps break out all over her.

"What do you want?" I ask, my gaze traveling down to her breasts.

They're bruised from my fingers, my teeth, my lips. It's the only part of her that bears my marks any longer. My mother saw the bruising on her neck a month ago and reprimanded me for it. No visible marks. That's what she told me, and that's what I'm trying to abide by.

Just another rule for me to follow. As if I don't have enough of them.

"You, Wells."

"I'm yours, cupcake."

It's true. I am hers. Always.

Stepping forward, I reach out and wrap my fingers around the side of her neck. "I love you, Parker. I'm sorry about that note today. I will handle it, and I will find out who sent it."

"I know you will, Wells. I know."

Leaning down, I touch my mouth to hers, slipping my tongue into her mouth and swirling it around to taste her. Sliding my hand between her legs, I glide my fingers through her folds before I swirl her clit, then dip two inside.

"Please," she whimpers.

Taking my hand from between her legs, I reach around to

grip the backs of her thighs and pick her up. I set her down on the edge of the railing and guide myself inside of her. "Yes," she hisses.

I fuck her against the railing of the balcony, outside for the world to see. The world could all be watching us with binoculars, and it wouldn't matter because we are the only two people in our own world.

It is only us.

Just us.

Touching my mouth to hers, I fuck her with my tongue and my cock at the same time until we both come.

Hard.

There is only Parker for me.

I was wrong to think that this relationship and commitment between the two of us was too soon. The timing is perfect, and I cannot imagine my life without her at my back, at my side, in my bed.

I just pray that she never learns the truth, that the group, the person behind her parents' deaths, is never revealed. This is a secret that needs to remain until my death. I could not live a life without Parker, and nothing could keep her with me if she were to discover the truth.

So she can never find out.

Not fucking ever.

Moving inside of her, I slip my hand between us and draw firm circles against her clit until I know she's on the edge, the verge of her release. When she comes, it's hard, her pussy clenching around me, and I move hard and fast, chasing my own release.

Burying myself deep inside of her, I shove my face into her neck and come.

Hard.

So fucking hard that I see stars. Once I catch my breath, I

lift my head and look into Parker's eyes. Searching her gaze, I smile at the sight of her.

"I love you, Wells," she whispers.

"More than life itself, cupcake. More than fucking life itself. I cannot wait for the future. Two months, Parker. Two months, and you're mine forever. Until the day we die."

Her lips curve up into a lazy smile. "Until the day we die, my love."

My heart could not be fuller.

My mind could not be clearer.

I love her.

WHAT'S NEXT

Get the next book in the series here
Enticing the Monster

ABOUT THE AUTHOR

As an only child, Hayley Faiman had to entertain herself somehow. She started writing stories at the age of six and never really stopped.

Born in California, she met her now husband at the age of sixteen and married him at the age of twenty in 2004. After all of these years together, he's still the love of her life.

She now lives in East Texas with her family!

Most of Hayley's days are spent taking care of her two boys, going to sports practices, or helping them with homework. Her evenings are spent with her husband and her nights—those are spent creating alpha book boyfriends.

Also by Hayley Faiman

Men of Baseball Series—

Pitching for Amalie

Catching Maggie

Forced Play for Libby

Sweet Spot for Victoria

Russian Bratva Series —

Owned by the Badman

Seducing the Badman

Dancing for the Badman

Living for the Badman

Tempting the Badman

Protected by the Badman

Forever my Badman

Betrothed to the Badman

Chosen by the Badman

Bought by the Badman

Collared by the Badman

Notorious Devils MC —

Rough & Rowdy

Rough & Raw

Rough & Rugged

Rough & Ruthless

Rough & Ready

Rough & Rich

Rough & Real

Cash Bar Series —

Laced with Fear

Chased with Strength

Flamed with Courage

Blended with Pain

Twisted with Chaos

Mixed with trouble

SAVAGE BEAST MC —

UnScrew Me

UnBreak Me

UnChain Me

UnLeash Me

UnTouch Me

UnHinge Me

UnWreck Me

UnCage Me

Unfit Hero Series —

CONVICT

HERO

FRAUD

KILLER

COWBOY

Zanetti Famiglia Series —

Becoming the Boss

Becoming his Mistress

Becoming his Possession

Becoming the Street Boss

Becoming the Hitman

Becoming his Wife

Becoming her Salvation

Prophecy Sisters Series —

Bride of the Traitor

Bride of the Sea

Bride of the Frontier

Bride of the Emperor

Astor Family Series —

Hypocritically Yours

Egotistically Yours

Matrimonially Yours

Occasionally Yours

Nasty Bastards MC —

Ruin My Life

Tame My Life

Start My Life

Dance into My Life

Shake Up My Life

Repair My Life

Sweeten My Life

Wrap Up My Life

Underworld Sinners—

Stolen by the Sinner

Bound to the Sinner

Caught by the Sinner

F*cked by the Sinner

Stripped by the Sinner

Rejecting the Sinner

Loved by the Sinner

Devil's Hellions MC —

Dirty Perfect Storm

Cocky Perfect Storm

Taboo Perfect Storm

Wicked Perfect Storm

Midnight Stalkers—

Tempting the Monster

Enticing the Monster

Watching the Monster

Awakened Curses —

Vow to a King

Vow to a Tyrant

Vow to a Rogue

Offspring Legends—

Between Flaming Stars

Beautiful Unwanted Wildflower

Esquire Black Duet Series –

DISCOVERY

APPEAL

Forbidden Love Series —

Personal Foul

Kinetic Energy

Standalone Titles

Royally Relinquished: A Modern Day Fairy Tale

Made in the USA
Middletown, DE
25 October 2023